BIZARRE ADVENTURES

Writer: **Jeff Parker**
Pencils: **Juan Santacruz**

Inks: **Raul Fernandez**
Colors: **Impacto Studios' Adriano Lucas**
Letters: **Dave Sharpe**
Cover Art: **Cameron Stewart and Guru eFX**
Assistant Editor: **Nathan Cosby**
Editor: **Mark Paniccia**

Captain America created by **Joe Simon & Jack Kirby**

Collection Editor: **Jennifer Grünwald**
Assistant Editors: **Cory Levine & Michael Short**
Associate Editor: **Mark D. Beazley**
Senior Editor, Special Projects: **Jeff Youngquist**
Senior Vice President of Sales: **David Gabriel**
Production: **Jerron Quality Color**
Vice President of Creative: **Tom Marvelli**

Editor in Chief: **Joe Quesada**
Publisher: **Dan Buckley**

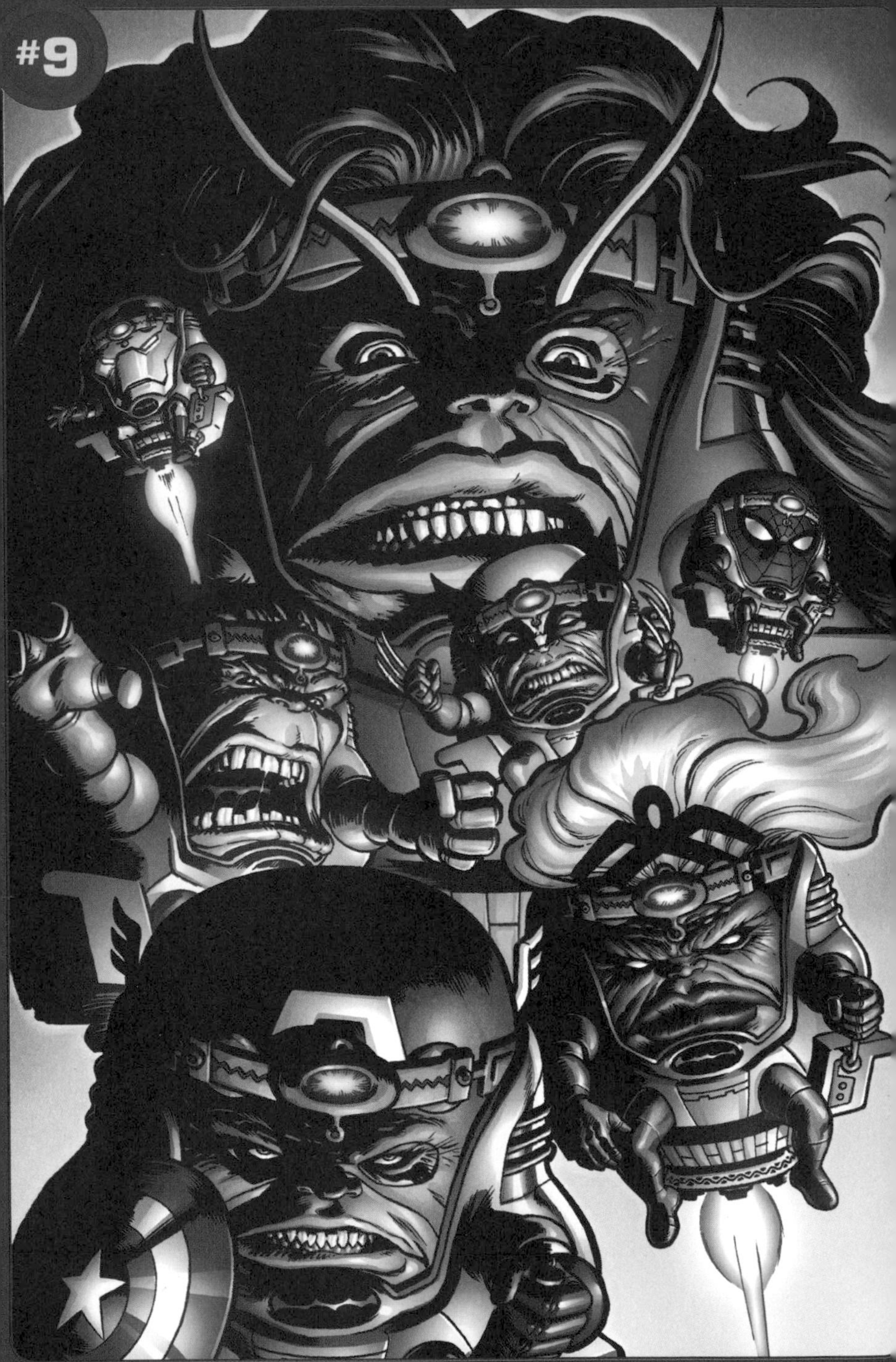
#9

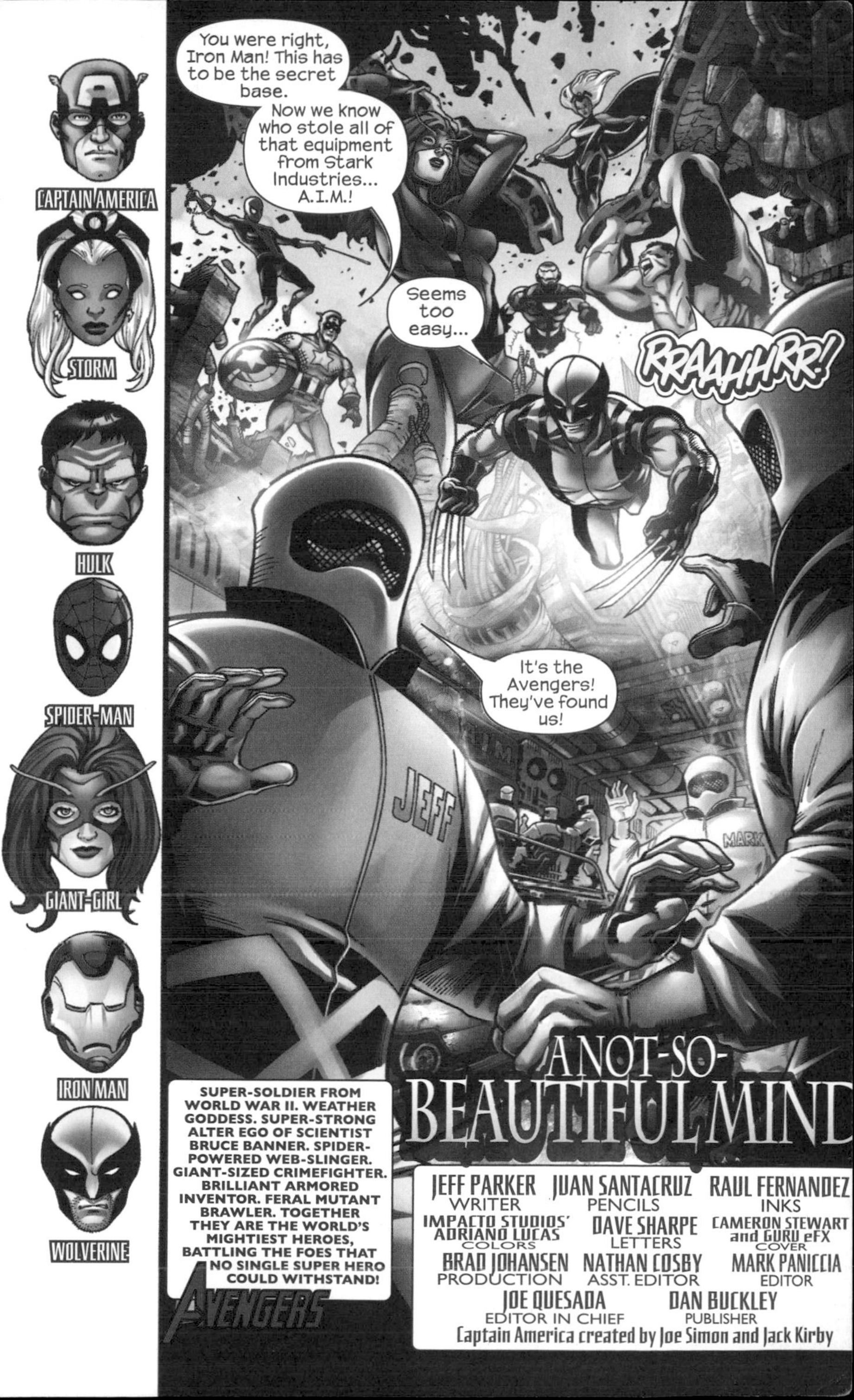
CAPTAIN AMERICA
STORM
HULK
SPIDER-MAN
GIANT-GIRL
IRON MAN
WOLVERINE
You were right, Iron Man! This has to be the secret base.
Now we know who stole all of that equipment from Stark Industries... A.I.M.!
Seems too easy...
RRAAHHRR!
It's the Avengers! They've found us!
JEFF
MARK
A NOT-SO-
BEAUTIFUL MIND
SUPER-SOLDIER FROM WORLD WAR II. WEATHER GODDESS. SUPER-STRONG ALTER EGO OF SCIENTIST BRUCE BANNER. SPIDER-POWERED WEB-SLINGER. GIANT-SIZED CRIMEFIGHTER. BRILLIANT ARMORED INVENTOR. FERAL MUTANT BRAWLER. TOGETHER THEY ARE THE WORLD'S MIGHTIEST HEROES, BATTLING THE FOES THAT NO SINGLE SUPER HERO COULD WITHSTAND!
AVENGERS
JEFF PARKER WRITER
JUAN SANTACRUZ PENCILS
RAUL FERNANDEZ INKS
IMPACTO STUDIOS' ADRIANO LUCAS COLORS
DAVE SHARPE LETTERS
CAMERON STEWART and GURU eFX COVER
BRAD JOHANSEN PRODUCTION
NATHAN COSBY ASST. EDITOR
MARK PANICCIA EDITOR
JOE QUESADA EDITOR IN CHIEF
DAN BUCKLEY PUBLISHER
Captain America created by Joe Simon and Jack Kirby

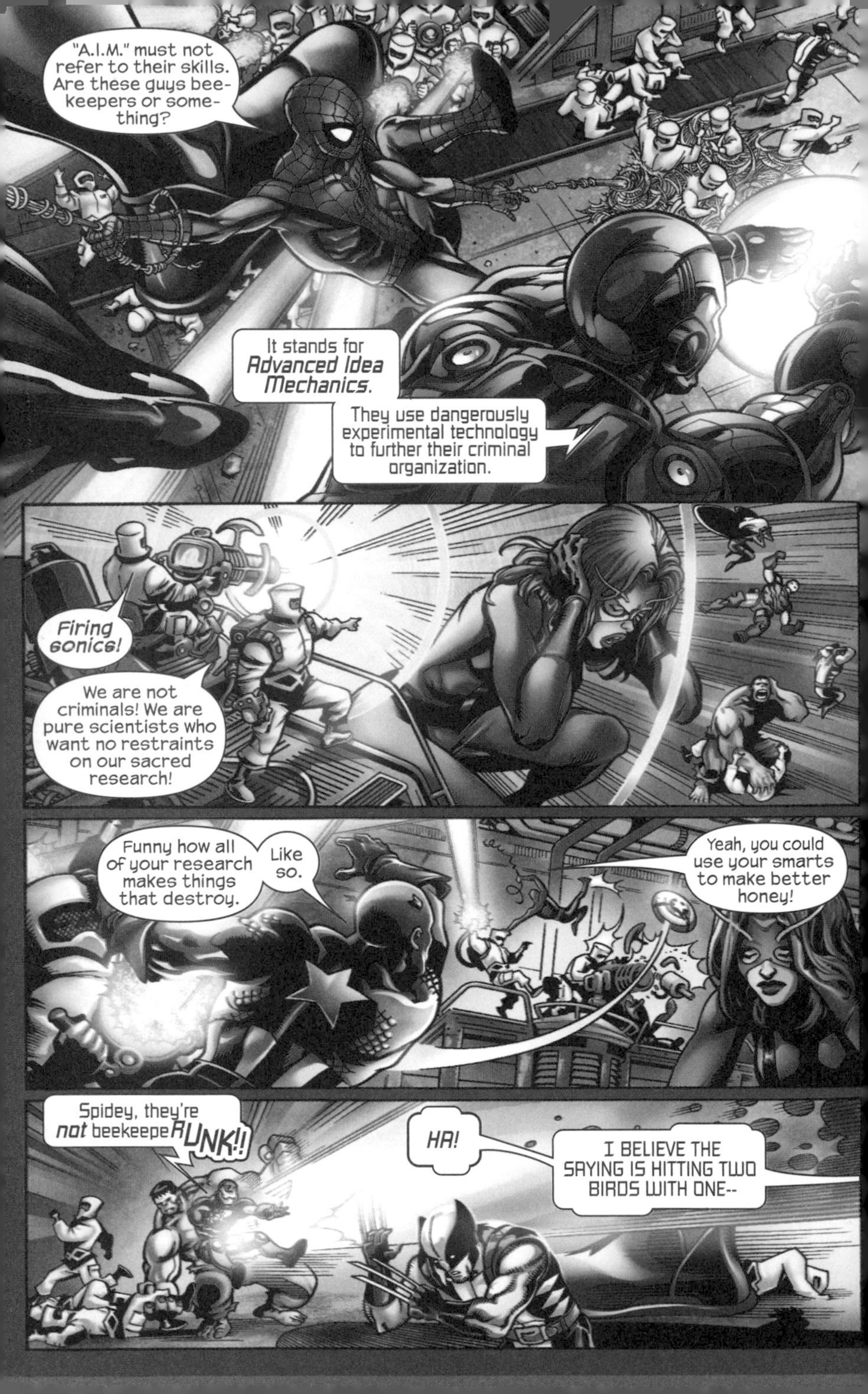
"A.I.M." must not refer to their skills. Are these guys bee-keepers or some-thing?
It stands for *Advanced Idea Mechanics.*
They use dangerously experimental technology to further their criminal organization.
Firing sonics!
We are not criminals! We are pure scientists who want no restraints on our sacred research!
Funny how all of your research makes things that destroy.
Like so.
Yeah, you could use your smarts to make better honey!
Spidey, they're *not* beekeepeRUNK!!
HA!
I BELIEVE THE SAYING IS HITTING TWO BIRDS WITH ONE--

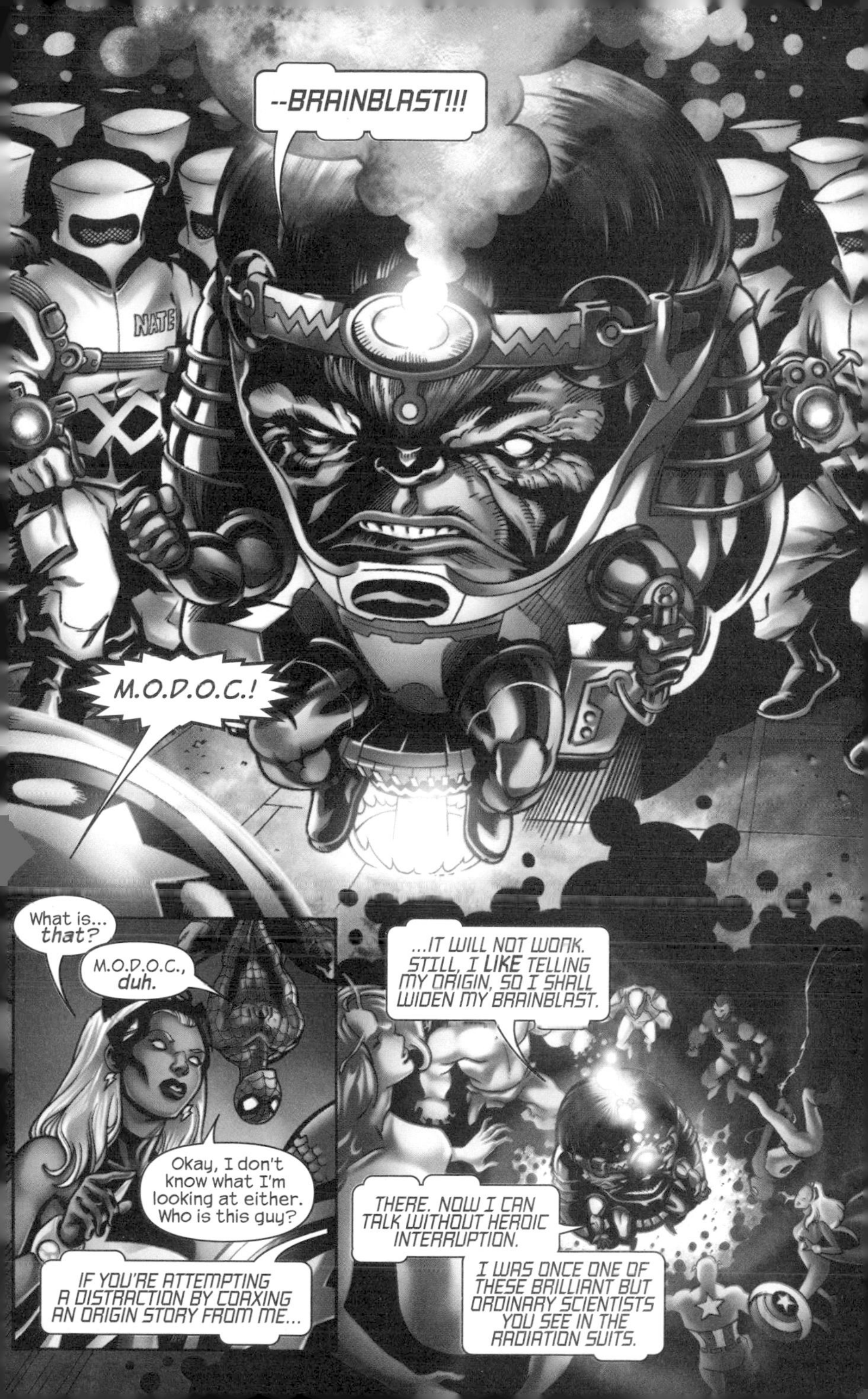
--BRAINBLAST!!!
NATE
M.O.D.O.C.!
What is... that?
M.O.D.O.C., duh.
Okay, I don't know what I'm looking at either. Who is this guy?
IF YOU'RE ATTEMPTING A DISTRACTION BY COAXING AN ORIGIN STORY FROM ME...
...IT WILL NOT WORK. STILL, I LIKE TELLING MY ORIGIN, SO I SHALL WIDEN MY BRAINBLAST.
THERE. NOW I CAN TALK WITHOUT HEROIC INTERRUPTION.
I WAS ONCE ONE OF THESE BRILLIANT BUT ORDINARY SCIENTISTS YOU SEE IN THE RADIATION SUITS.

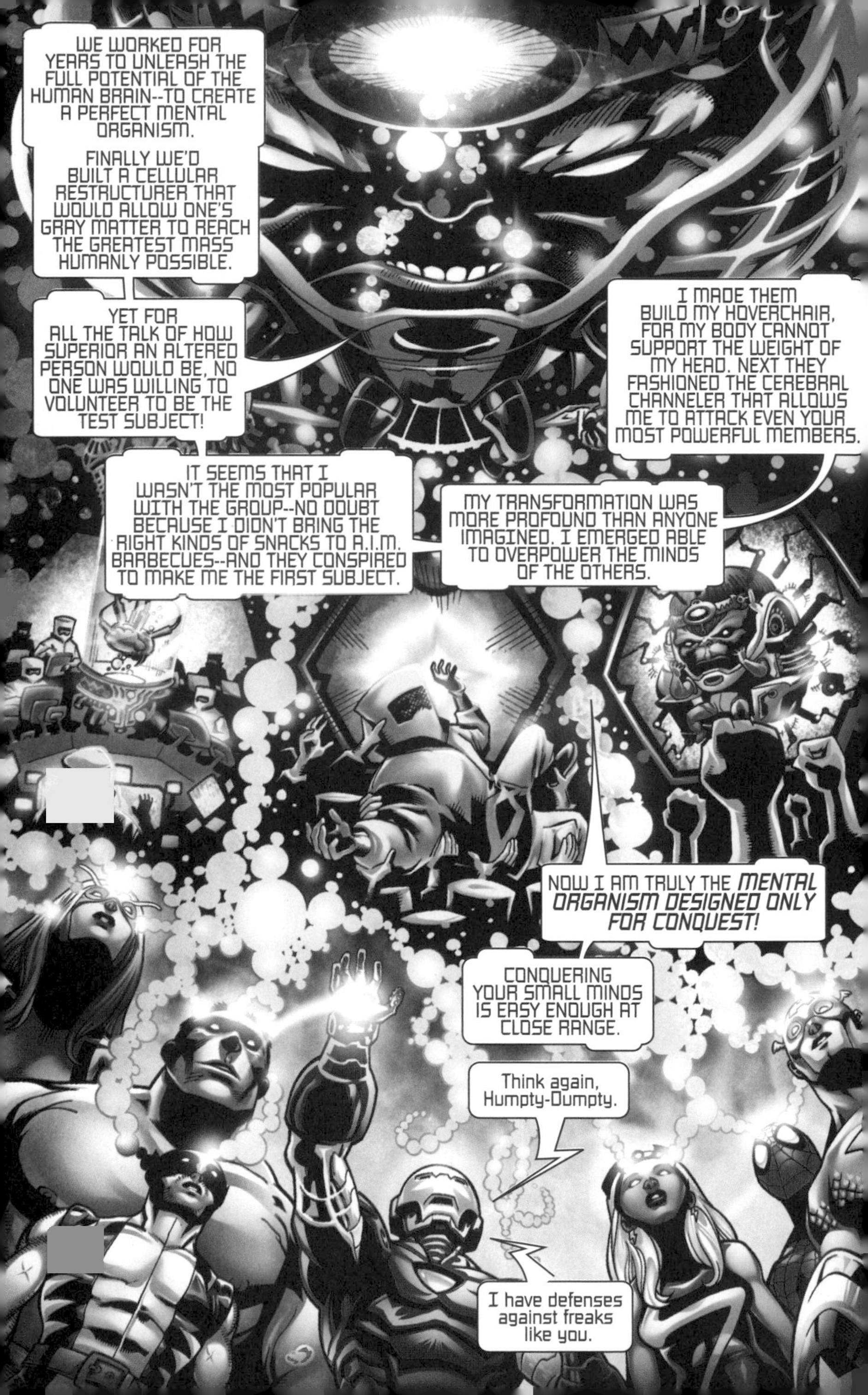
WE WORKED FOR YEARS TO UNLEASH THE FULL POTENTIAL OF THE HUMAN BRAIN--TO CREATE A PERFECT MENTAL ORGANISM.
FINALLY WE'D BUILT A CELLULAR RESTRUCTURER THAT WOULD ALLOW ONE'S GRAY MATTER TO REACH THE GREATEST MASS HUMANLY POSSIBLE.
YET FOR ALL THE TALK OF HOW SUPERIOR AN ALTERED PERSON WOULD BE, NO ONE WAS WILLING TO VOLUNTEER TO BE THE TEST SUBJECT!
IT SEEMS THAT I WASN'T THE MOST POPULAR WITH THE GROUP--NO DOUBT BECAUSE I DIDN'T BRING THE RIGHT KINDS OF SNACKS TO A.I.M. BARBECUES--AND THEY CONSPIRED TO MAKE ME THE FIRST SUBJECT.
MY TRANSFORMATION WAS MORE PROFOUND THAN ANYONE IMAGINED. I EMERGED ABLE TO OVERPOWER THE MINDS OF THE OTHERS.
I MADE THEM BUILD MY HOVERCHAIR, FOR MY BODY CANNOT SUPPORT THE WEIGHT OF MY HEAD. NEXT THEY FASHIONED THE CEREBRAL CHANNELER THAT ALLOWS ME TO ATTACK EVEN YOUR MOST POWERFUL MEMBERS.
NOW I AM TRULY THE MENTAL ORGANISM DESIGNED ONLY FOR CONQUEST!
CONQUERING YOUR SMALL MINDS IS EASY ENOUGH AT CLOSE RANGE.
Think again, Humpty-Dumpty.
I have defenses against freaks like you.

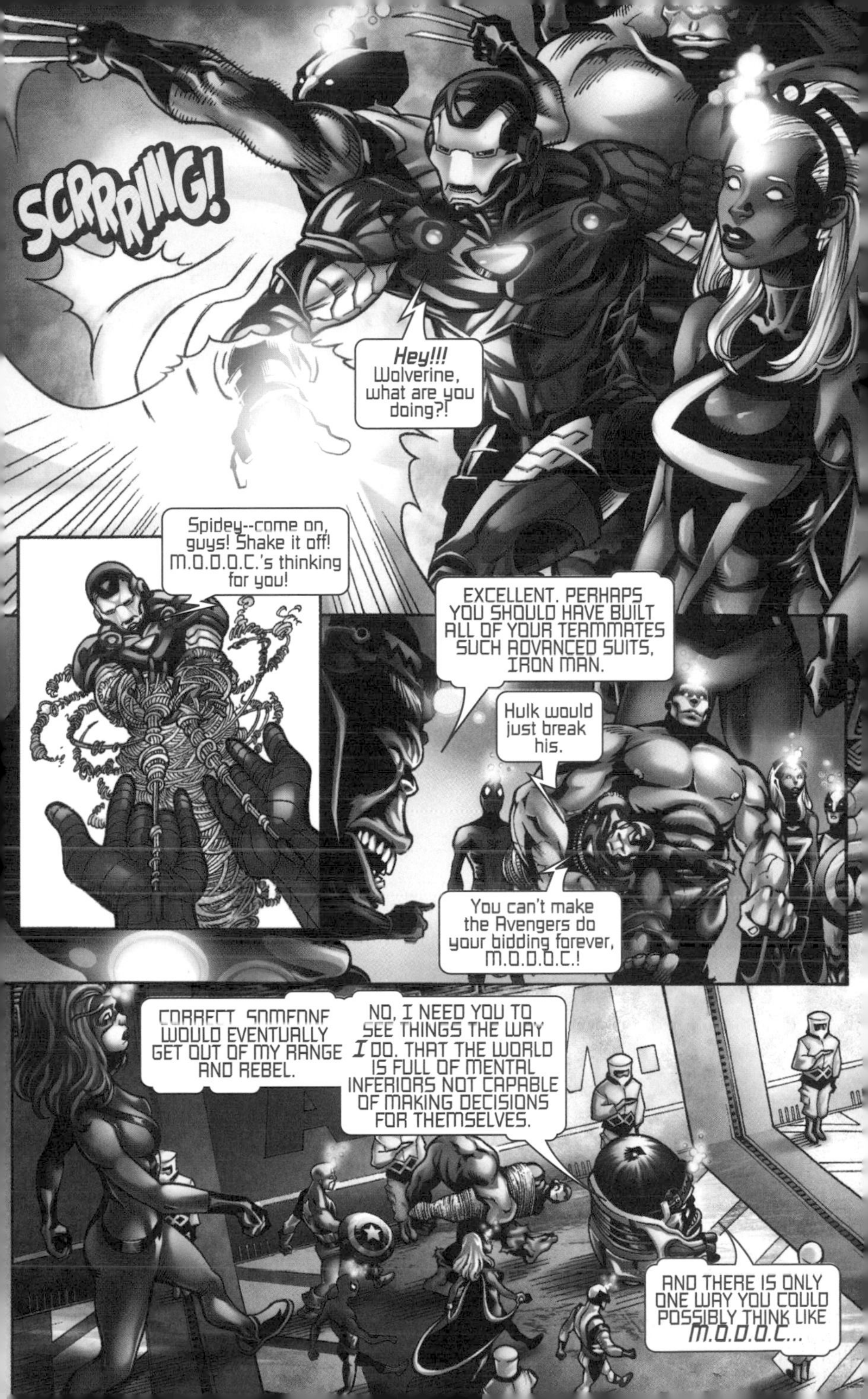
SCRRRING!
Hey!!! Wolverine, what are you doing?!
Spidey--come on, guys! Shake it off! M.O.D.O.C.'s thinking for you!
EXCELLENT. PERHAPS YOU SHOULD HAVE BUILT ALL OF YOUR TEAMMATES SUCH ADVANCED SUITS, IRON MAN.
Hulk would just break his.
You can't make the Avengers do your bidding forever, M.O.D.O.C.!
CORRECT. SOMEONE WOULD EVENTUALLY GET OUT OF MY RANGE AND REBEL.
NO, I NEED YOU TO SEE THINGS THE WAY I DO. THAT THE WORLD IS FULL OF MENTAL INFERIORS NOT CAPABLE OF MAKING DECISIONS FOR THEMSELVES.
AND THERE IS ONLY ONE WAY YOU COULD POSSIBLY THINK LIKE M.O.D.O.C...

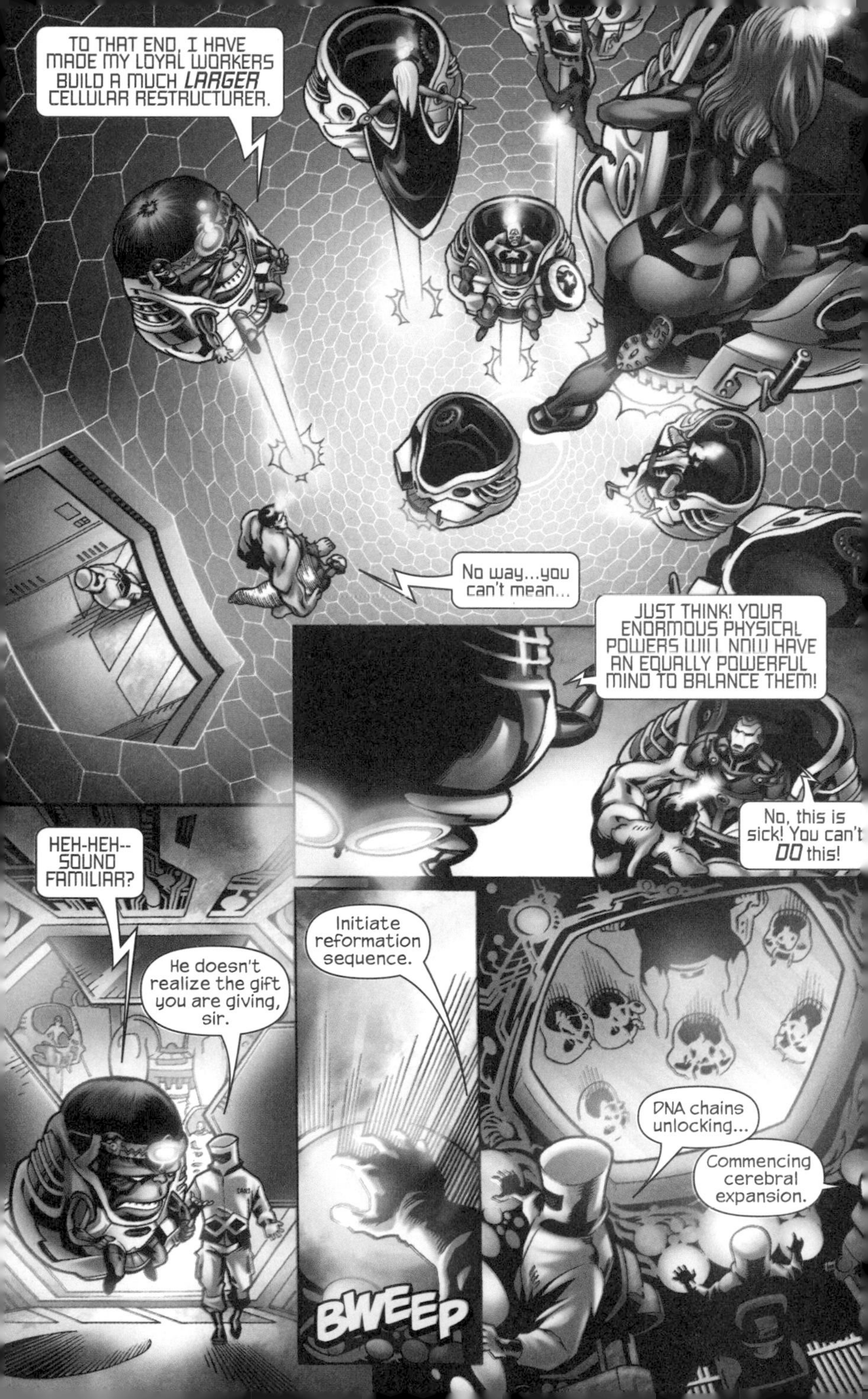
TO THAT END, I HAVE MADE MY LOYAL WORKERS BUILD A MUCH LARGER CELLULAR RESTRUCTURER.
No way...you can't mean...
JUST THINK! YOUR ENORMOUS PHYSICAL POWERS WILL NOW HAVE AN EQUALLY POWERFUL MIND TO BALANCE THEM!
No, this is sick! You can't DO this!
HEH-HEH-- SOUND FAMILIAR?
He doesn't realize the gift you are giving, sir.
Initiate reformation sequence.
BWEEP
DNA chains unlocking...
Commencing cerebral expansion.

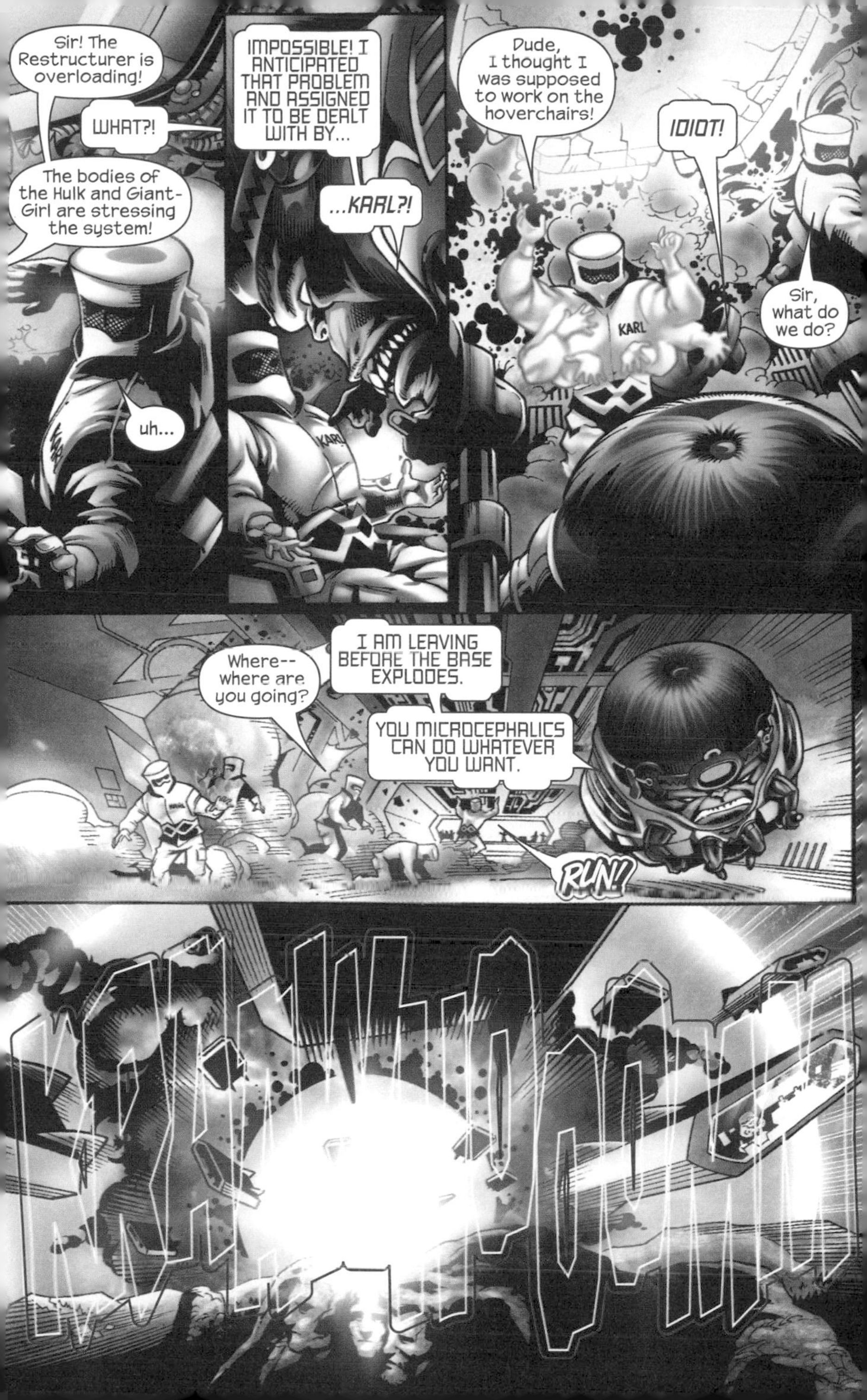
Sir! The Restructurer is overloading!
WHAT?!
The bodies of the Hulk and Giant-Girl are stressing the system!
uh...
IMPOSSIBLE! I ANTICIPATED THAT PROBLEM AND ASSIGNED IT TO BE DEALT WITH BY...
...KARL?!
Dude, I thought I was supposed to work on the hoverchairs!
IDIOT!
Sir, what do we do?
Where-- where are you going?
I AM LEAVING BEFORE THE BASE EXPLODES.
YOU MICROCEPHALICS CAN DO WHATEVER YOU WANT.
RUN!!

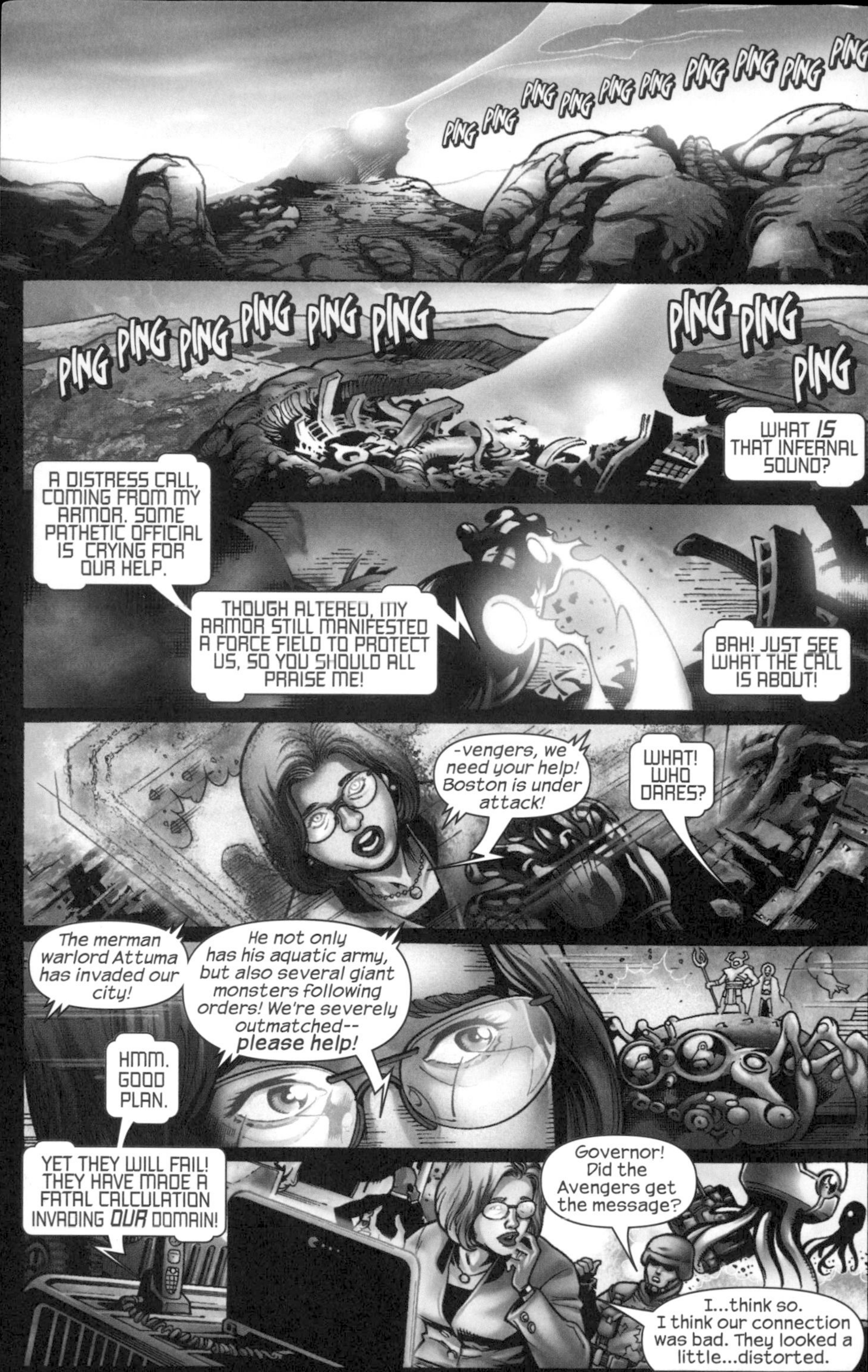
PING PING PING PING PING PING PING PING PING PING PING
PING PING PING PING PING PING
PING PING
PING
WHAT IS THAT INFERNAL SOUND?
A DISTRESS CALL, COMING FROM MY ARMOR. SOME PATHETIC OFFICIAL IS CRYING FOR OUR HELP.
THOUGH ALTERED, MY ARMOR STILL MANIFESTED A FORCE FIELD TO PROTECT US, SO YOU SHOULD ALL PRAISE ME!
BAH! JUST SEE WHAT THE CALL IS ABOUT!
-vengers, we need your help! Boston is under attack!
WHAT! WHO DARES?
The merman warlord Attuma has invaded our city!
He not only has his aquatic army, but also several giant monsters following orders! We're severely outmatched-- please help!
HMM. GOOD PLAN.
YET THEY WILL FAIL! THEY HAVE MADE A FATAL CALCULATION INVADING OUR DOMAIN!
Governor! Did the Avengers get the message?
I...think so. I think our connection was bad. They looked a little...distorted.

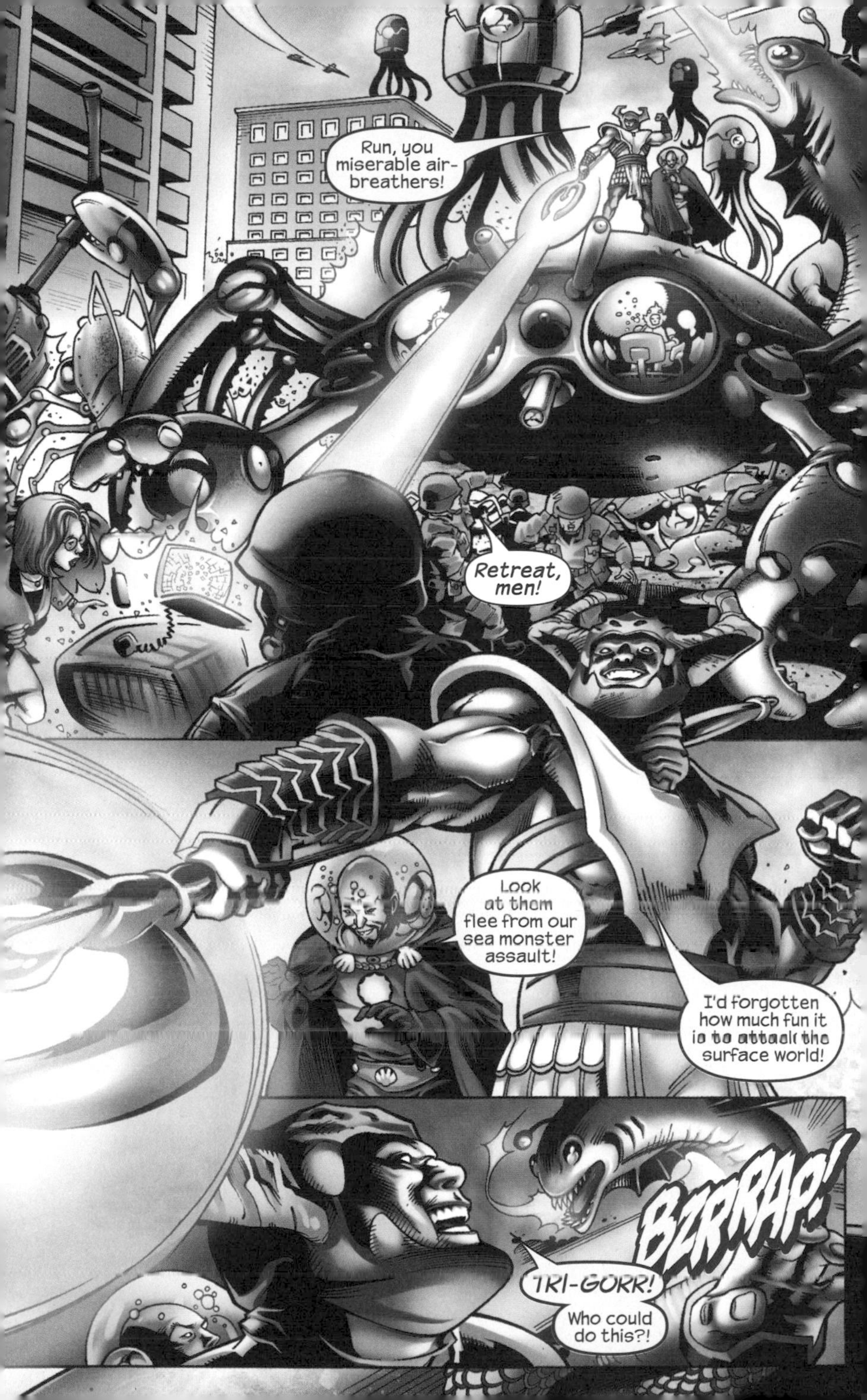
Run, you miserable air-breathers!
Retreat, men!
Look at them flee from our sea monster assault!
I'd forgotten how much fun it is to attack the surface world!
BZRRAP!
TRI-GORR!
Who could do this?!

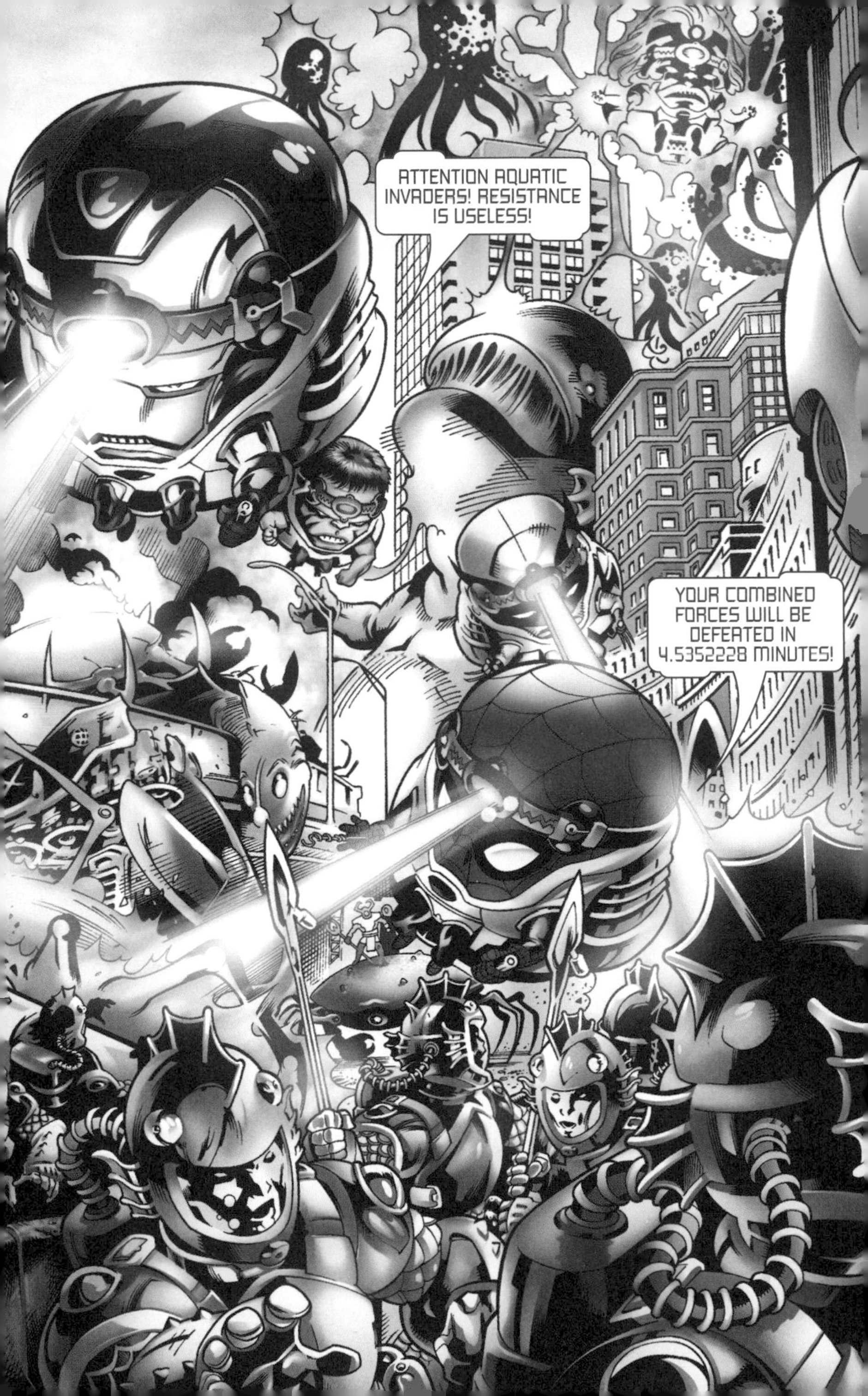
ATTENTION AQUATIC INVADERS! RESISTANCE IS USELESS!
YOUR COMBINED FORCES WILL BE DEFEATED IN 4.5352228 MINUTES!

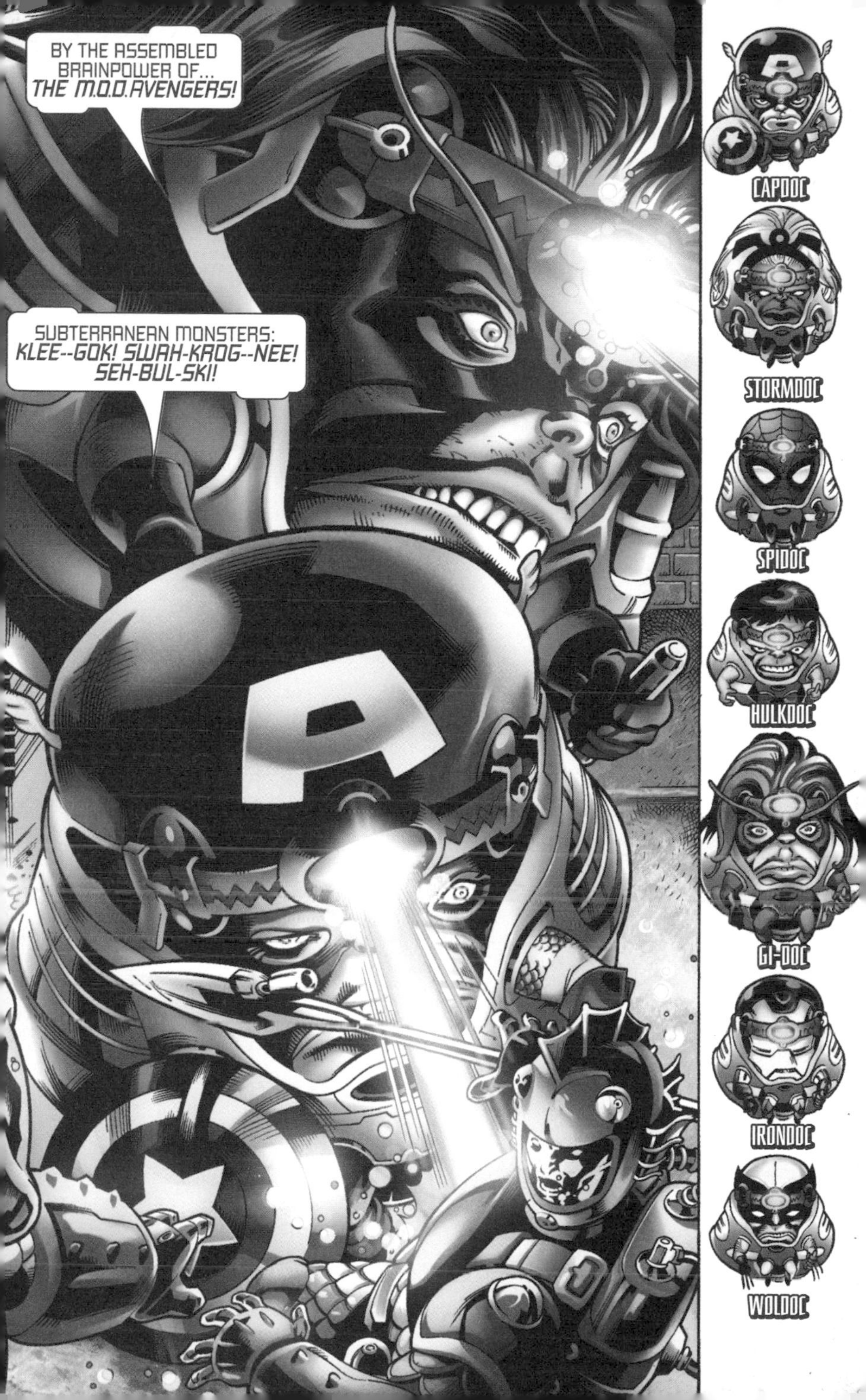
BY THE ASSEMBLED BRAINPOWER OF... THE M.O.D.AVENGERS!
SUBTERRANEAN MONSTERS: KLEE--GOK! SWAH-KROG--NEE! SEH-BUL-SKI!
CAPDOC
STORMDOC
SPIDOC
HULKDOC
GI-DOC
IRONDOC
WOLDOC

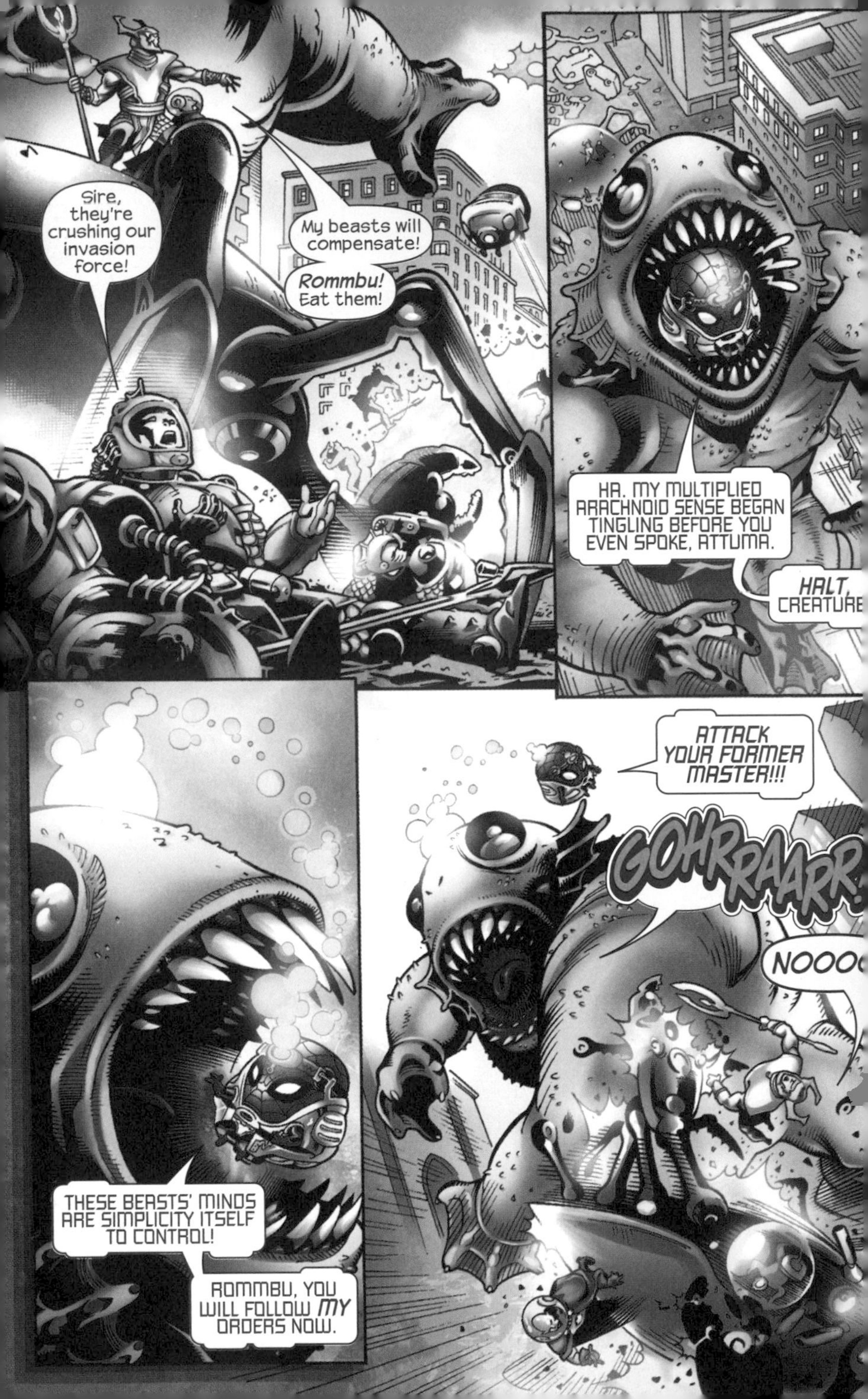
Sire, they're crushing our invasion force!
My beasts will compensate!
Rommbu! Eat them!
HA. MY MULTIPLIED ARACHNOID SENSE BEGAN TINGLING BEFORE YOU EVEN SPOKE, ATTUMA.
HALT, CREATURE
THESE BEASTS' MINDS ARE SIMPLICITY ITSELF TO CONTROL!
ROMMBU, YOU WILL FOLLOW MY ORDERS NOW.
ATTACK YOUR FORMER MASTER!!!
GOHRRAARR
NOOO

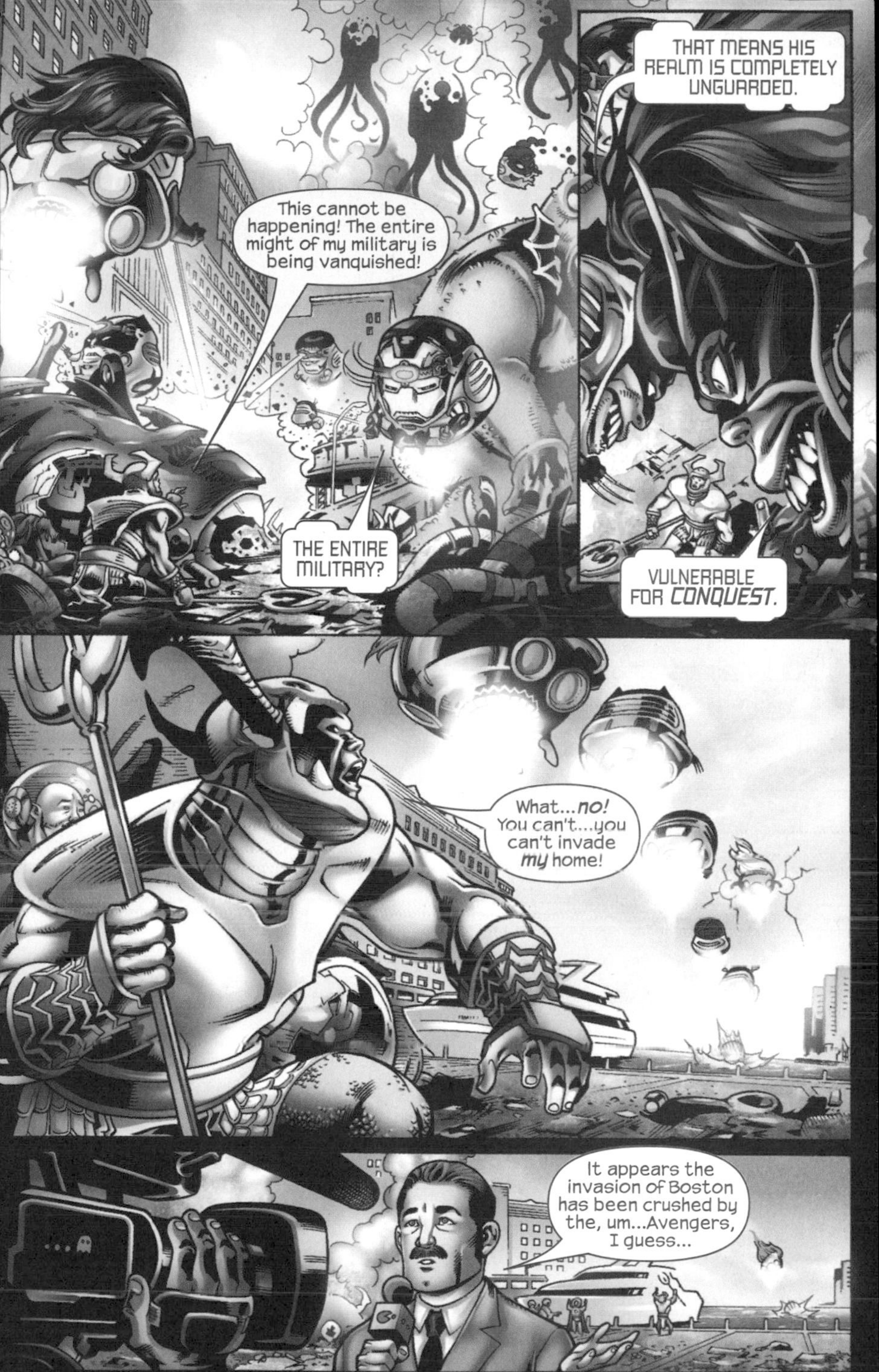
This cannot be happening! The entire might of my military is being vanquished!
THE ENTIRE MILITARY?
THAT MEANS HIS REALM IS COMPLETELY UNGUARDED.
VULNERABLE FOR *CONQUEST*.
What...*no!* You can't...you can't invade *my* home!
It appears the invasion of Boston has been crushed by the, um...Avengers, I guess...

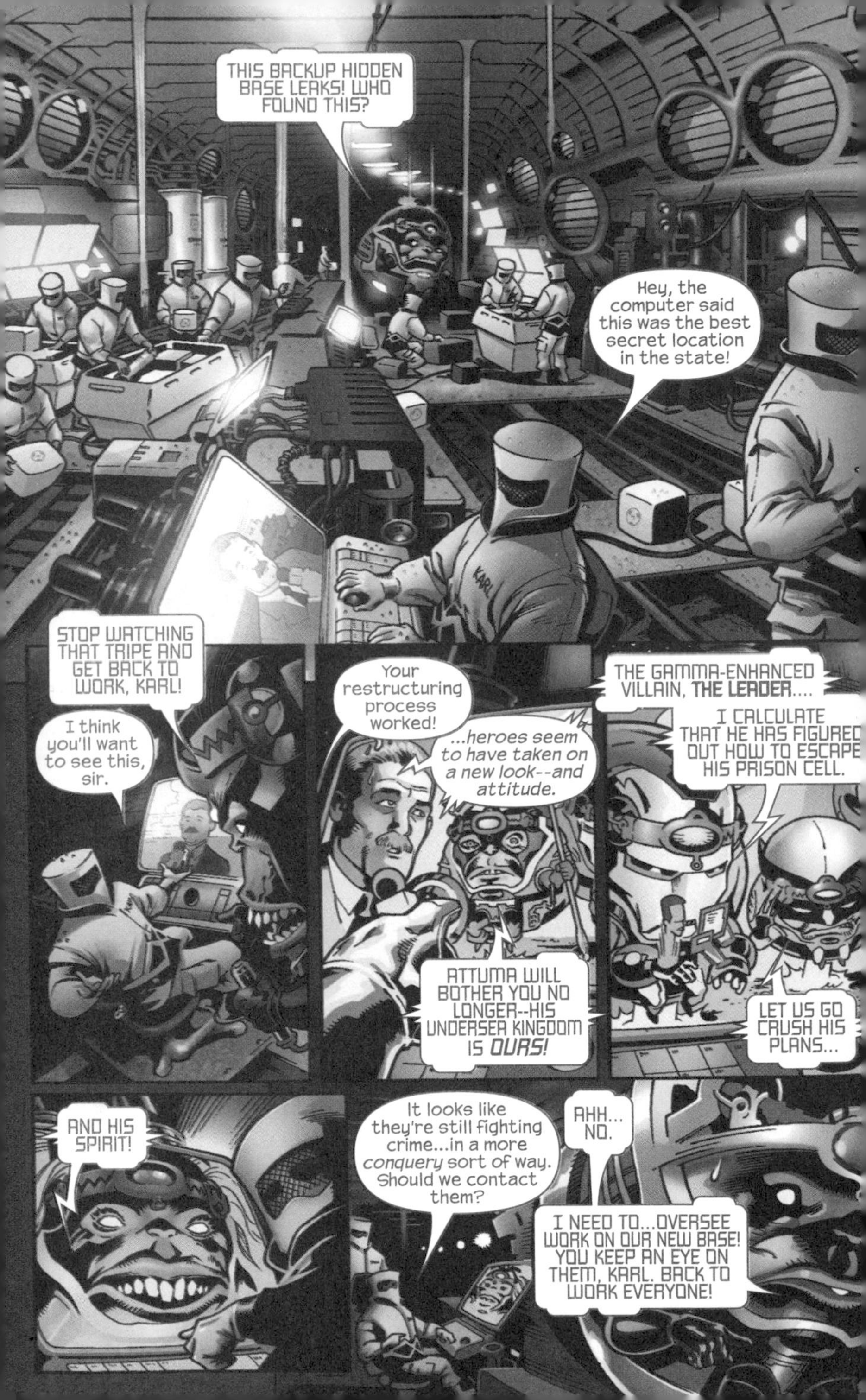
THIS BACKUP HIDDEN BASE LEAKS! WHO FOUND THIS?
Hey, the computer said this was the best secret location in the state!
KARL
STOP WATCHING THAT TRIPE AND GET BACK TO WORK, KARL!
I think you'll want to see this, sir.
Your restructuring process worked!
...heroes seem to have taken on a new look--and attitude.
ATTUMA WILL BOTHER YOU NO LONGER--HIS UNDERSEA KINGDOM IS OURS!
THE GAMMA-ENHANCED VILLAIN, THE LEADER....
I CALCULATE THAT HE HAS FIGURED OUT HOW TO ESCAPE HIS PRISON CELL.
LET US GO CRUSH HIS PLANS...
AND HIS SPIRIT!
It looks like they're still fighting crime...in a more conquery sort of way. Should we contact them?
AHH... NO.
I NEED TO...OVERSEE WORK ON OUR NEW BASE! YOU KEEP AN EYE ON THEM, KARL. BACK TO WORK EVERYONE!

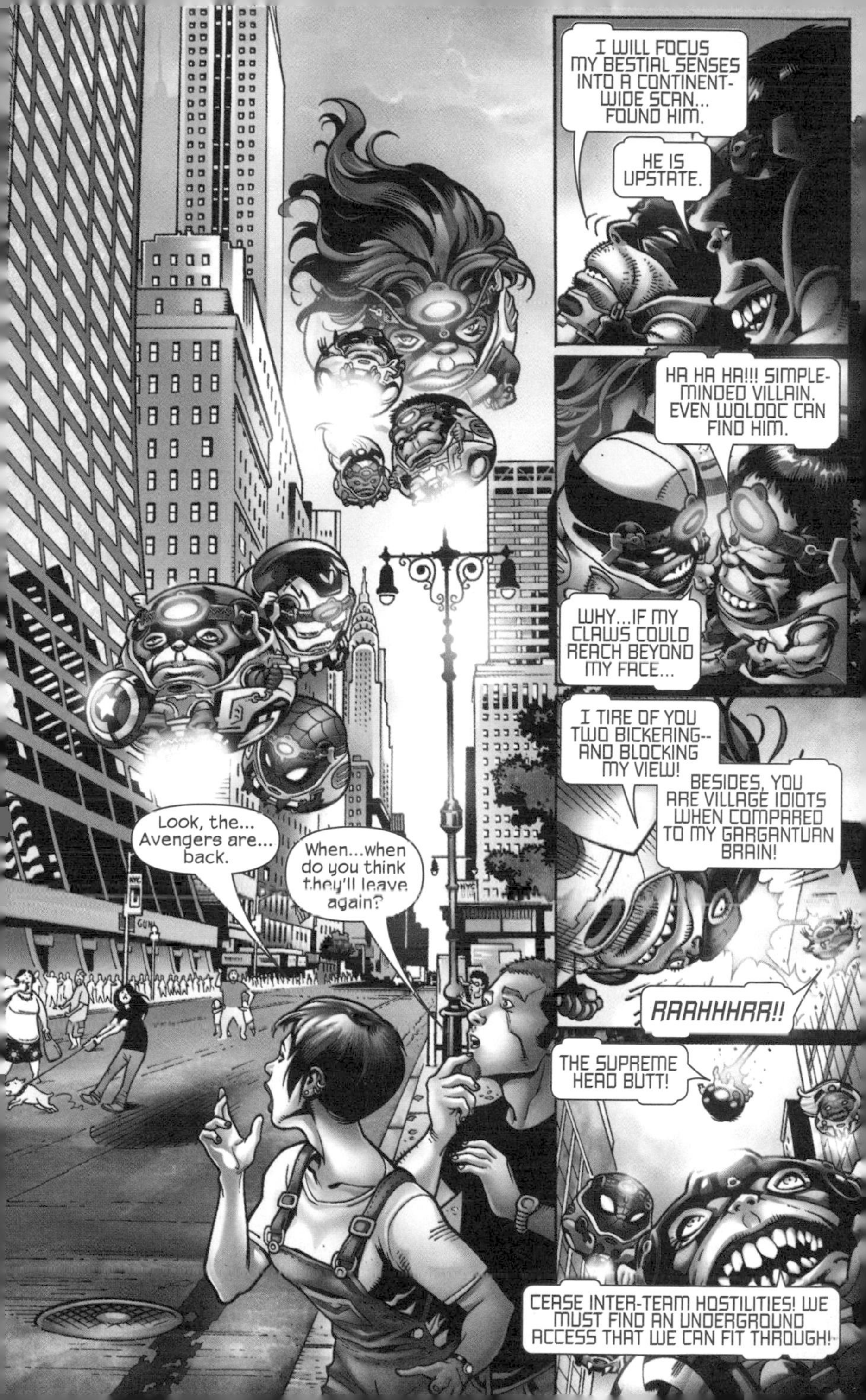
Look, the... Avengers are... back.
When...when do you think they'll leave again?
I WILL FOCUS MY BESTIAL SENSES INTO A CONTINENT-WIDE SCAN... FOUND HIM.
HE IS UPSTATE.
HA HA HA!!! SIMPLE-MINDED VILLAIN. EVEN WOLDOC CAN FIND HIM.
WHY...IF MY CLAWS COULD REACH BEYOND MY FACE...
I TIRE OF YOU TWO BICKERING-- AND BLOCKING MY VIEW!
BESIDES, YOU ARE VILLAGE IDIOTS WHEN COMPARED TO MY GARGANTUAN BRAIN!
RAAHHHAR!!
THE SUPREME HEAD BUTT!
CEASE INTER-TEAM HOSTILITIES! WE MUST FIND AN UNDERGROUND ACCESS THAT WE CAN FIT THROUGH!

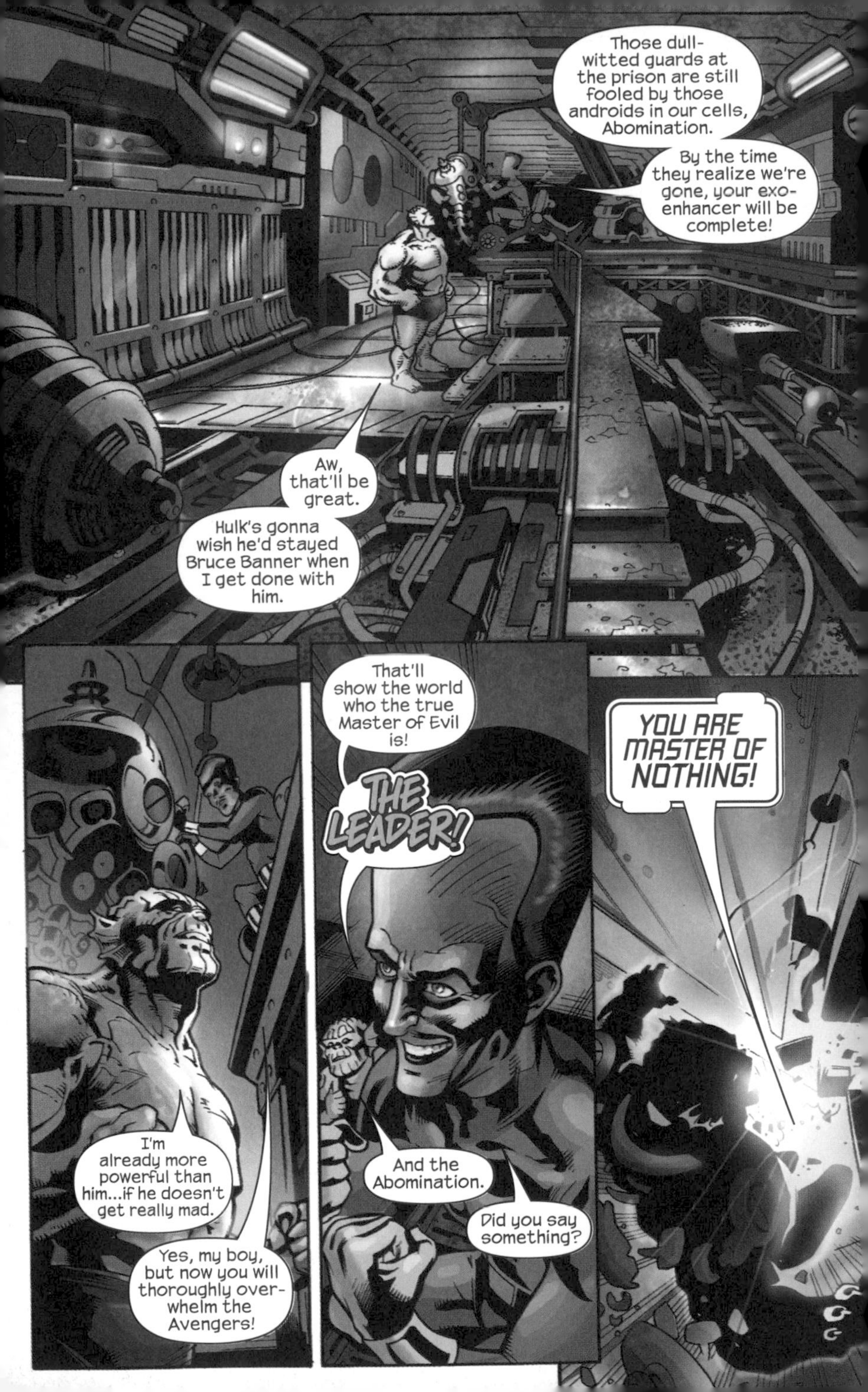
Those dull-witted guards at the prison are still fooled by those androids in our cells, Abomination.
By the time they realize we're gone, your exo-enhancer will be complete!
Aw, that'll be great.
Hulk's gonna wish he'd stayed Bruce Banner when I get done with him.
I'm already more powerful than him...if he doesn't get really mad.
Yes, my boy, but now you will thoroughly over-whelm the Avengers!
That'll show the world who the true Master of Evil is!
THE LEADER!
And the Abomination.
Did you say something?
YOU ARE MASTER OF NOTHING!

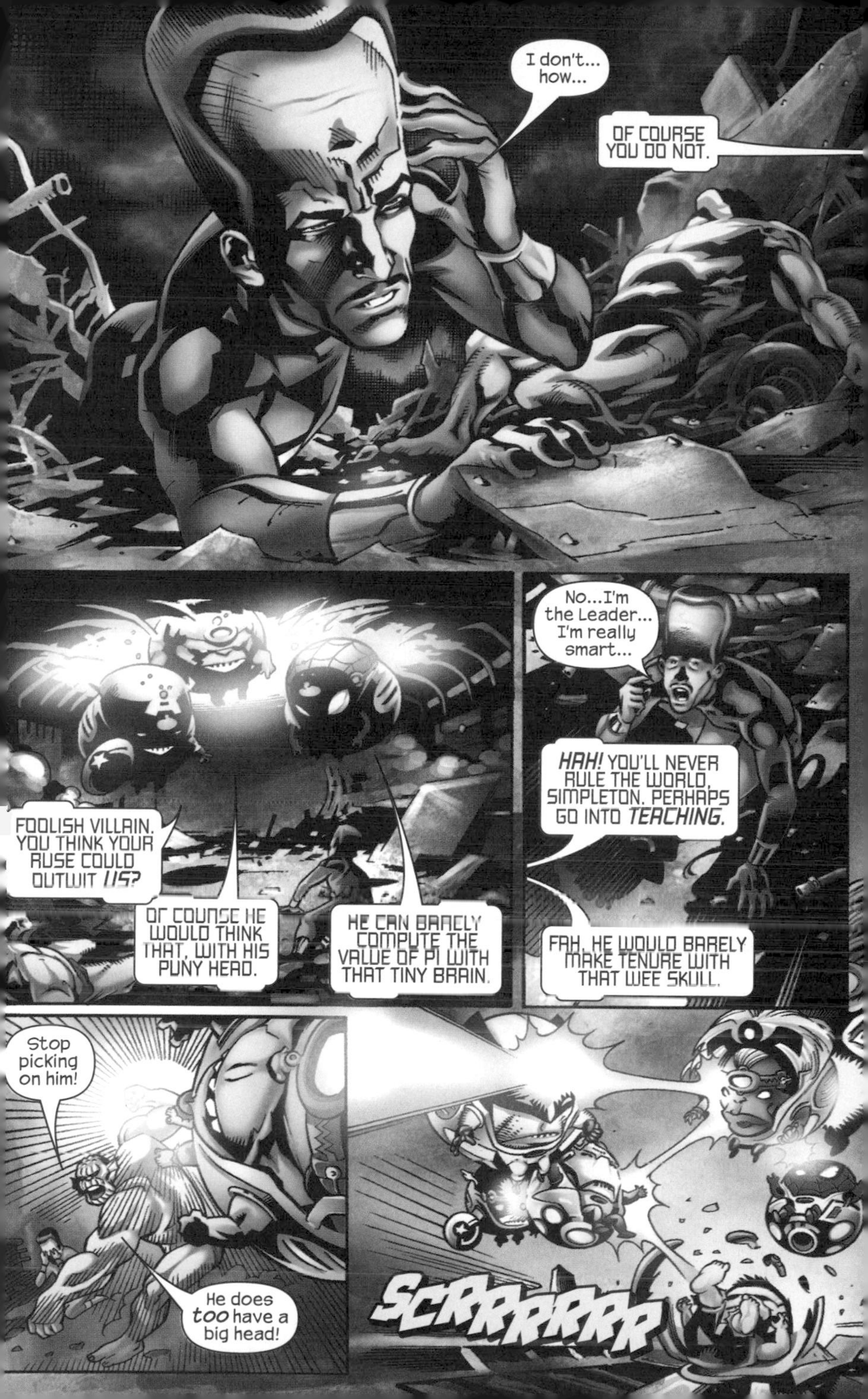
I don't... how...
OF COURSE YOU DO NOT.
FOOLISH VILLAIN. YOU THINK YOUR RUSE COULD OUTWIT *US?*
OF COURSE HE WOULD THINK THAT, WITH HIS PUNY HEAD.
HE CAN BARELY COMPUTE THE VALUE OF PI WITH THAT TINY BRAIN.
No...I'm the Leader... I'm really smart...
HAH! YOU'LL NEVER RULE THE WORLD, SIMPLETON. PERHAPS GO INTO *TEACHING*.
FAH. HE WOULD BARELY MAKE TENURE WITH THAT WEE SKULL.
Stop picking on him!
He does *too* have a big head!
SCRRRRRRR

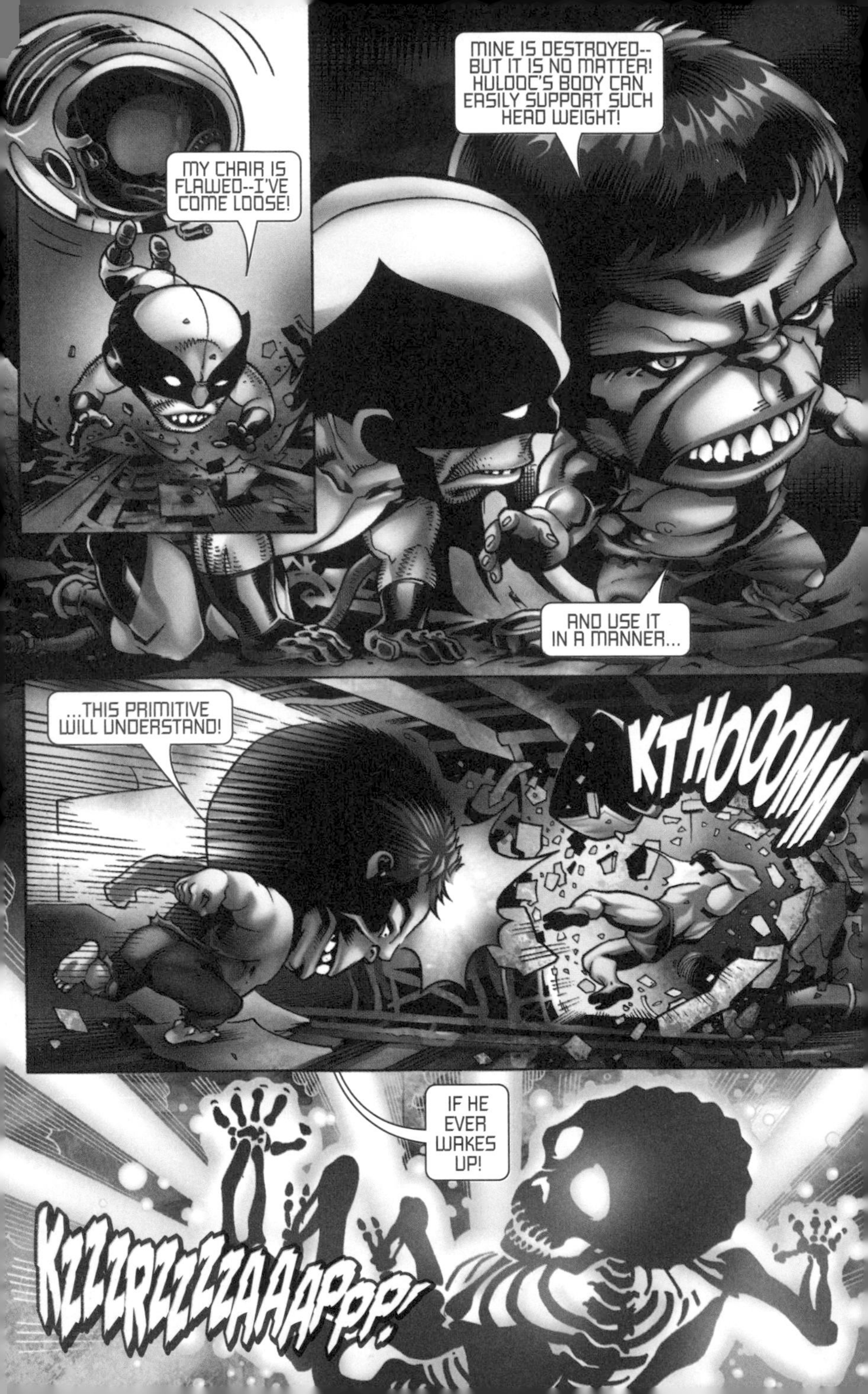

MY CHAIR IS FLAWED--I'VE COME LOOSE!
MINE IS DESTROYED-- BUT IT IS NO MATTER! HULDOC'S BODY CAN EASILY SUPPORT SUCH HEAD WEIGHT!
AND USE IT IN A MANNER...
...THIS PRIMITIVE WILL UNDERSTAND!
KTHOOOMM
IF HE EVER WAKES UP!
KZZZRZZZZAAAPPP!

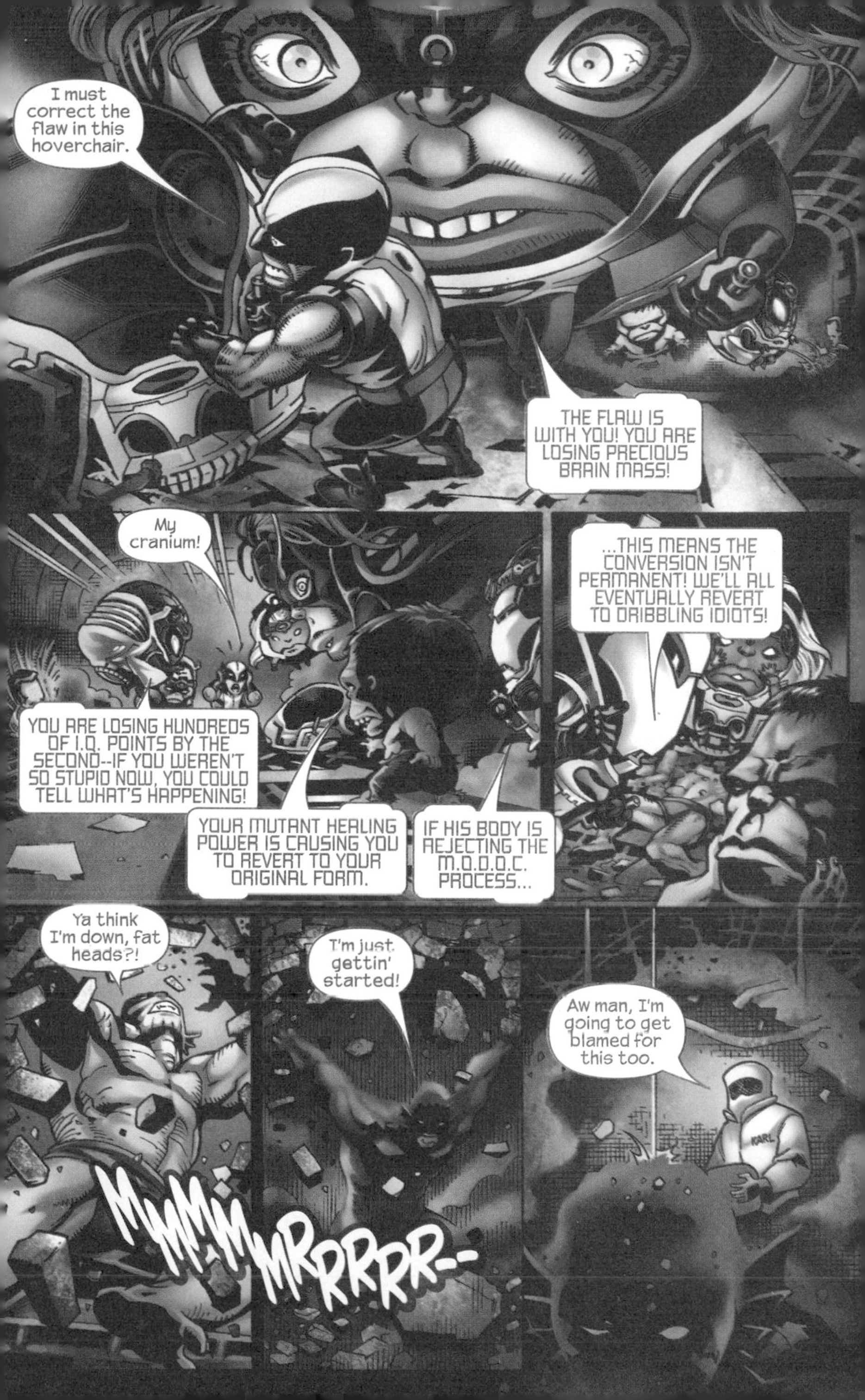
I must correct the flaw in this hoverchair.
THE FLAW IS WITH YOU! YOU ARE LOSING PRECIOUS BRAIN MASS!
My cranium!
YOU ARE LOSING HUNDREDS OF I.Q. POINTS BY THE SECOND--IF YOU WEREN'T SO STUPID NOW, YOU COULD TELL WHAT'S HAPPENING!
YOUR MUTANT HEALING POWER IS CAUSING YOU TO REVERT TO YOUR ORIGINAL FORM.
IF HIS BODY IS REJECTING THE M.O.D.O.C. PROCESS...
...THIS MEANS THE CONVERSION ISN'T PERMANENT! WE'LL ALL EVENTUALLY REVERT TO DRIBBLING IDIOTS!
Ya think I'm down, fat heads?!
I'm just gettin' started!
MMMMMRRRRR--
Aw man, I'm going to get blamed for this too.
KARL

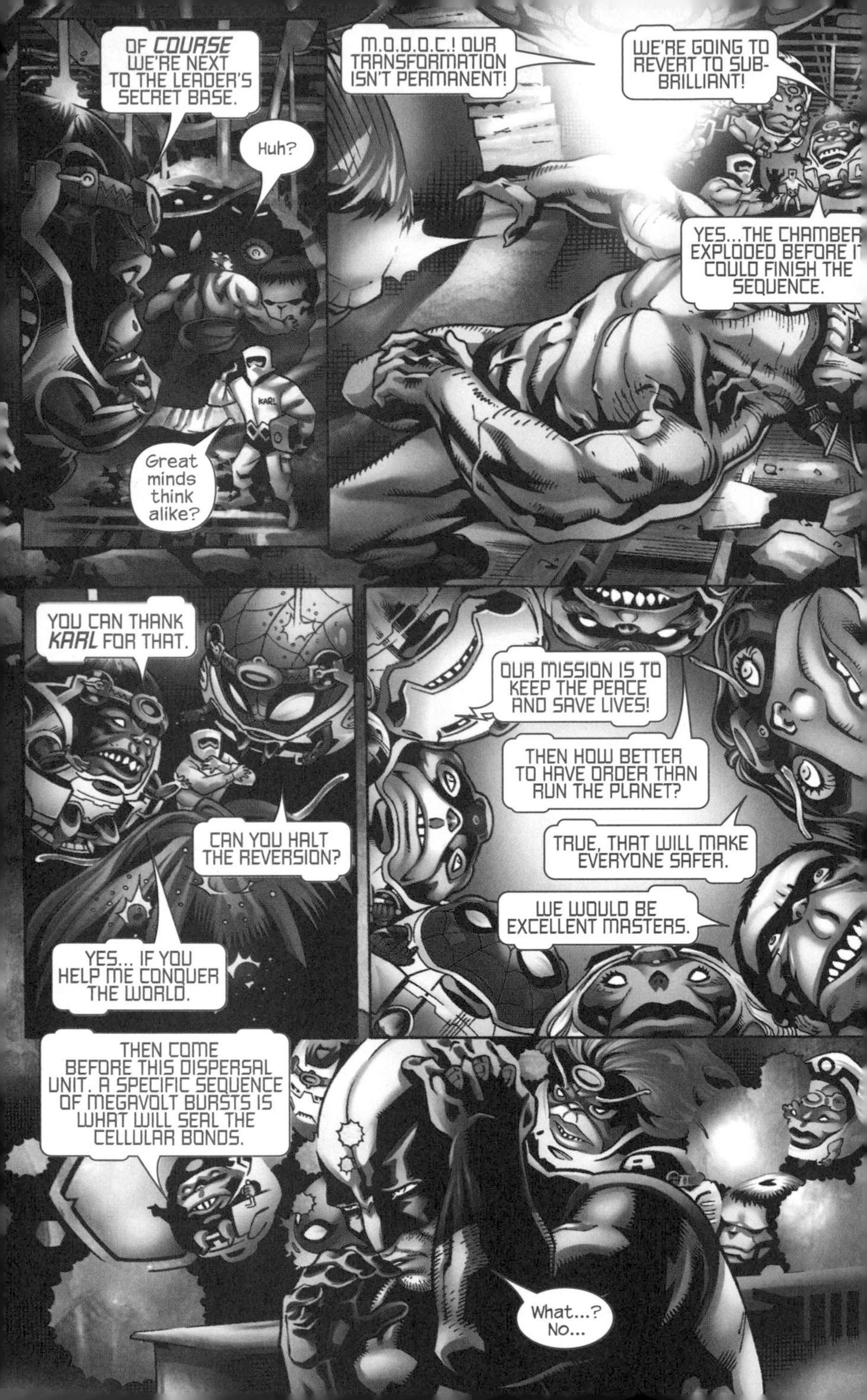
OF COURSE WE'RE NEXT TO THE LEADER'S SECRET BASE.
Huh?
Great minds think alike?
M.O.D.O.C.! OUR TRANSFORMATION ISN'T PERMANENT!
WE'RE GOING TO REVERT TO SUB-BRILLIANT!
YES...THE CHAMBER EXPLODED BEFORE IT COULD FINISH THE SEQUENCE.
YOU CAN THANK KARL FOR THAT.
CAN YOU HALT THE REVERSION?
YES... IF YOU HELP ME CONQUER THE WORLD.
OUR MISSION IS TO KEEP THE PEACE AND SAVE LIVES!
THEN HOW BETTER TO HAVE ORDER THAN RUN THE PLANET?
TRUE, THAT WILL MAKE EVERYONE SAFER.
WE WOULD BE EXCELLENT MASTERS.
THEN COME BEFORE THIS DISPERSAL UNIT. A SPECIFIC SEQUENCE OF MEGAVOLT BURSTS IS WHAT WILL SEAL THE CELLULAR BONDS.
What...? No...

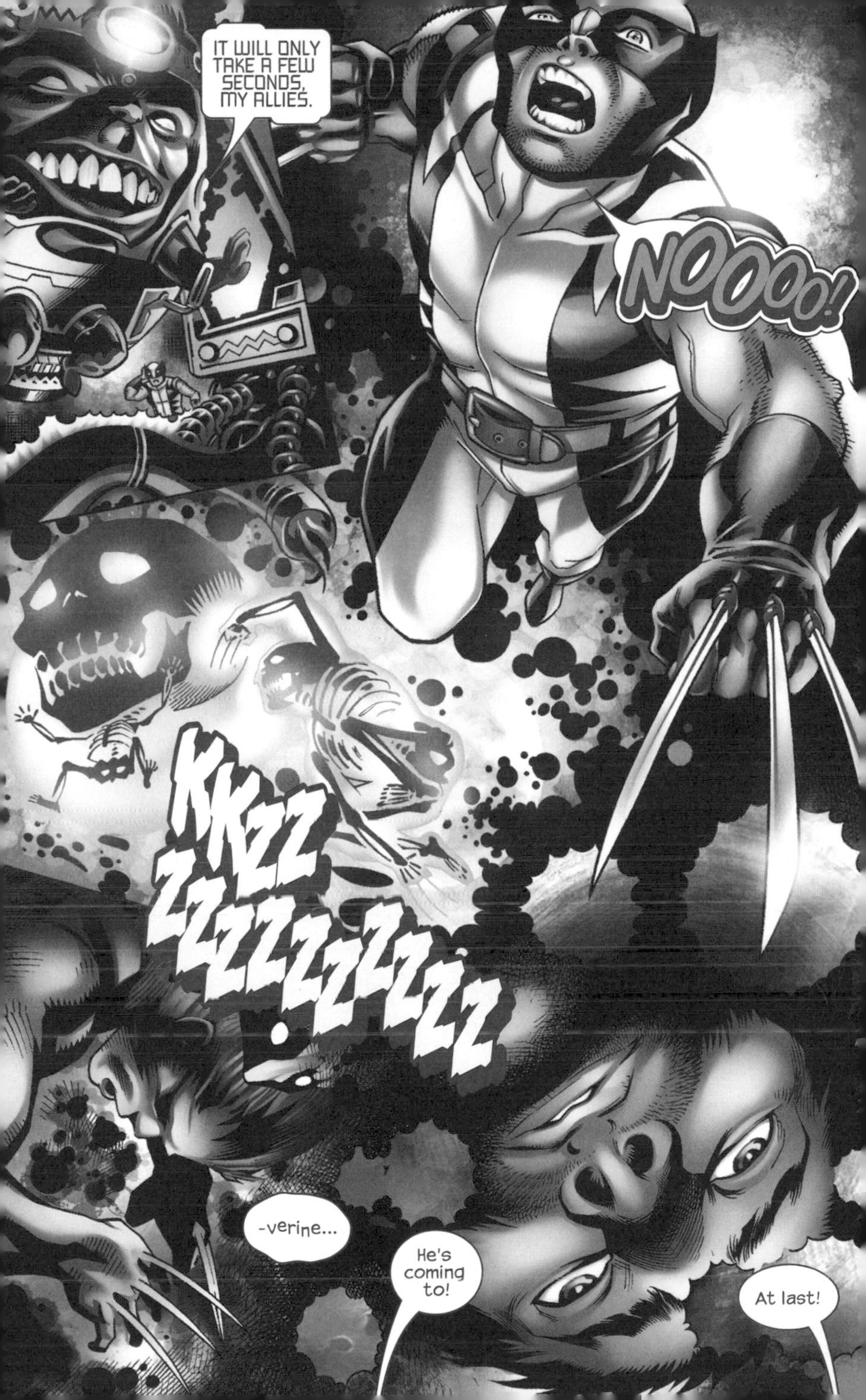
IT WILL ONLY TAKE A FEW SECONDS, MY ALLIES.
NOOOO!
KKZZZZZZZZZZZZ
-verine...
He's coming to!
At last!

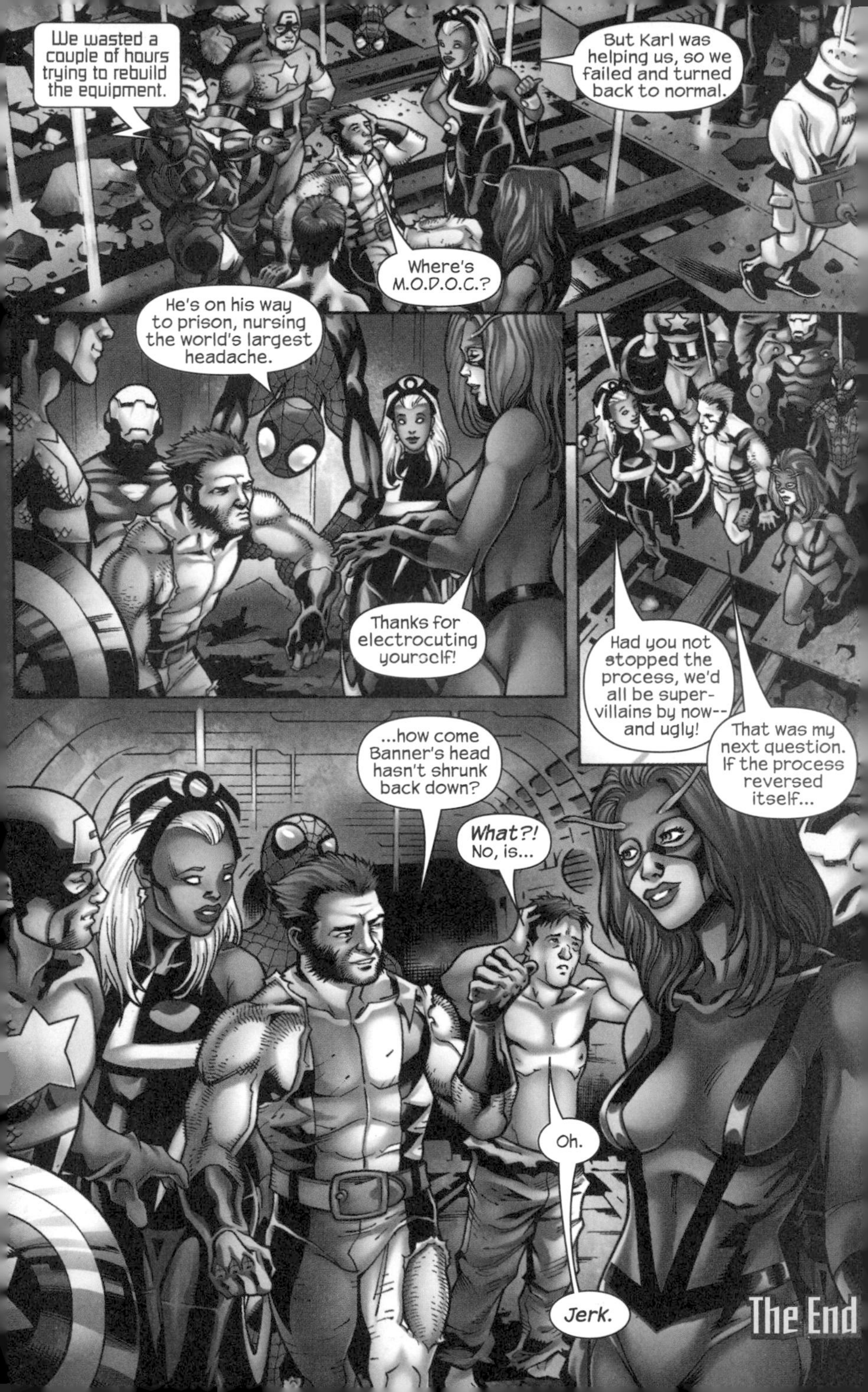
We wasted a couple of hours trying to rebuild the equipment.
But Karl was helping us, so we failed and turned back to normal.
Where's M.O.D.O.C.?
He's on his way to prison, nursing the world's largest headache.
Thanks for electrocuting yourself!
Had you not stopped the process, we'd all be super-villains by now-- and ugly!
That was my next question. If the process reversed itself...
...how come Banner's head hasn't shrunk back down?
What?! No, is...
Oh.
Jerk.
The End

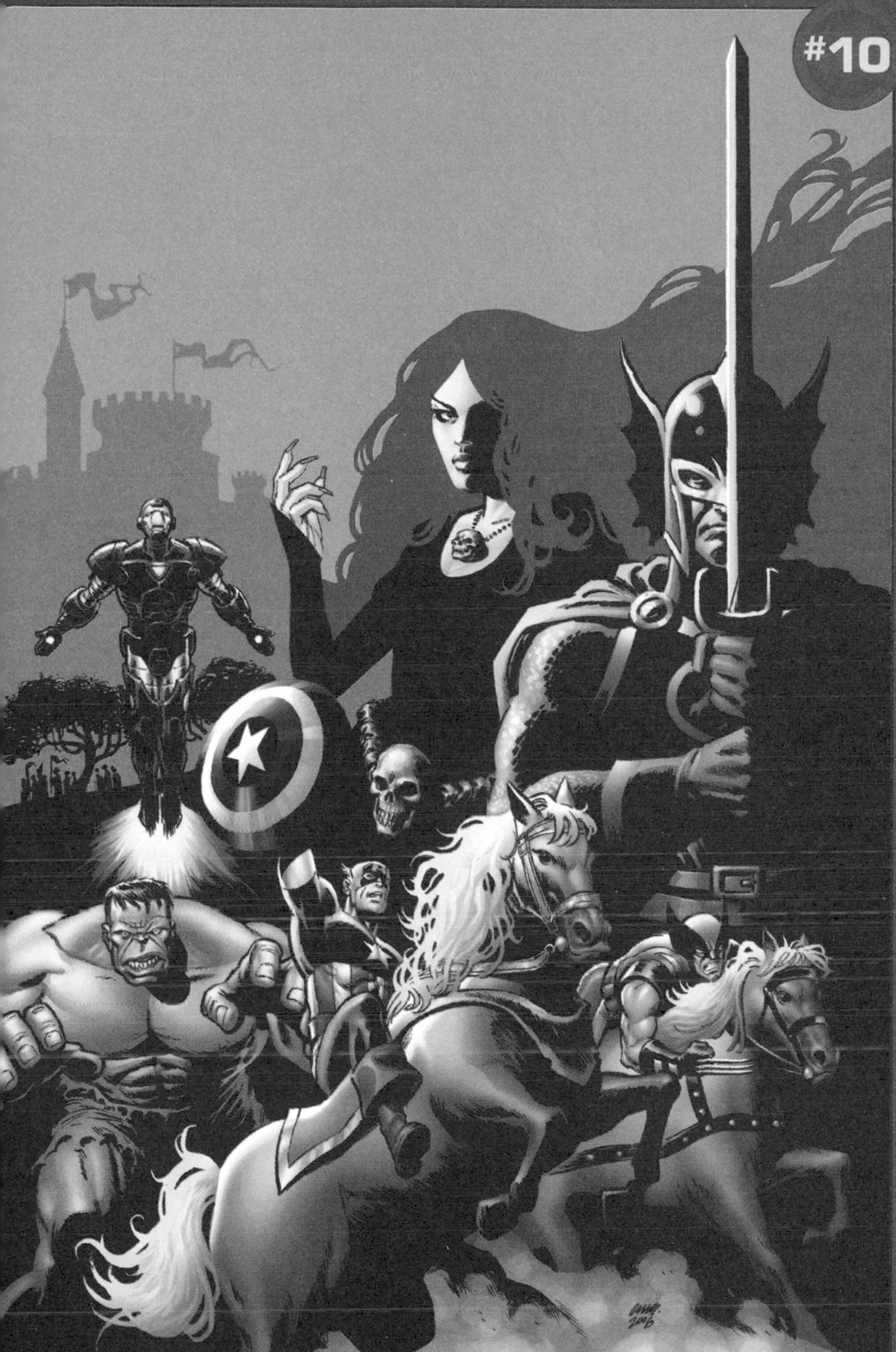
#10

CAPTAIN AMERICA

STORM

HULK

SPIDER-MAN

GIANT-GIRL

IRON MAN

WOLVERINE

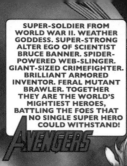

SUPER-SOLDIER FROM WORLD WAR II. WEATHER GODDESS. SUPER-STRONG ALTER EGO OF SCIENTIST BRUCE BANNER. SPIDER-POWERED WEB-SLINGER. GIANT-SIZED CRIMEFIGHTER. BRILLIANT ARMORED INVENTOR. FERAL MUTANT BRAWLER. TOGETHER THEY ARE THE WORLD'S MIGHTIEST HEROES, BATTLING THE FOES THAT NO SINGLE SUPER HERO COULD WITHSTAND!

AVENGERS

The Black Knight has unseated the Red Knight! The Avengers are slaves within the realm of Avalon forever!

Harken, ye seekers of adventure! 'Twas at the greatest tournament in two worlds did this battle take place! On that day did four mighty heroes face a most ancient and beautiful evil!

MEDIEVAL WOMEN

JEFF PARKER
SCRIBE

JUAN SANTACRUZ
KNIGHT

RAUL FERNANDEZ
SQUIRE OF INK

IMPACTO STUDIOS'
ADRIANO LUCAS
COLORS

DAVE SHARPE
SCRIVENER

CAMERON STEWART
and GURU eFX
COVER MAGES

BRAD JOHANSEN
BLACKSMITH

NATHAN COSBY
KNAVE

MARK PANICCIA
WIZARD

JOE QUESADA
WIZARD SUPREME

DAN BUCKLEY
KING

Captain America created by Joe Simon and Jack Kirby

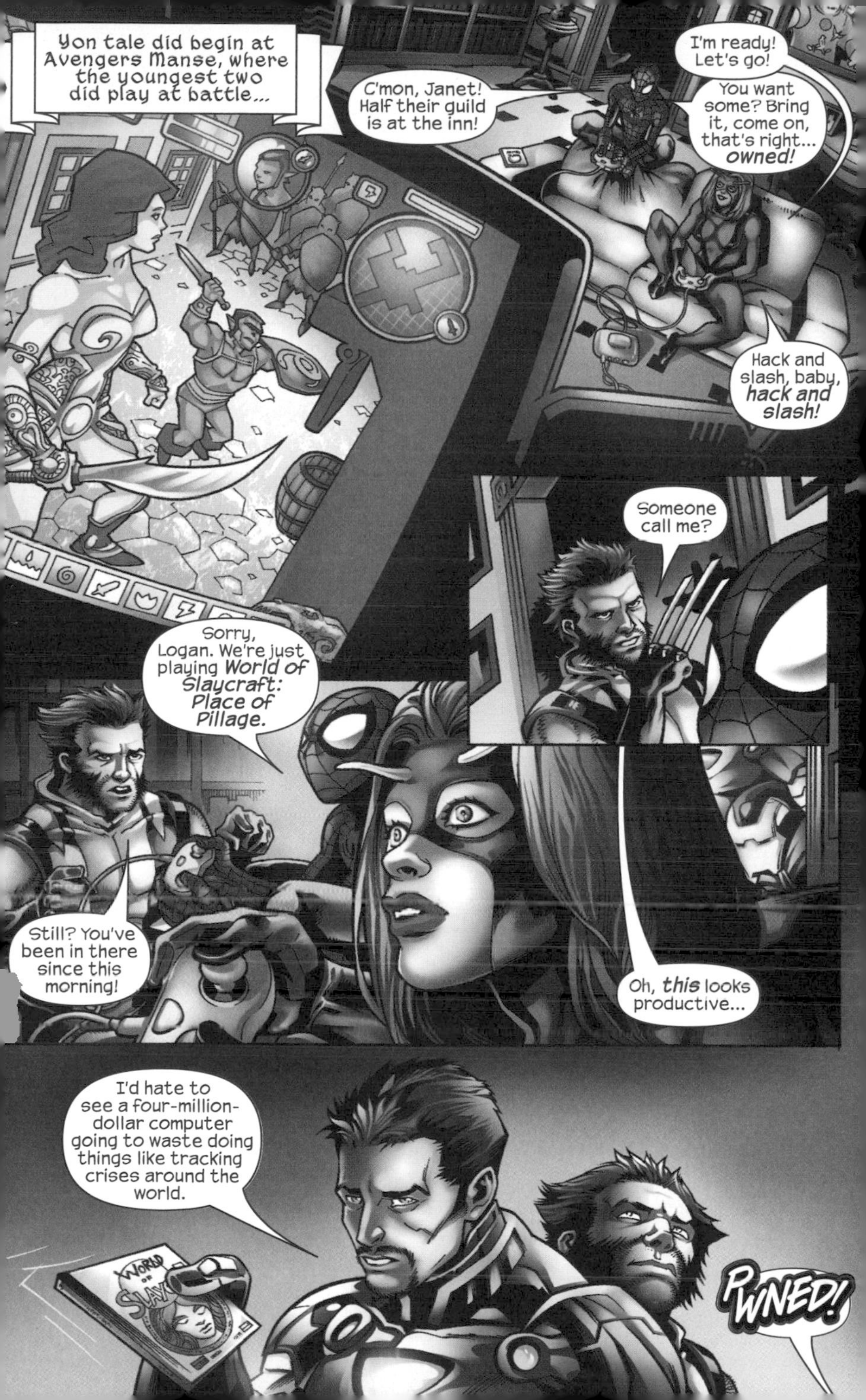

Yon tale did begin at Avengers Manse, where the youngest two did play at battle...
C'mon, Janet! Half their guild is at the inn!
I'm ready! Let's go!
You want some? Bring it, come on, that's right... *owned!*
Hack and slash, baby, *hack and slash!*
Someone call me?
Sorry, Logan. We're just playing *World of Slaycraft: Place of Pillage.*
Still? You've been in there since this morning!
Oh, *this* looks productive...
I'd hate to see a four-million-dollar computer going to waste doing things like tracking crises around the world.
PWNED!

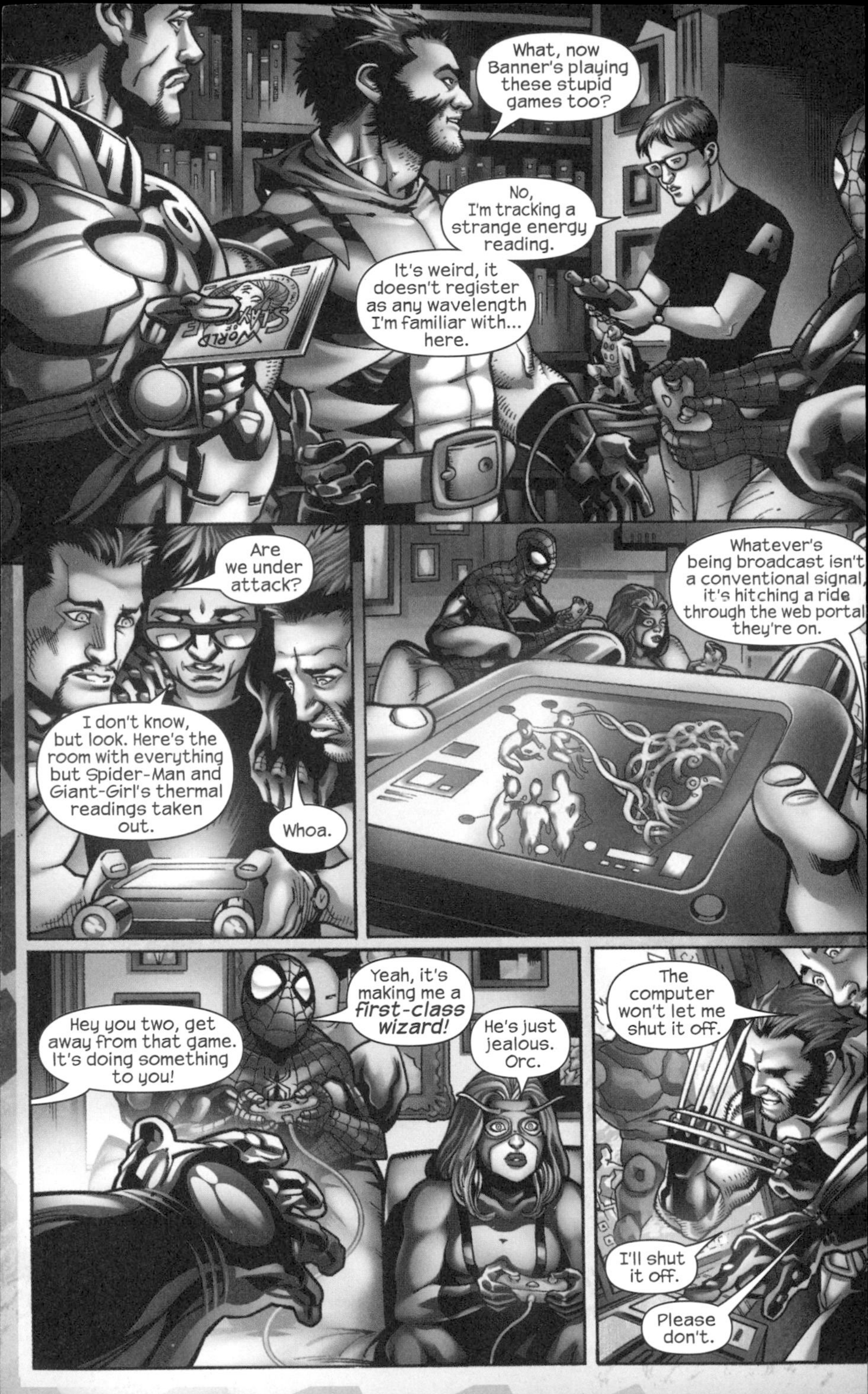
What, now Banner's playing these stupid games too?
No, I'm tracking a strange energy reading.
It's weird, it doesn't register as any wavelength I'm familiar with... here.
WORLD SLAYCRAFT
Are we under attack?
I don't know, but look. Here's the room with everything but Spider-Man and Giant-Girl's thermal readings taken out.
Whoa.
Whatever's being broadcast isn't a conventional signal, it's hitching a ride through the web portal they're on.
Hey you two, get away from that game. It's doing something to you!
Yeah, it's making me a *first-class wizard!*
He's just jealous. Orc.
The computer won't let me shut it off.
I'll shut it off.
Please don't.

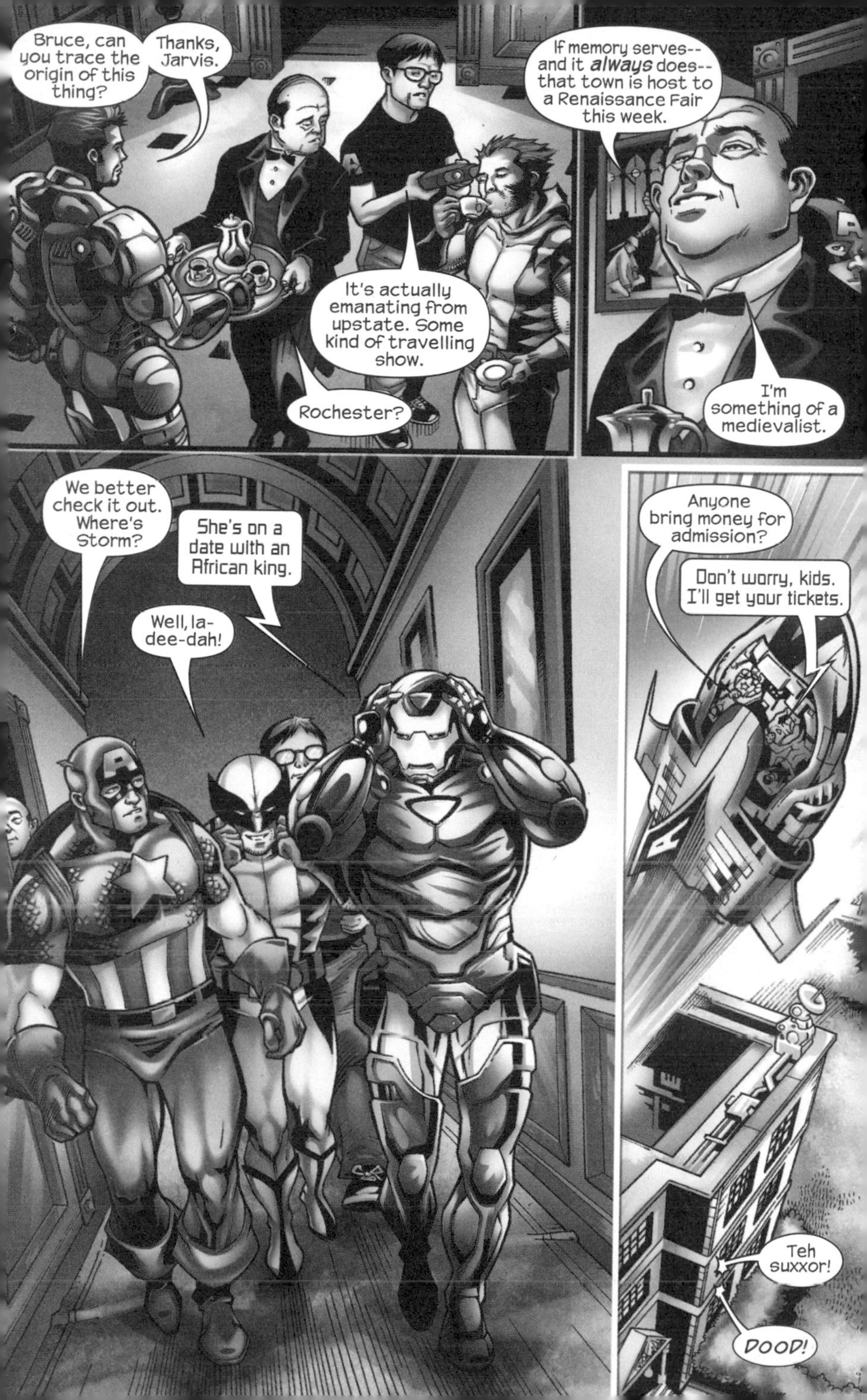
Bruce, can you trace the origin of this thing?
Thanks, Jarvis.
It's actually emanating from upstate. Some kind of travelling show.
Rochester?
If memory serves-- and it *always* does-- that town is host to a Renaissance Fair this week.
I'm something of a medievalist.
We better check it out. Where's Storm?
She's on a date with an African king.
Well, la-dee-dah!
Anyone bring money for admission?
Don't worry, kids. I'll get your tickets.
Teh suxxor!
DOOD!

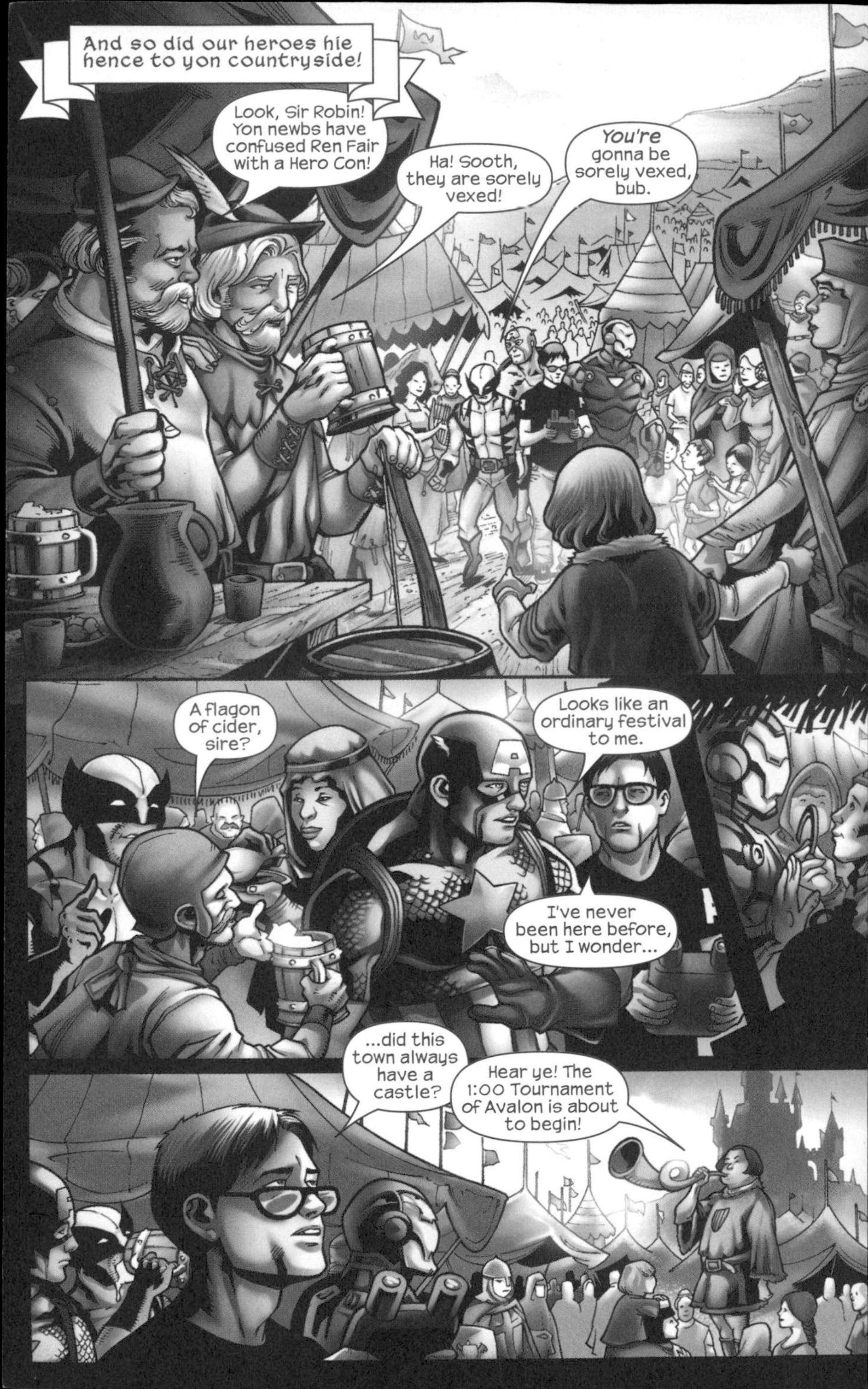
And so did our heroes hie hence to yon countryside!
Look, Sir Robin! Yon newbs have confused Ren Fair with a Hero Con!
Ha! Sooth, they are sorely vexed!
You're gonna be sorely vexed, bub.
A flagon of cider, sire?
Looks like an ordinary festival to me.
I've never been here before, but I wonder...
...did this town always have a castle?
Hear ye! The 1:00 Tournament of Avalon is about to begin!

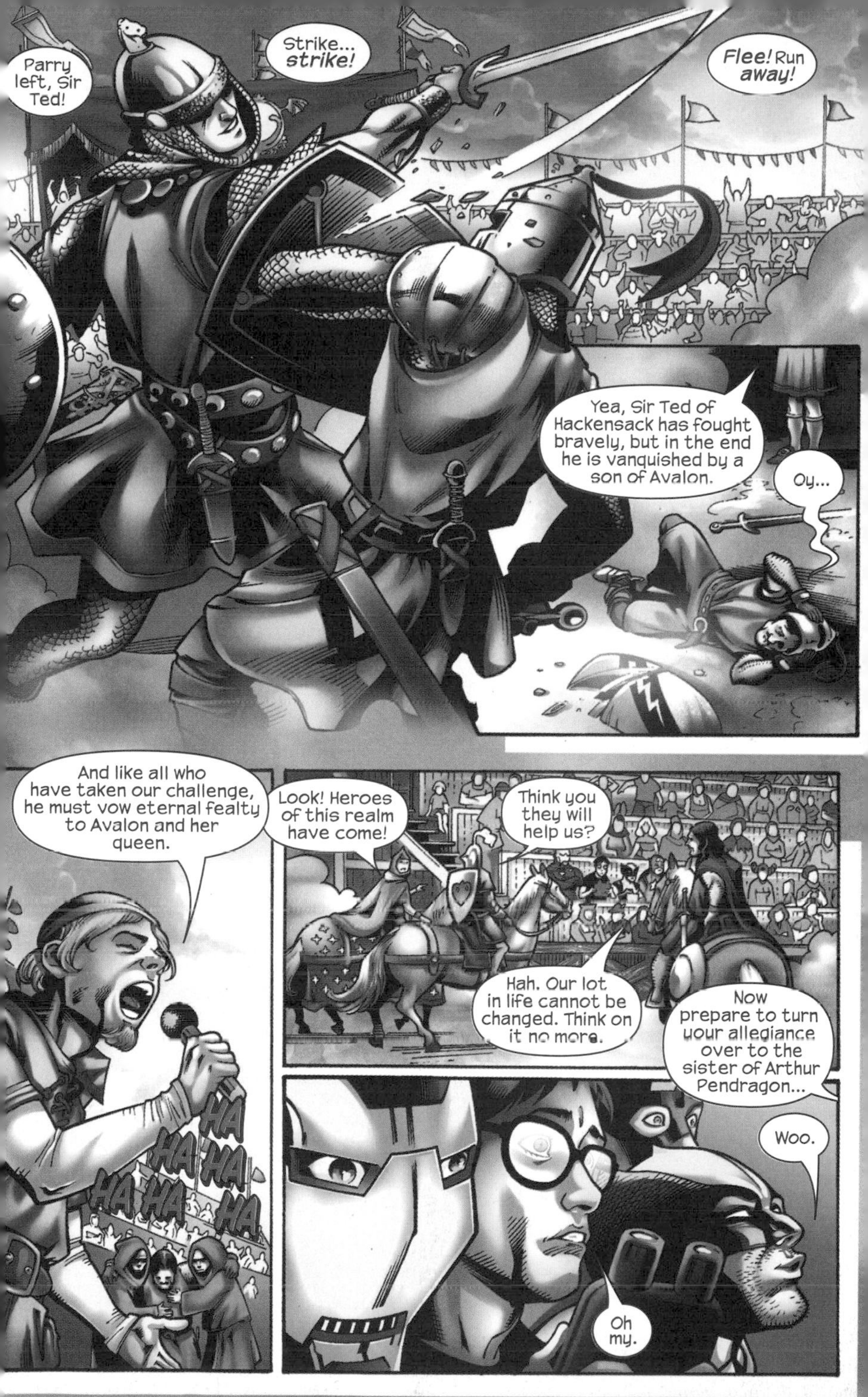
Parry left, Sir Ted!
Strike... strike!
Flee! Run away!
Yea, Sir Ted of Hackensack has fought bravely, but in the end he is vanquished by a son of Avalon.
Oy...
And like all who have taken our challenge, he must vow eternal fealty to Avalon and her queen.
HA HA HA HA HA HA HA
Look! Heroes of this realm have come!
Think you they will help us?
Hah. Our lot in life cannot be changed. Think on it no more.
Now prepare to turn your allegiance over to the sister of Arthur Pendragon...
Woo.
Oh my.

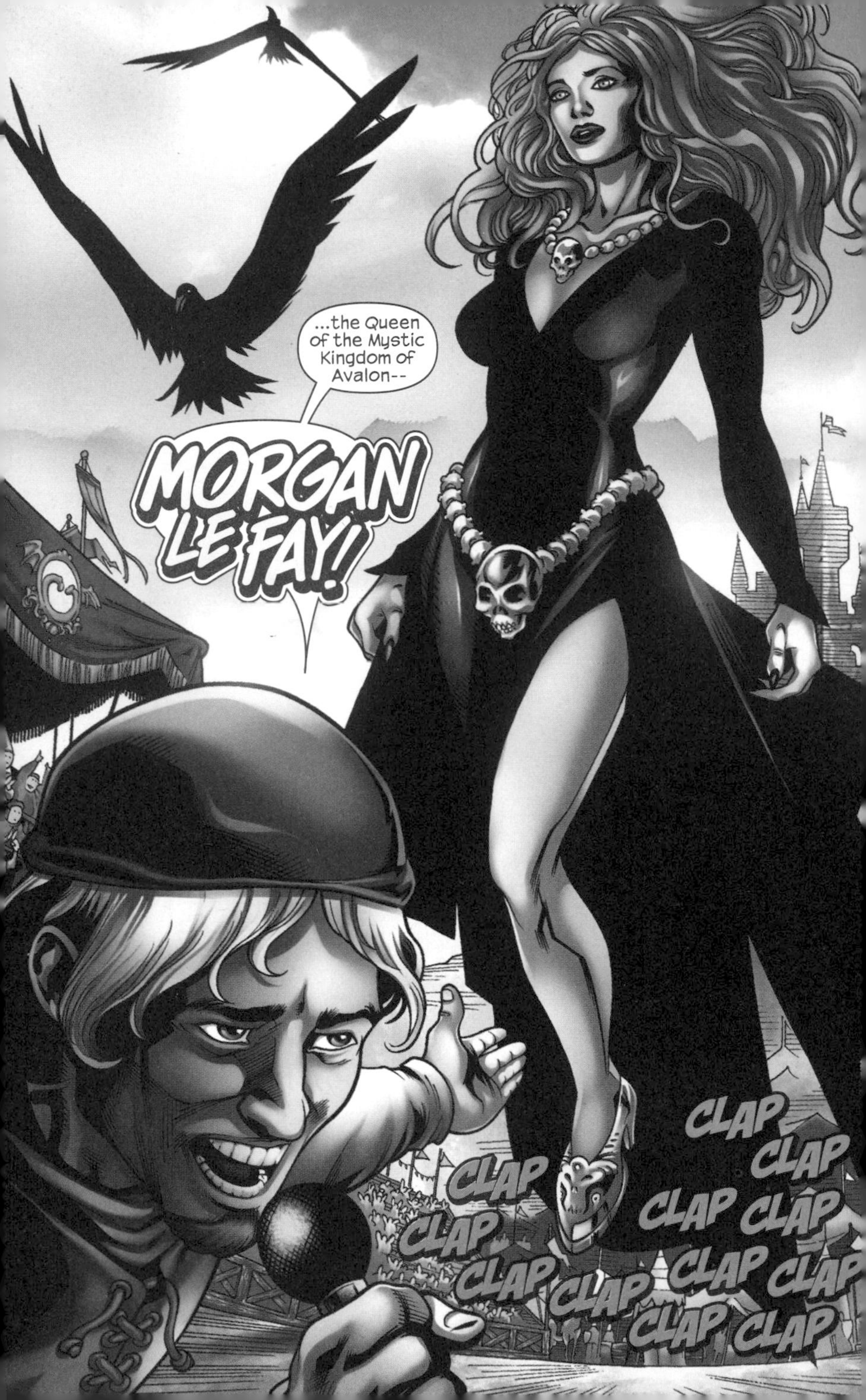
...the Queen of the Mystic Kingdom of Avalon--
MORGAN LE FAY!
CLAP
CLAP
CLAP
CLAP CLAP
CLAP
CLAP
CLAP
CLAP CLAP
CLAP CLAP

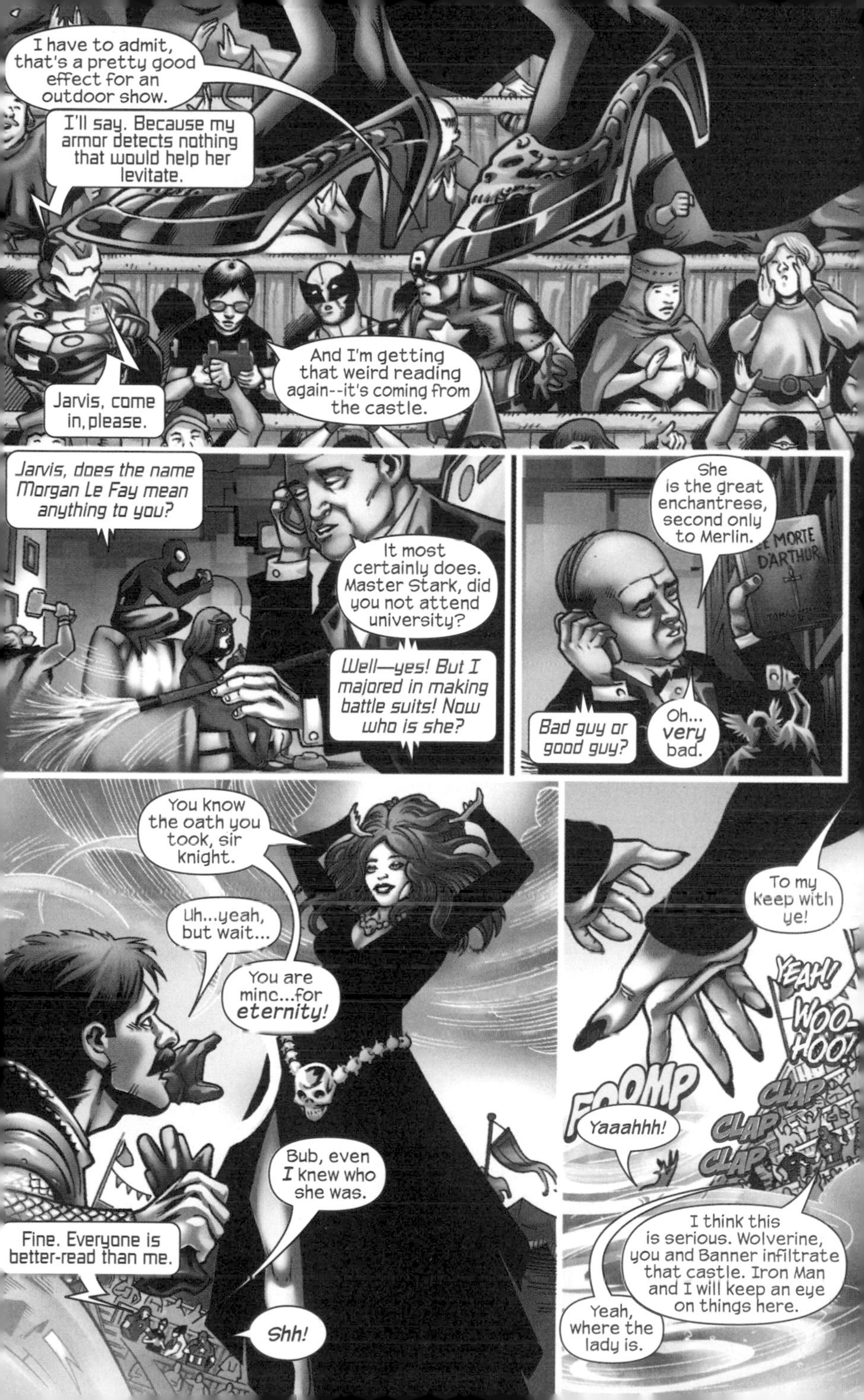
I have to admit, that's a pretty good effect for an outdoor show.
I'll say. Because my armor detects nothing that would help her levitate.
Jarvis, come in, please.
And I'm getting that weird reading again--it's coming from the castle.
Jarvis, does the name Morgan Le Fay mean anything to you?
It most certainly does. Master Stark, did you not attend university?
Well—yes! But I majored in making battle suits! Now who is she?
She is the great enchantress, second only to Merlin.
LE MORTE D'ARTHUR
Bad guy or good guy?
Oh... very bad.
You know the oath you took, sir knight.
Uh...yeah, but wait...
You are mine...for eternity!
Bub, even I knew who she was.
Fine. Everyone is better-read than me.
Shh!
To my keep with ye!
YEAH!
WOO-HOO!
FOOMP
Yaaahhh!
CLAP
CLAP
CLAP
I think this is serious. Wolverine, you and Banner infiltrate that castle. Iron Man and I will keep an eye on things here.
Yeah, where the lady is.

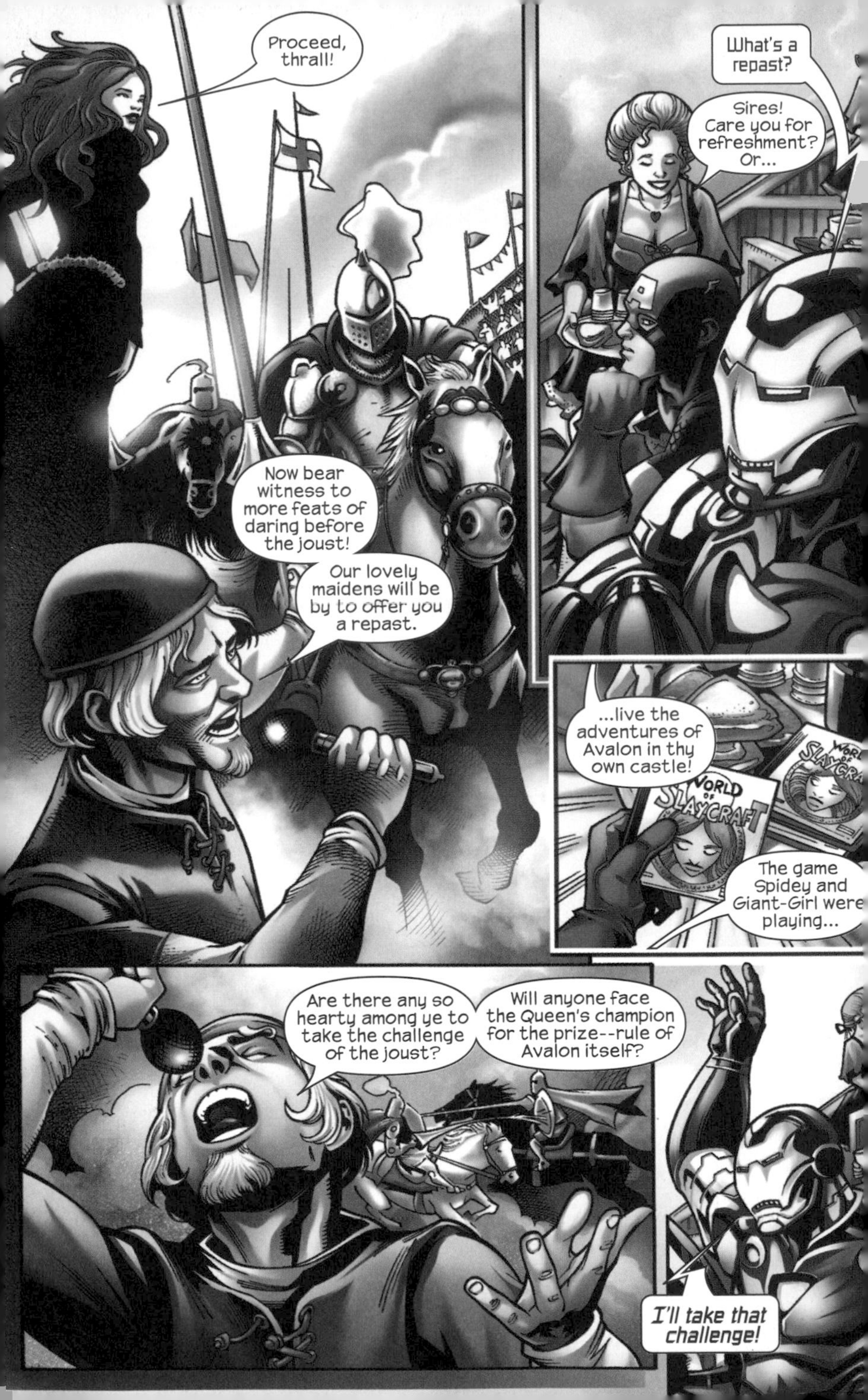
Proceed, thrall!
Now bear witness to more feats of daring before the joust!
Our lovely maidens will be by to offer you a repast.
What's a repast?
Sires! Care you for refreshment? Or...
...live the adventures of Avalon in thy own castle!
WORLD OF SLAYCRAFT
The game Spidey and Giant-Girl were playing...
Are there any so hearty among ye to take the challenge of the joust?
Will anyone face the Queen's champion for the prize--rule of Avalon itself?
I'll take that challenge!

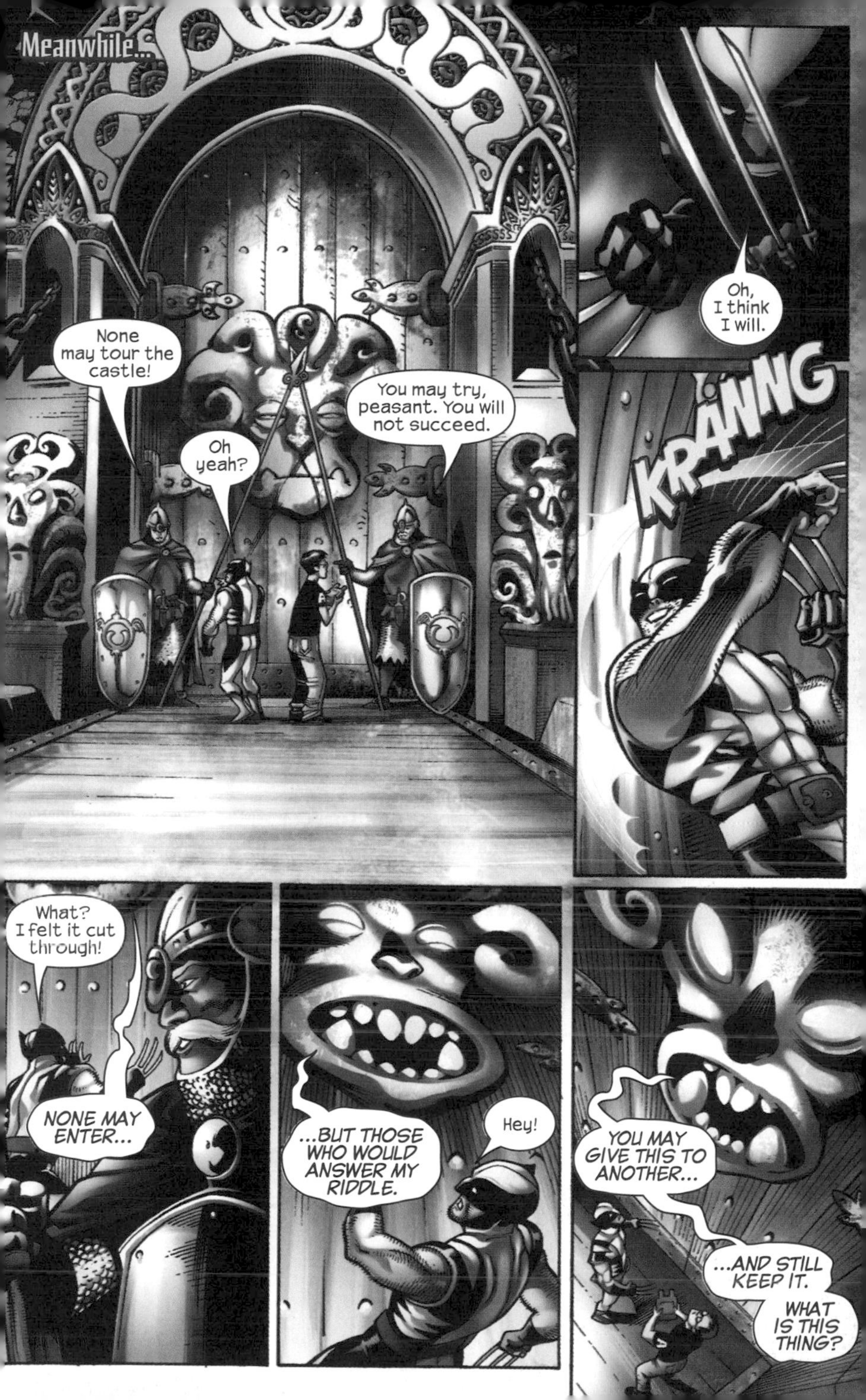
Meanwhile...
None may tour the castle!
You may try, peasant. You will not succeed.
Oh yeah?
Oh, I think I will.
KRANNG
What? I felt it cut through!
NONE MAY ENTER...
...BUT THOSE WHO WOULD ANSWER MY RIDDLE.
Hey!
YOU MAY GIVE THIS TO ANOTHER...
...AND STILL KEEP IT.
WHAT IS THIS THING?

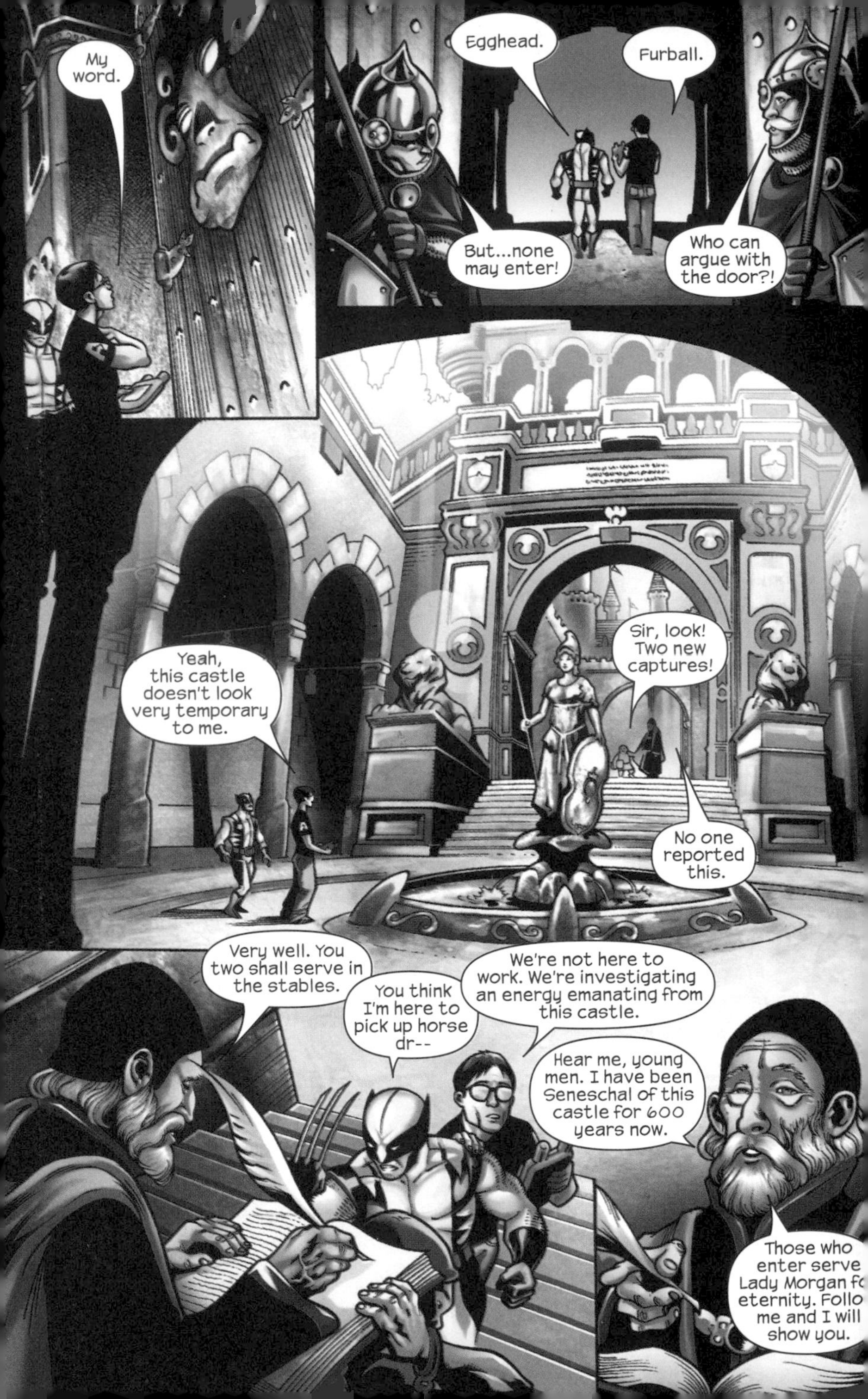
My word.
Egghead.
Furball.
But...none may enter!
Who can argue with the door?!
Yeah, this castle doesn't look very temporary to me.
Sir, look! Two new captures!
No one reported this.
Very well. You two shall serve in the stables.
You think I'm here to pick up horse dr--
We're not here to work. We're investigating an energy emanating from this castle.
Hear me, young men. I have been Seneschal of this castle for 600 years now.
Those who enter serve Lady Morgan fo eternity. Follo me and I will show you.

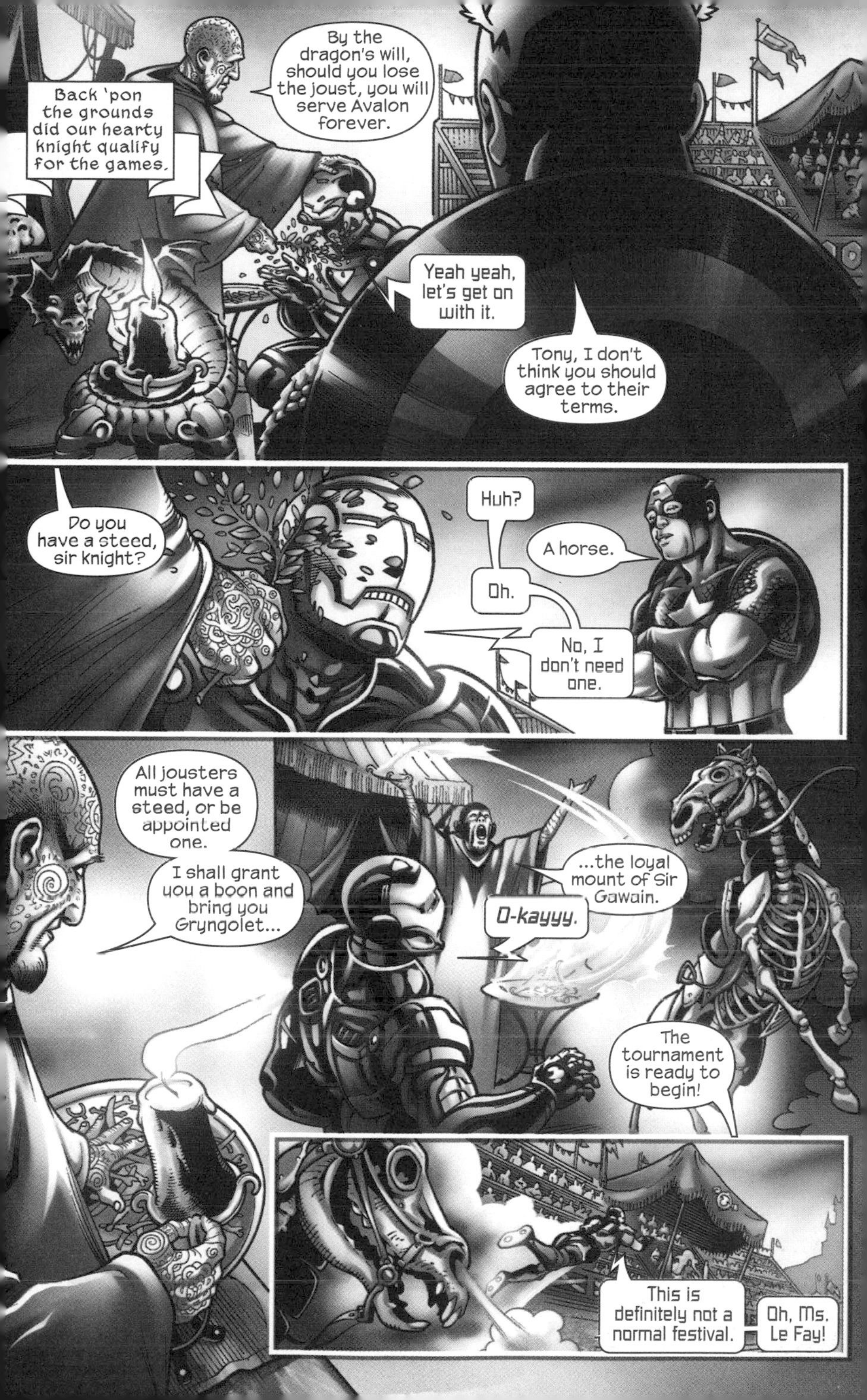

Back 'pon the grounds did our hearty knight qualify for the games.
By the dragon's will, should you lose the joust, you will serve Avalon forever.
Yeah yeah, let's get on with it.
Tony, I don't think you should agree to their terms.
Do you have a steed, sir knight?
Huh?
A horse.
Oh.
No, I don't need one.
All jousters must have a steed, or be appointed one.
I shall grant you a boon and bring you Gryngolet...
...the loyal mount of Sir Gawain.
O-kayyy.
The tournament is ready to begin!
This is definitely not a normal festival.
Oh, Ms. Le Fay!

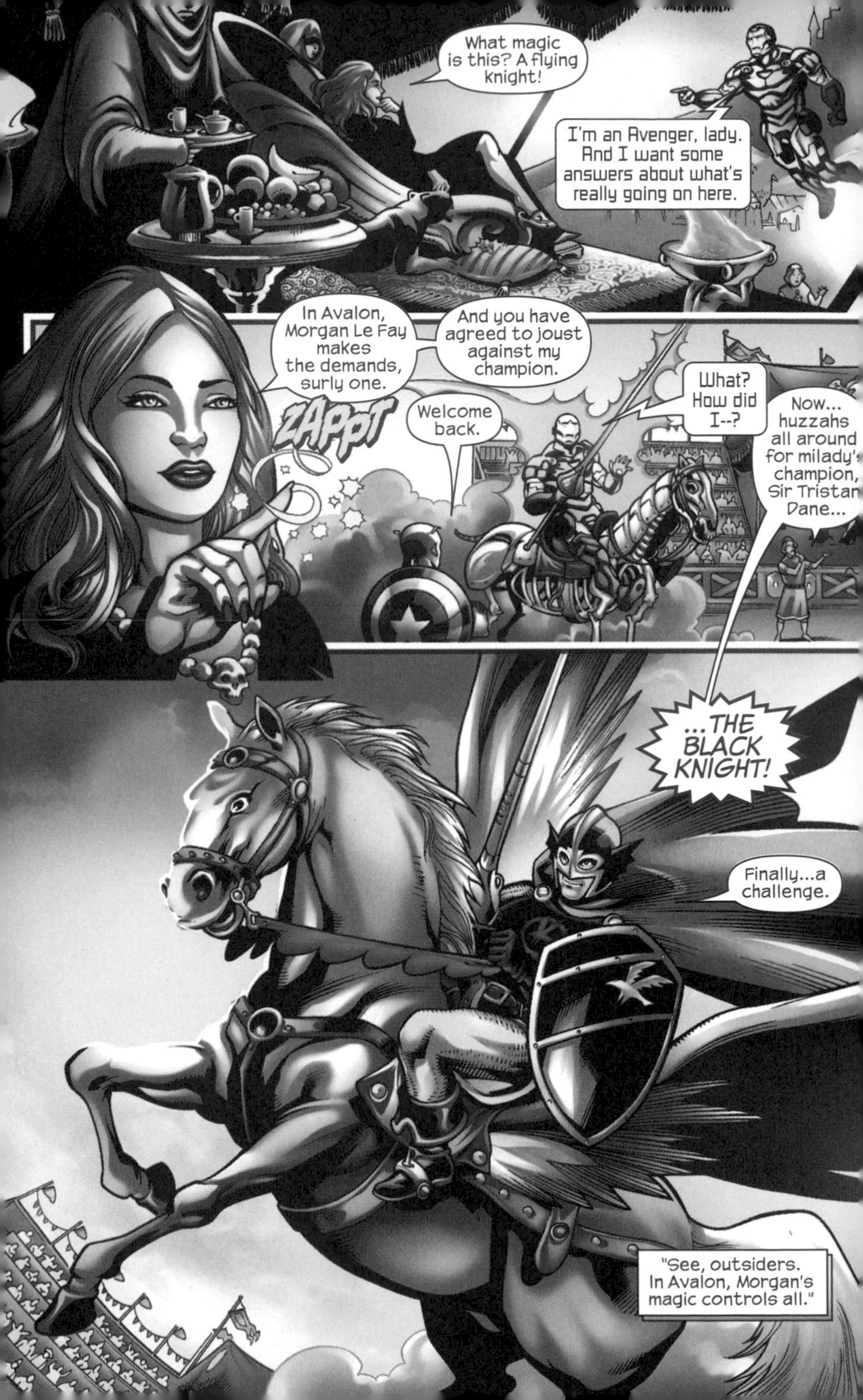
What magic is this? A flying knight!
I'm an Avenger, lady. And I want some answers about what's really going on here.
In Avalon, Morgan Le Fay makes the demands, surly one.
And you have agreed to joust against my champion.
ZAPPT
Welcome back.
What? How did I--?
Now... huzzahs all around for milady's champion, Sir Tristan Dane...
...THE BLACK KNIGHT!
Finally...a challenge.
"See, outsiders. In Avalon, Morgan's magic controls all."

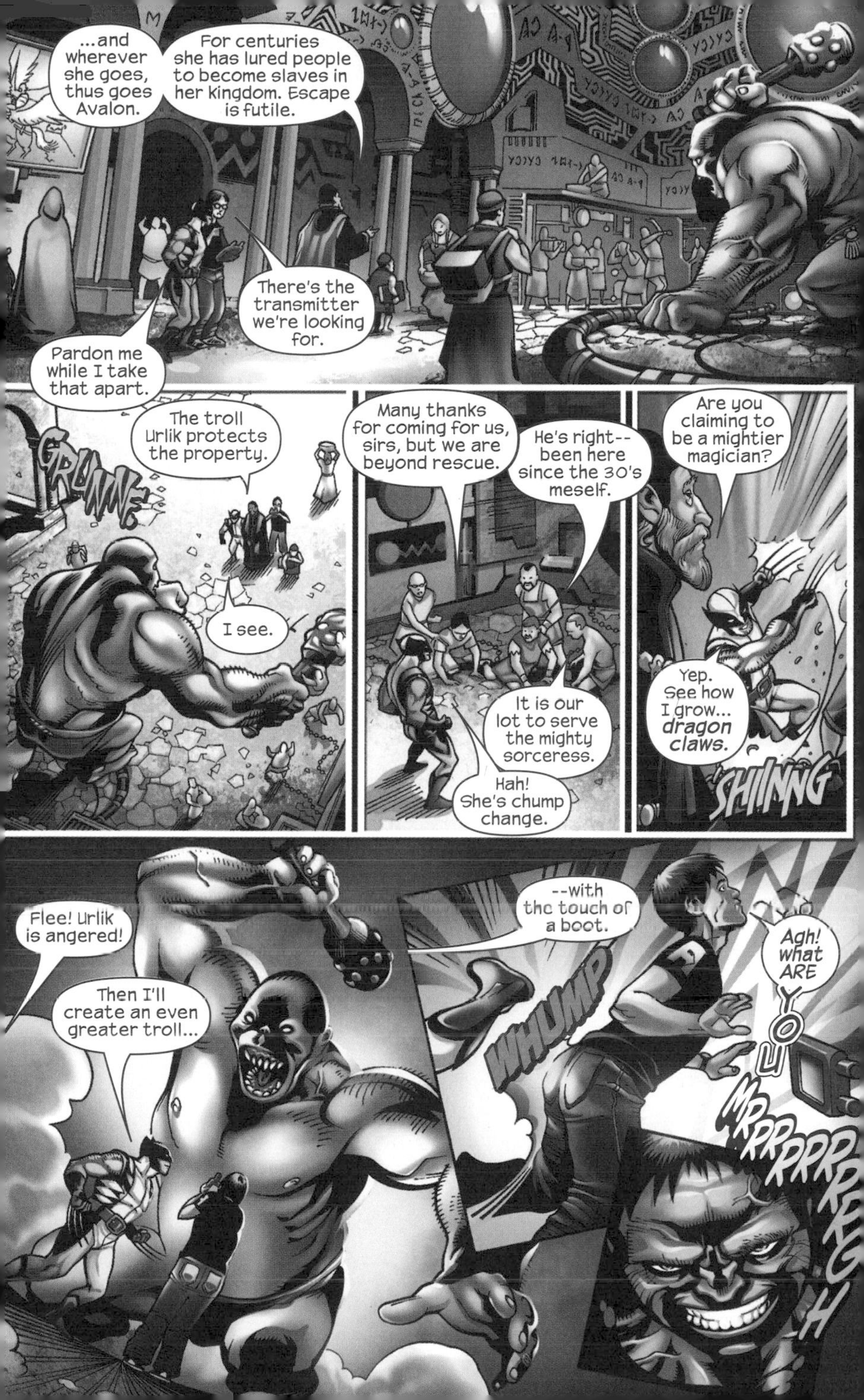
...and wherever she goes, thus goes Avalon.
For centuries she has lured people to become slaves in her kingdom. Escape is futile.
There's the transmitter we're looking for.
Pardon me while I take that apart.
The troll Urlik protects the property.
GRUNNE
I see.
Many thanks for coming for us, sirs, but we are beyond rescue.
He's right--been here since the 30's meself.
It is our lot to serve the mighty sorceress.
Hah! She's chump change.
Are you claiming to be a mightier magician?
Yep. See how I grow... dragon claws.
SHIINNG
Flee! Urlik is angered!
Then I'll create an even greater troll...
--with the touch of a boot.
WHUMP
Agh! What ARE YOU
MRRRRRREGH

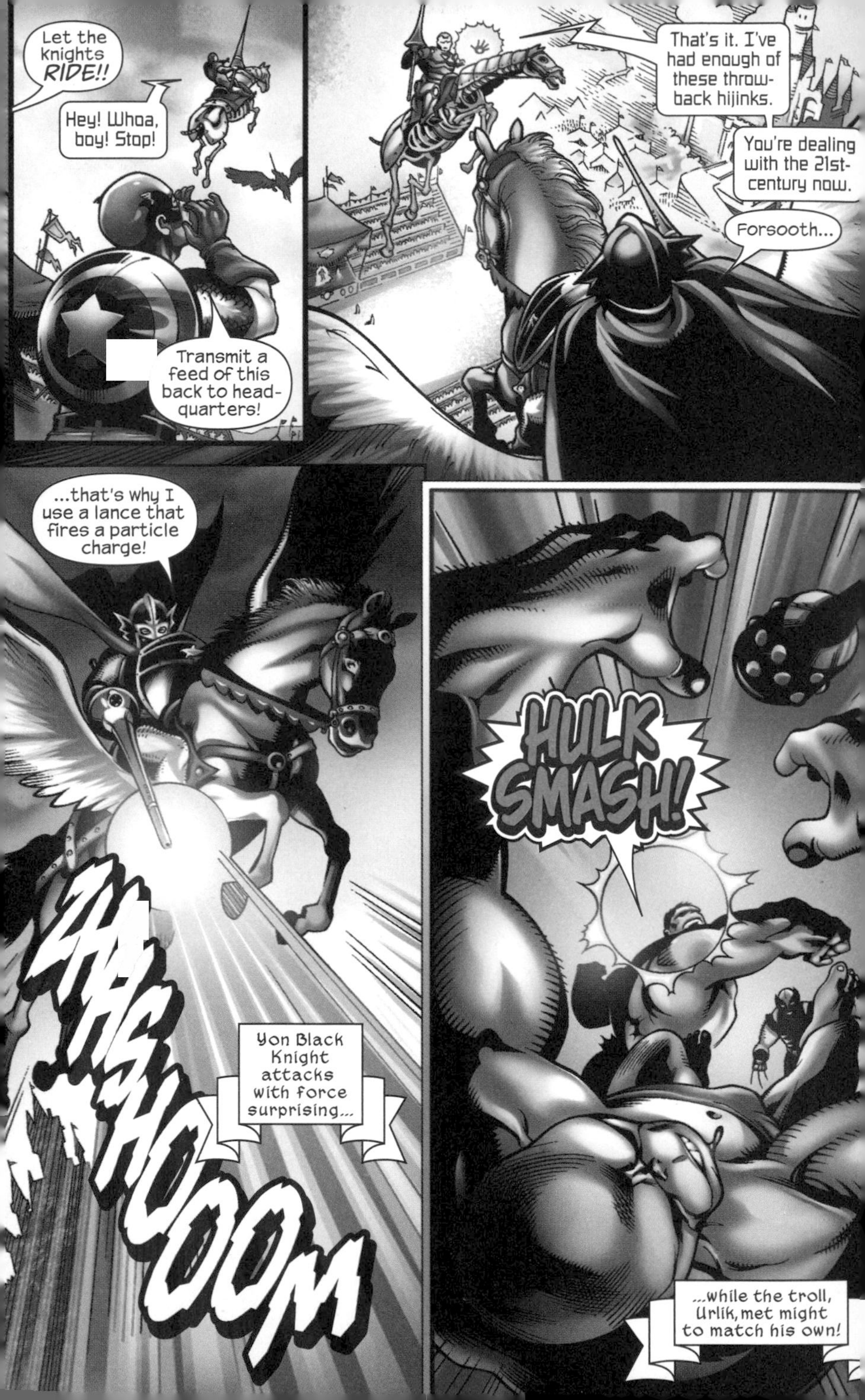

Let the knights RIDE!!
Hey! Whoa, boy! Stop!
Transmit a feed of this back to head-quarters!
That's it. I've had enough of these throw-back hijinks.
You're dealing with the 21st-century now.
Forsooth...
...that's why I use a lance that fires a particle charge!
ZHSHOOOM
Yon Black Knight attacks with force surprising...
HULK SMASH!
...while the troll, Urlik, met might to match his own!

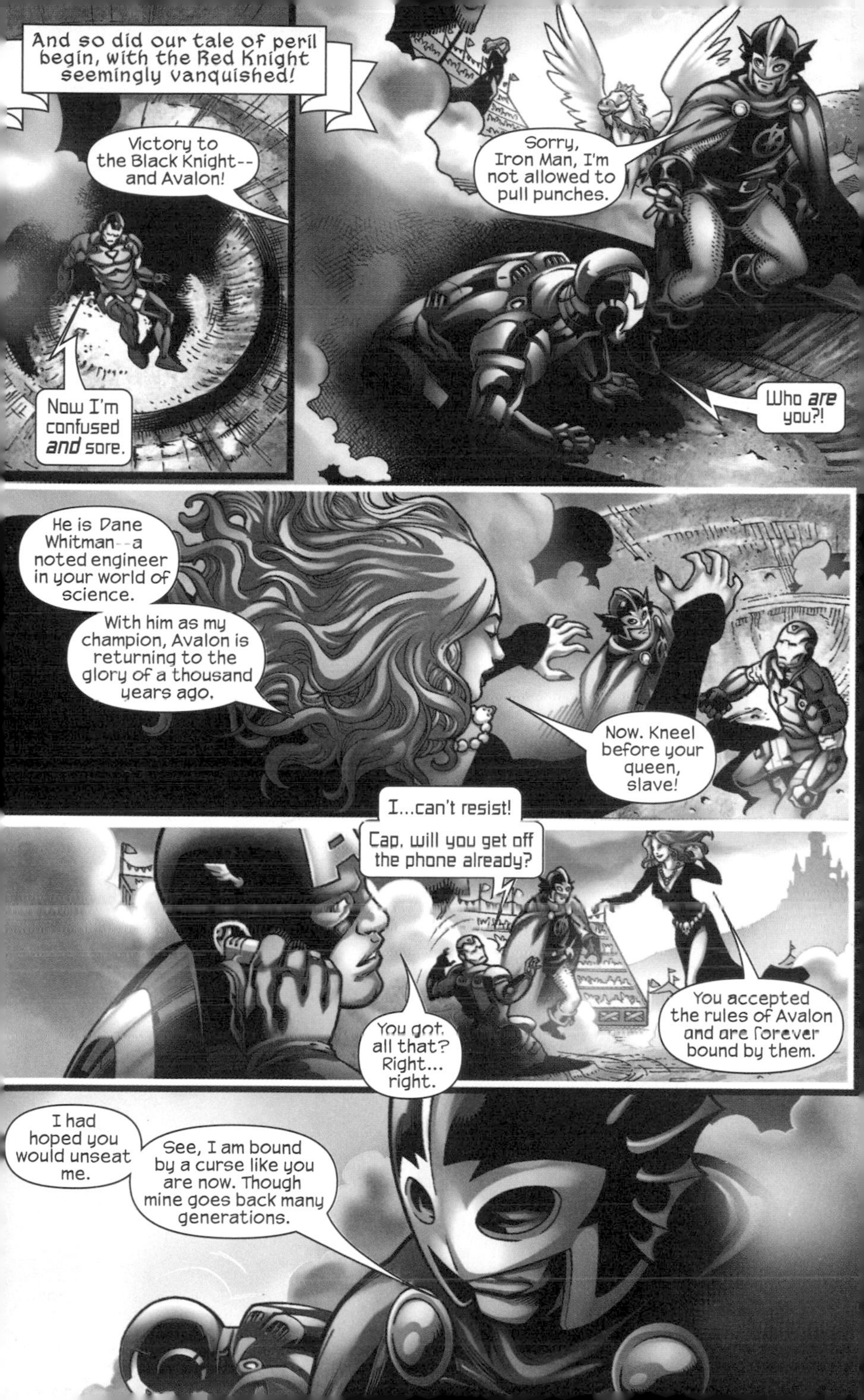
And so did our tale of peril begin, with the Red Knight seemingly vanquished!
Victory to the Black Knight--and Avalon!
Now I'm confused *and* sore.
Sorry, Iron Man, I'm not allowed to pull punches.
Who *are* you?!
He is Dane Whitman--a noted engineer in your world of science.
With him as my champion, Avalon is returning to the glory of a thousand years ago.
Now. Kneel before your queen, slave!
I...can't resist!
Cap, will you get off the phone already?
You got all that? Right... right.
You accepted the rules of Avalon and are forever bound by them.
I had hoped you would unseat me.
See, I am bound by a curse like you are now. Though mine goes back many generations.

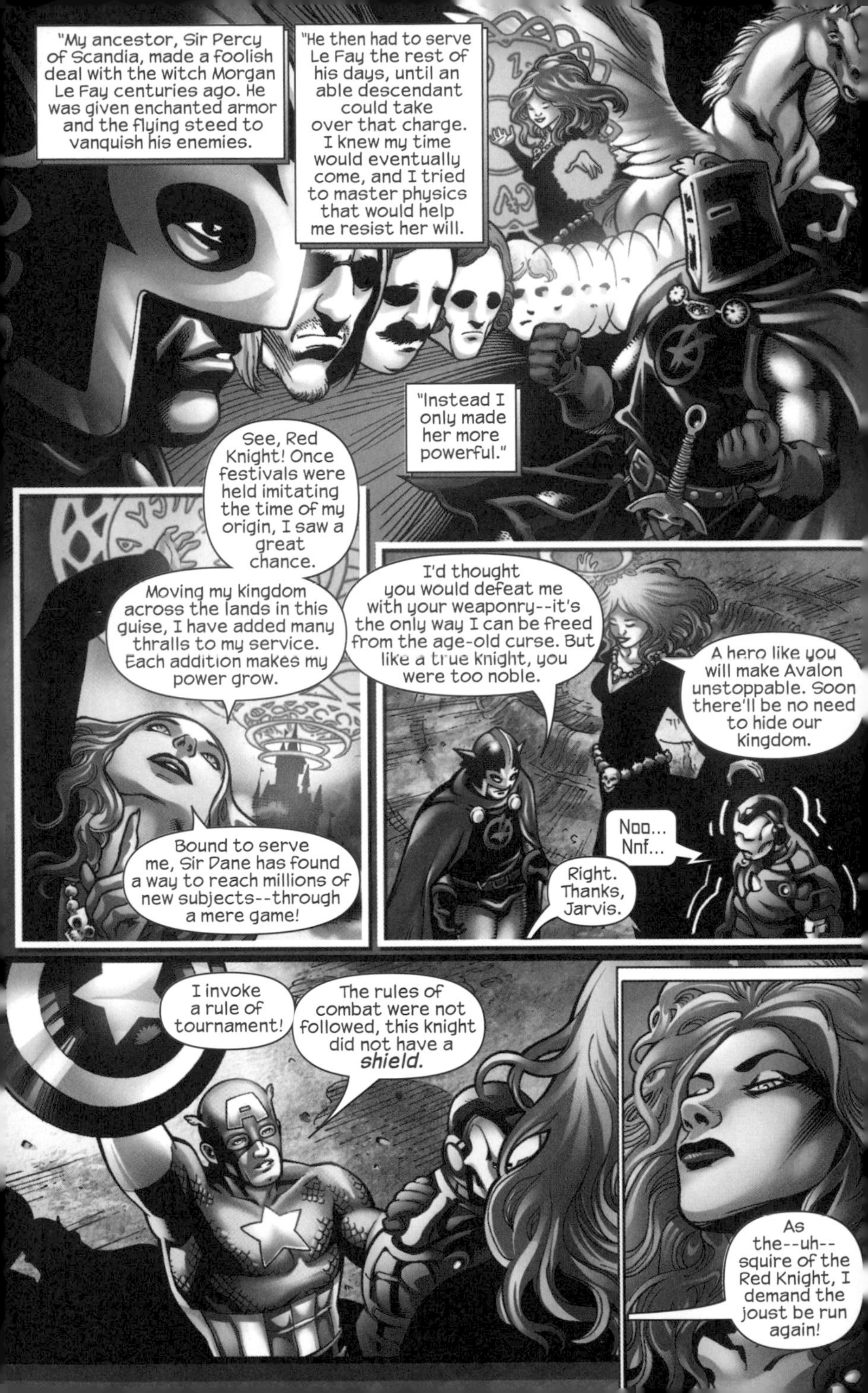
"My ancestor, Sir Percy of Scandia, made a foolish deal with the witch Morgan Le Fay centuries ago. He was given enchanted armor and the flying steed to vanquish his enemies.
"He then had to serve Le Fay the rest of his days, until an able descendant could take over that charge. I knew my time would eventually come, and I tried to master physics that would help me resist her will.
"Instead I only made her more powerful."
See, Red Knight! Once festivals were held imitating the time of my origin, I saw a great chance.
Moving my kingdom across the lands in this guise, I have added many thralls to my service. Each addition makes my power grow.
Bound to serve me, Sir Dane has found a way to reach millions of new subjects--through a mere game!
I'd thought you would defeat me with your weaponry--it's the only way I can be freed from the age-old curse. But like a true knight, you were too noble.
A hero like you will make Avalon unstoppable. Soon there'll be no need to hide our kingdom.
Noo... Nnf...
Right. Thanks, Jarvis.
I invoke a rule of tournament!
The rules of combat were not followed, this knight did not have a *shield.*
As the--uh--squire of the Red Knight, I demand the joust be run again!

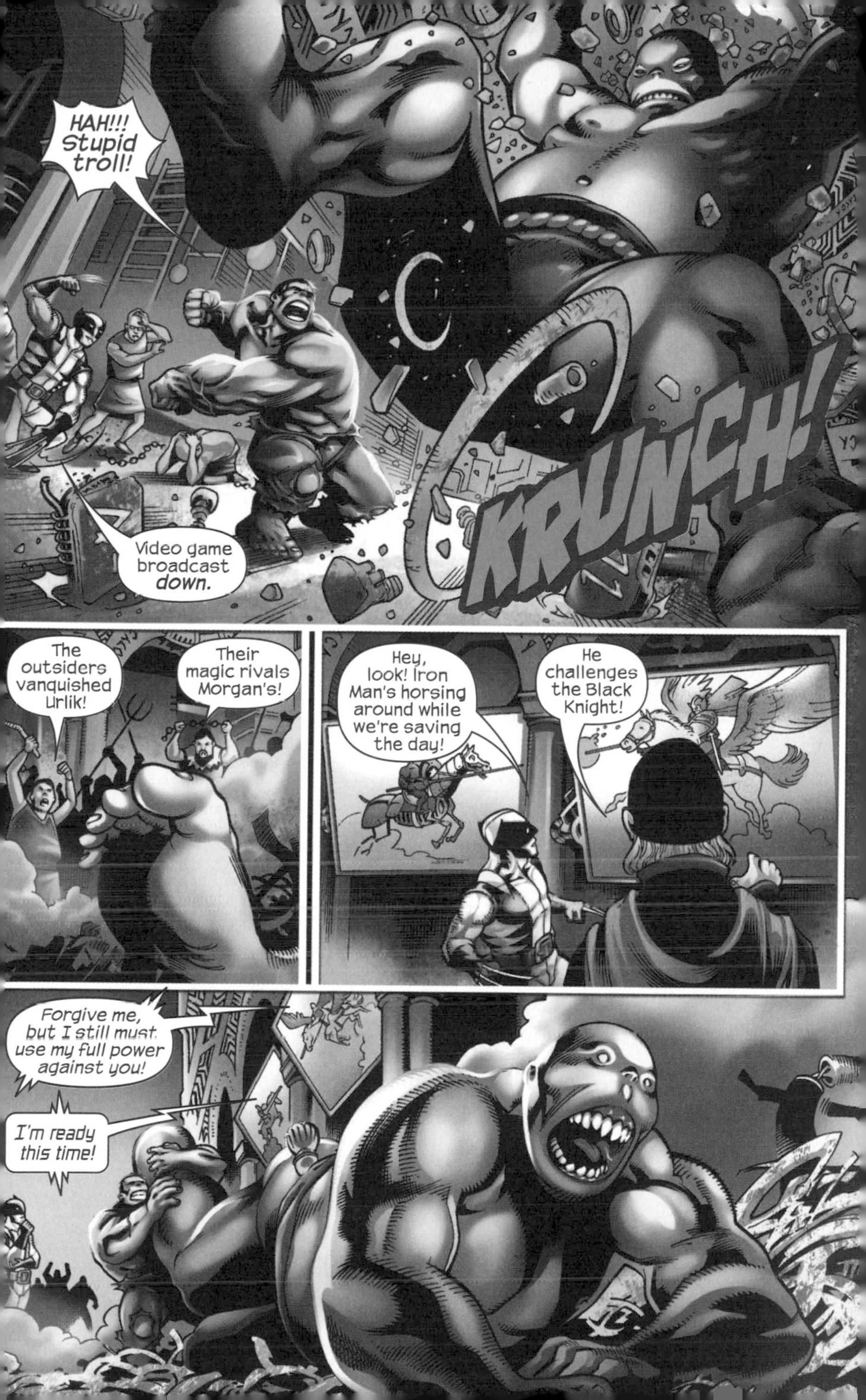
HAH!!! Stupid troll!
Video game broadcast **down.**
KRUNCH!
The outsiders vanquished Urlik!
Their magic rivals Morgan's!
Hey, look! Iron Man's horsing around while we're saving the day!
He challenges the Black Knight!
Forgive me, but I still must use my full power against you!
I'm ready this time!

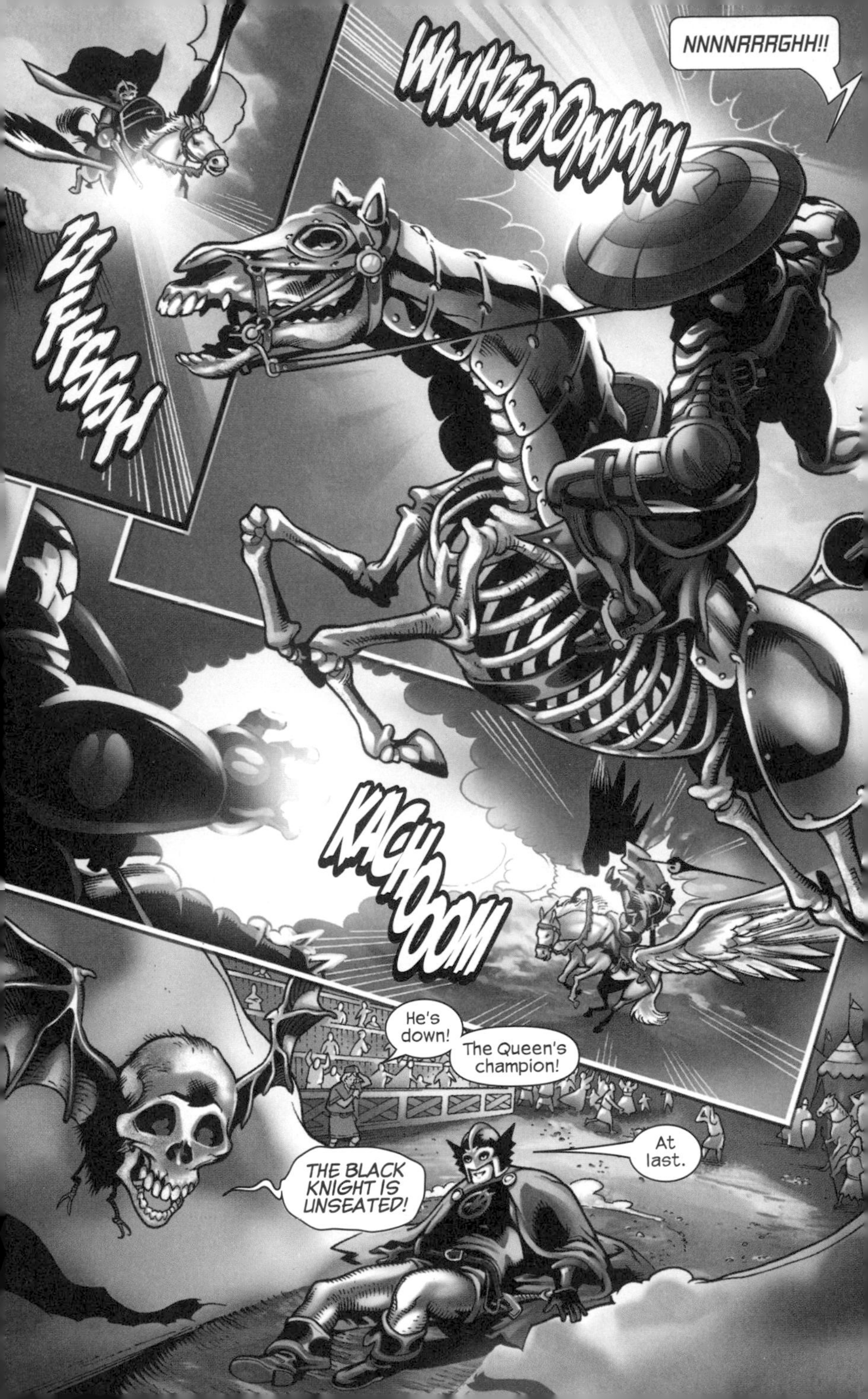
WWHZZOOMMM
NNNNRRRGHH!!
ZZFFSSSH
KACHOOOOM
He's down!
The Queen's champion!
THE BLACK KNIGHT IS UNSEATED!
At last.

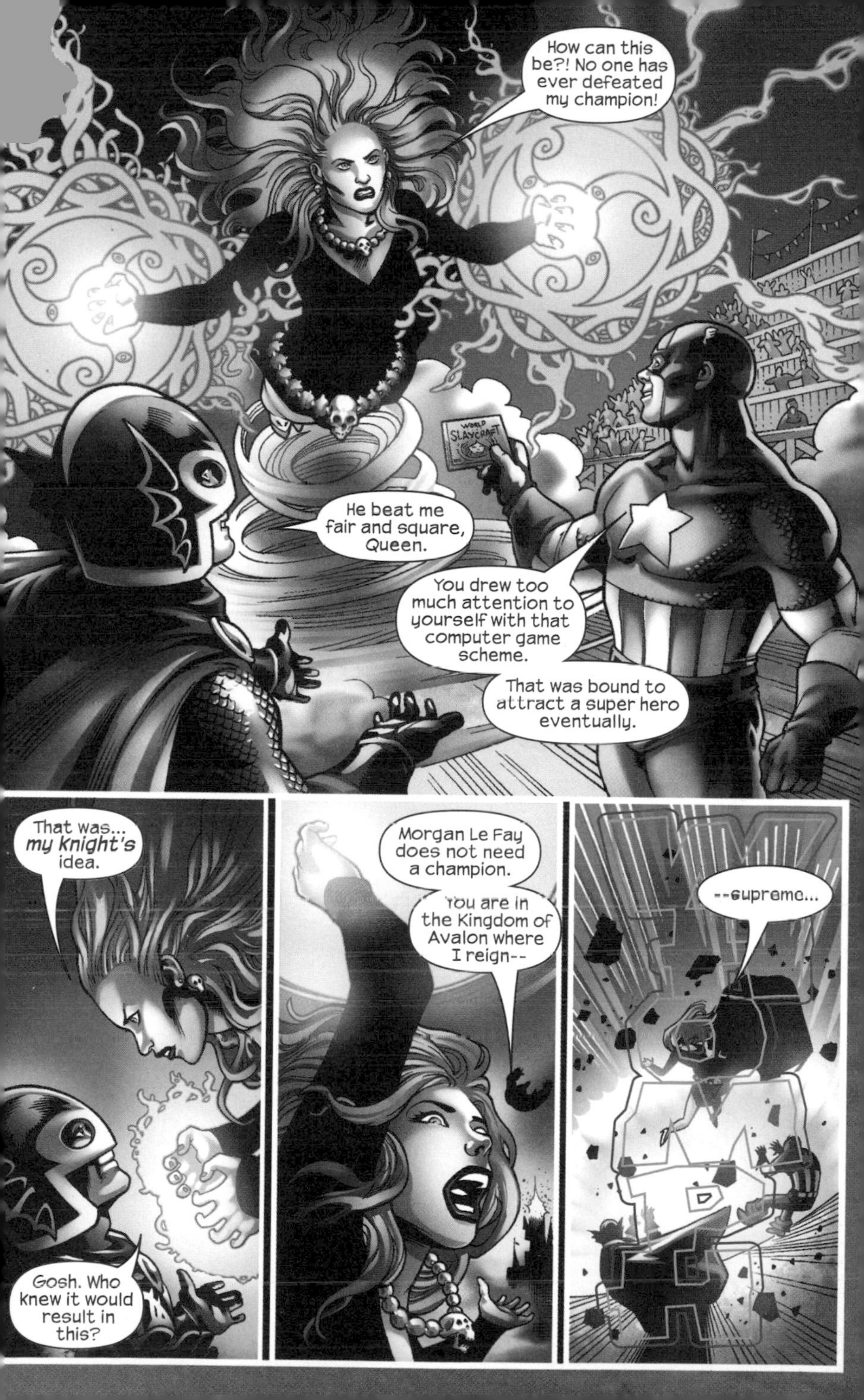
How can this be?! No one has ever defeated my champion!
WORLD SLAYCRAFT
He beat me fair and square, Queen.
You drew too much attention to yourself with that computer game scheme.
That was bound to attract a super hero eventually.
That was... *my knight's* idea.
Gosh. Who knew it would result in this?
Morgan Le Fay does not need a champion.
You are in the Kingdom of Avalon where I reign--
--supreme...

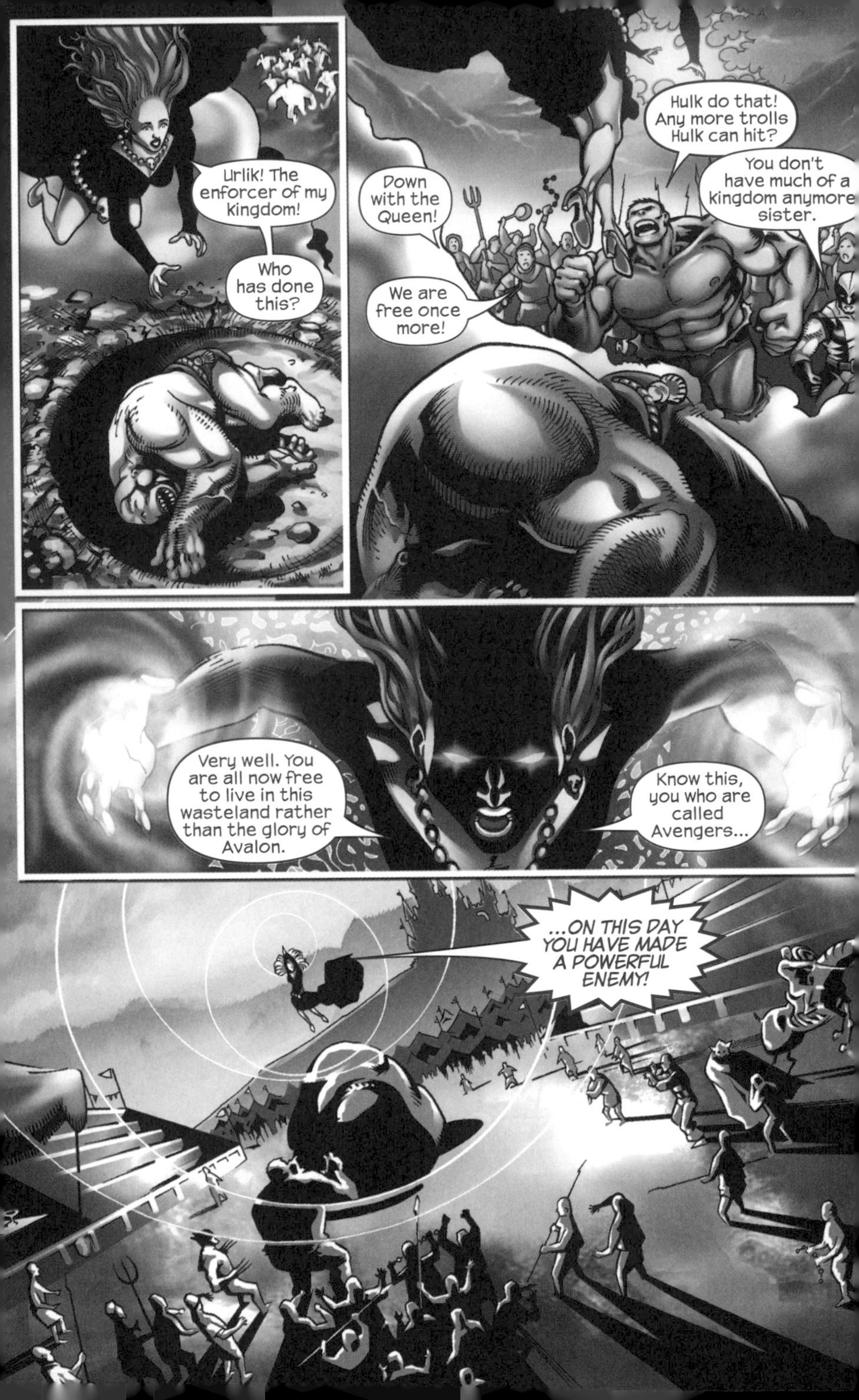

Urlik! The enforcer of my kingdom!
Who has done this?
Down with the Queen!
Hulk do that! Any more trolls Hulk can hit?
You don't have much of a kingdom anymore sister.
We are free once more!
Very well. You are all now free to live in this wasteland rather than the glory of Avalon.
Know this, you who are called Avengers...
...ON THIS DAY YOU HAVE MADE A POWERFUL ENEMY!

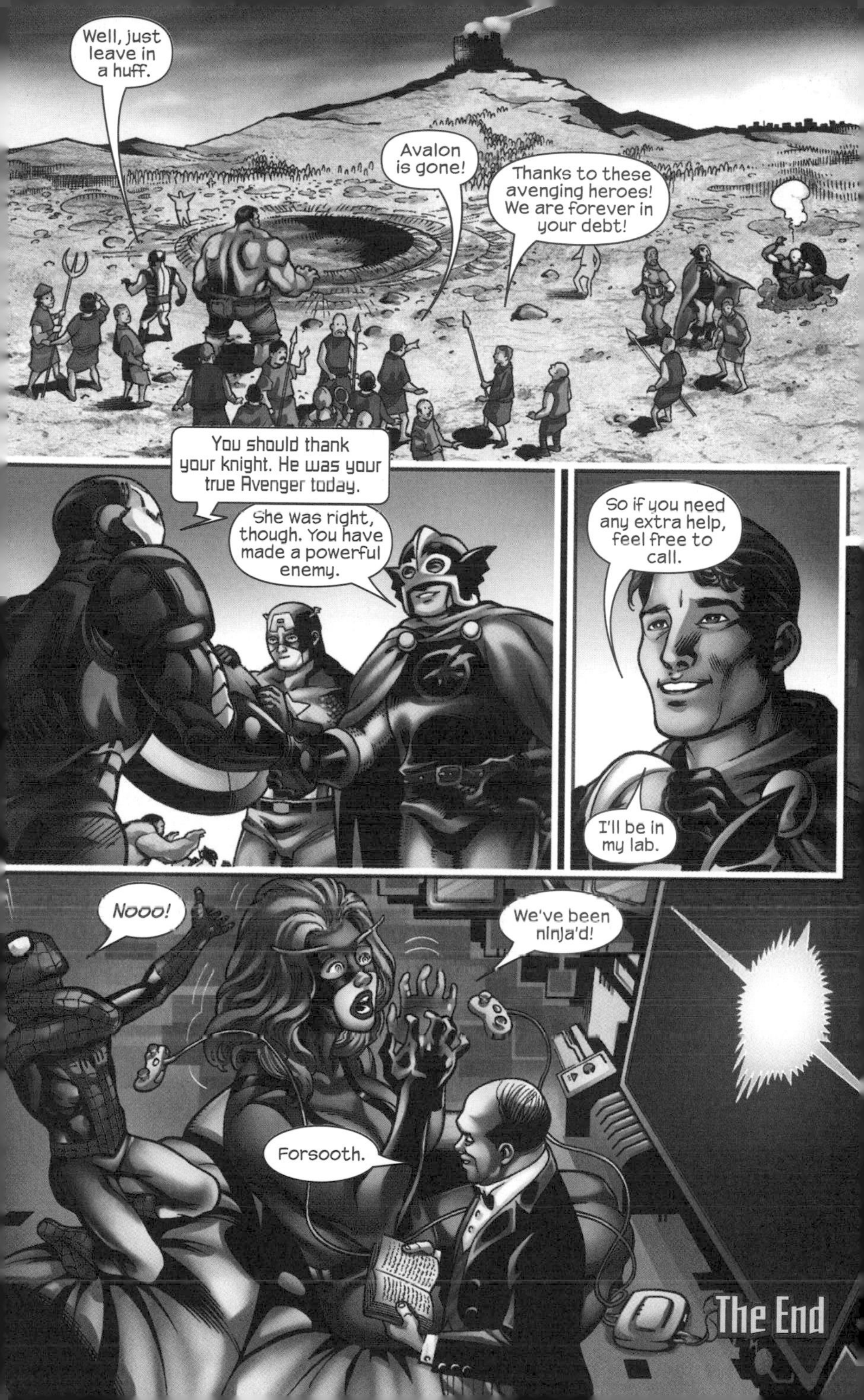
Well, just leave in a huff.
Avalon is gone!
Thanks to these avenging heroes! We are forever in your debt!
You should thank your knight. He was your true Avenger today.
She was right, though. You have made a powerful enemy.
So if you need any extra help, feel free to call.
I'll be in my lab.
Nooo!
We've been ninja'd!
Forsooth.
The End

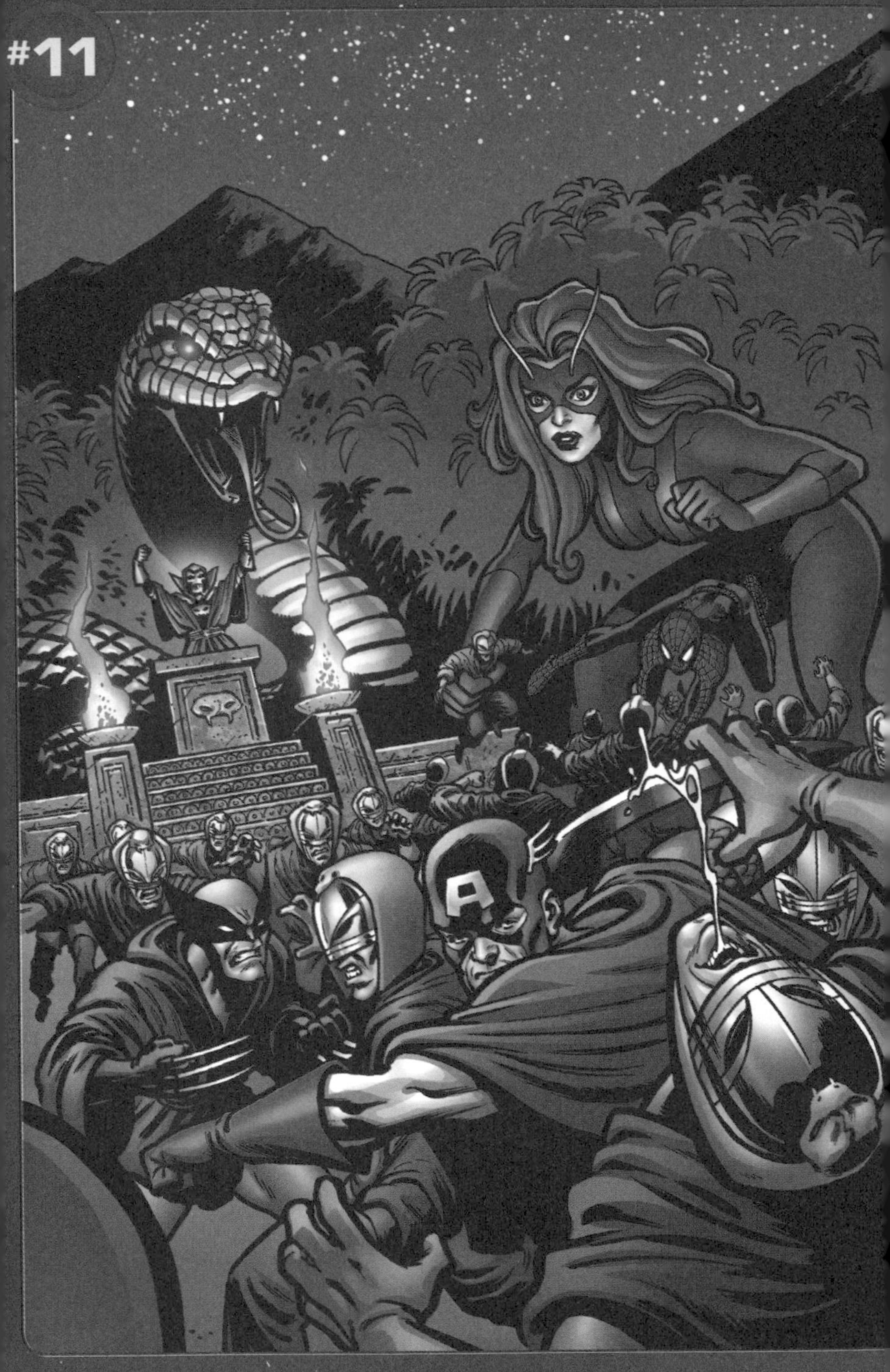
#11

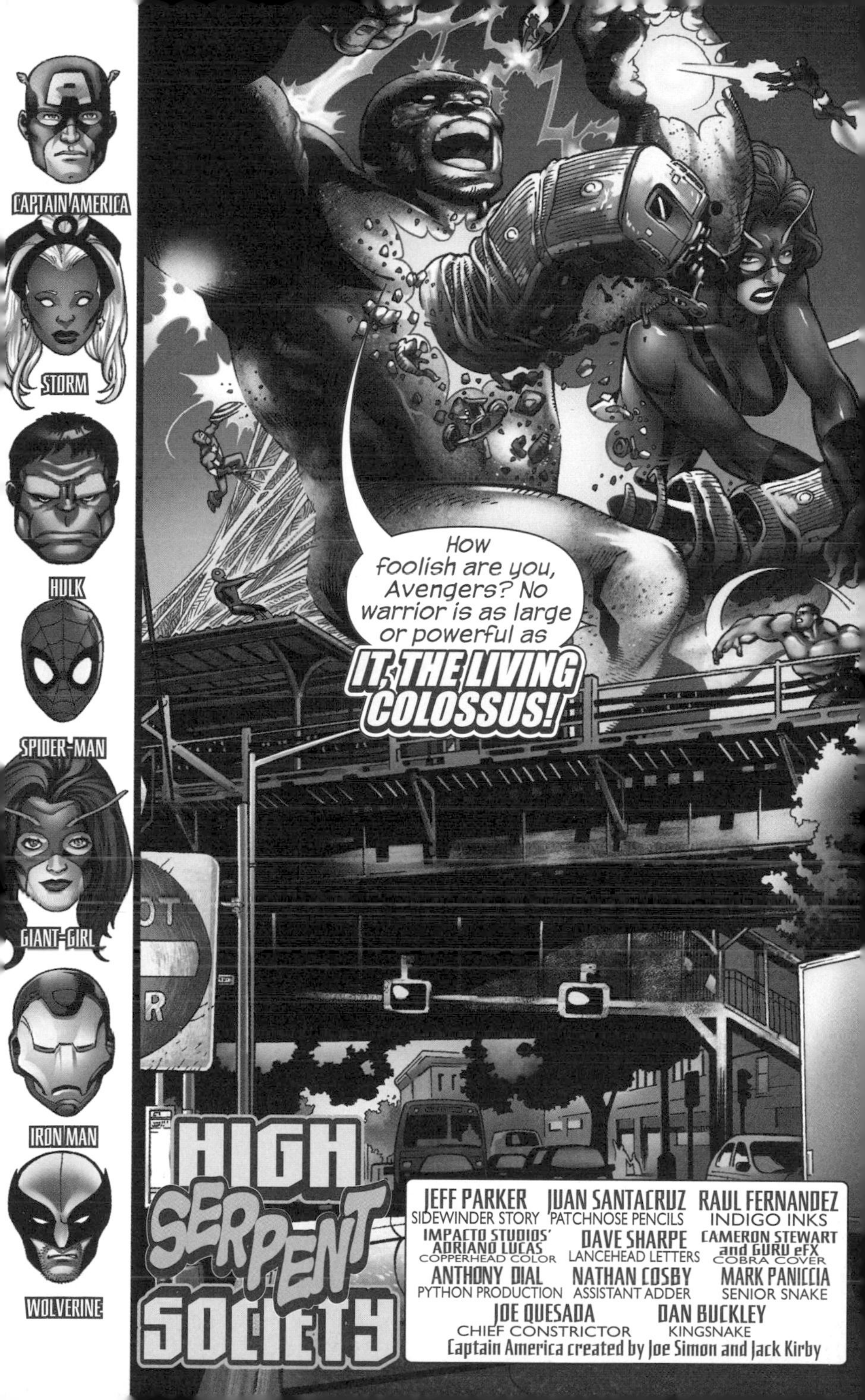

CAPTAIN AMERICA
STORM
HULK
SPIDER-MAN
GIANT-GIRL
IRON MAN
WOLVERINE
How foolish are you, Avengers? No warrior is as large or powerful as IT, THE LIVING COLOSSUS!
HIGH SERPENT SOCIETY
JEFF PARKER SIDEWINDER STORY
JUAN SANTACRUZ PATCHNOSE PENCILS
RAUL FERNANDEZ INDIGO INKS
IMPACTO STUDIOS' ADRIANO LUCAS COPPERHEAD COLOR
DAVE SHARPE LANCEHEAD LETTERS
CAMERON STEWART and GURU eFX COBRA COVER
ANTHONY DIAL PYTHON PRODUCTION
NATHAN COSBY ASSISTANT ADDER
MARK PANICCIA SENIOR SNAKE
JOE QUESADA CHIEF CONSTRICTOR
DAN BUCKLEY KINGSNAKE
Captain America created by Joe Simon and Jack Kirby

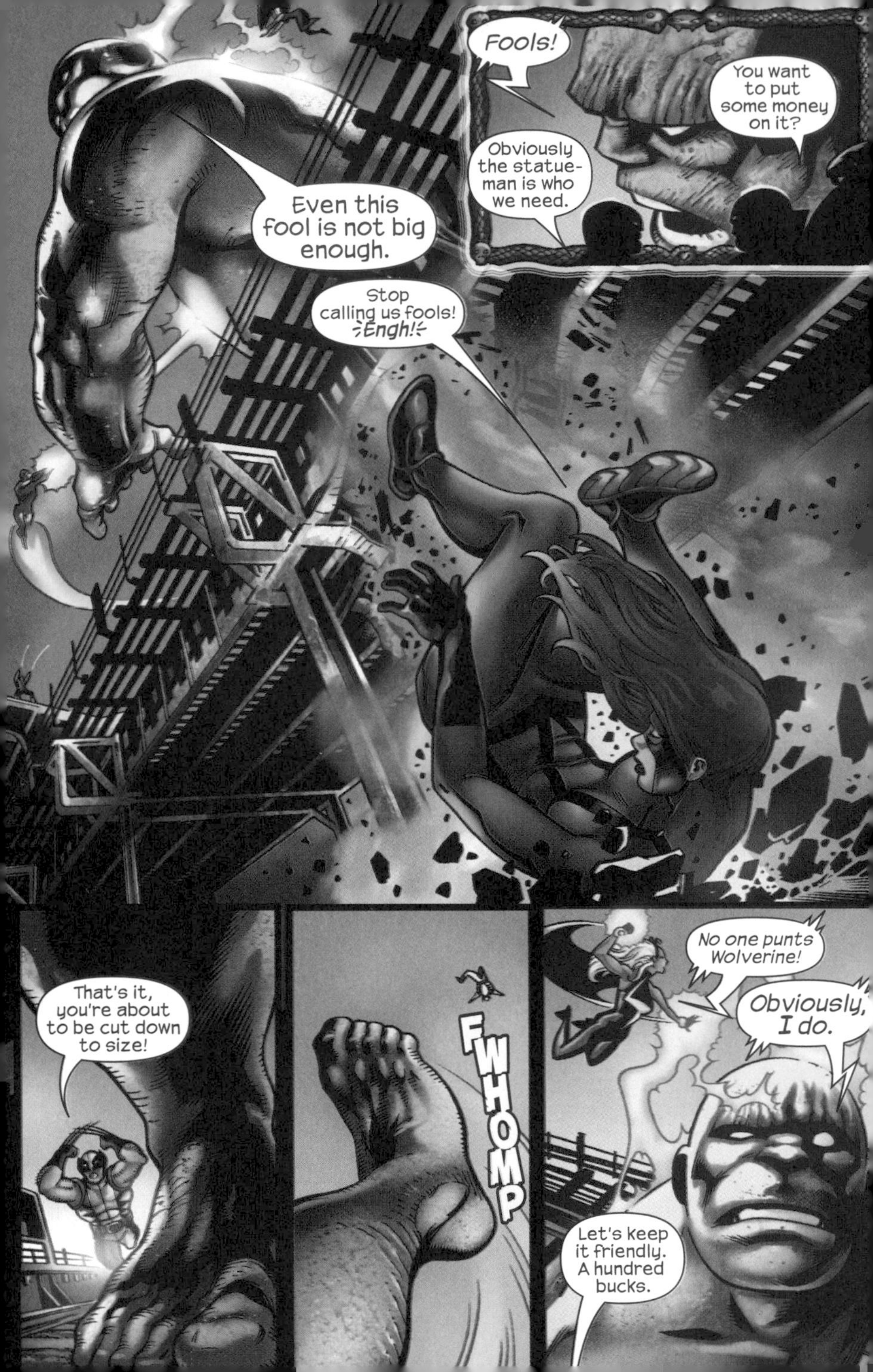
Fools!
You want to put some money on it?
Obviously the statue-man is who we need.
Even this fool is not big enough.
Stop calling us fools! Engh!
That's it, you're about to be cut down to size!
FWHOMP
No one punts Wolverine!
Obviously, I do.
Let's keep it friendly. A hundred bucks.

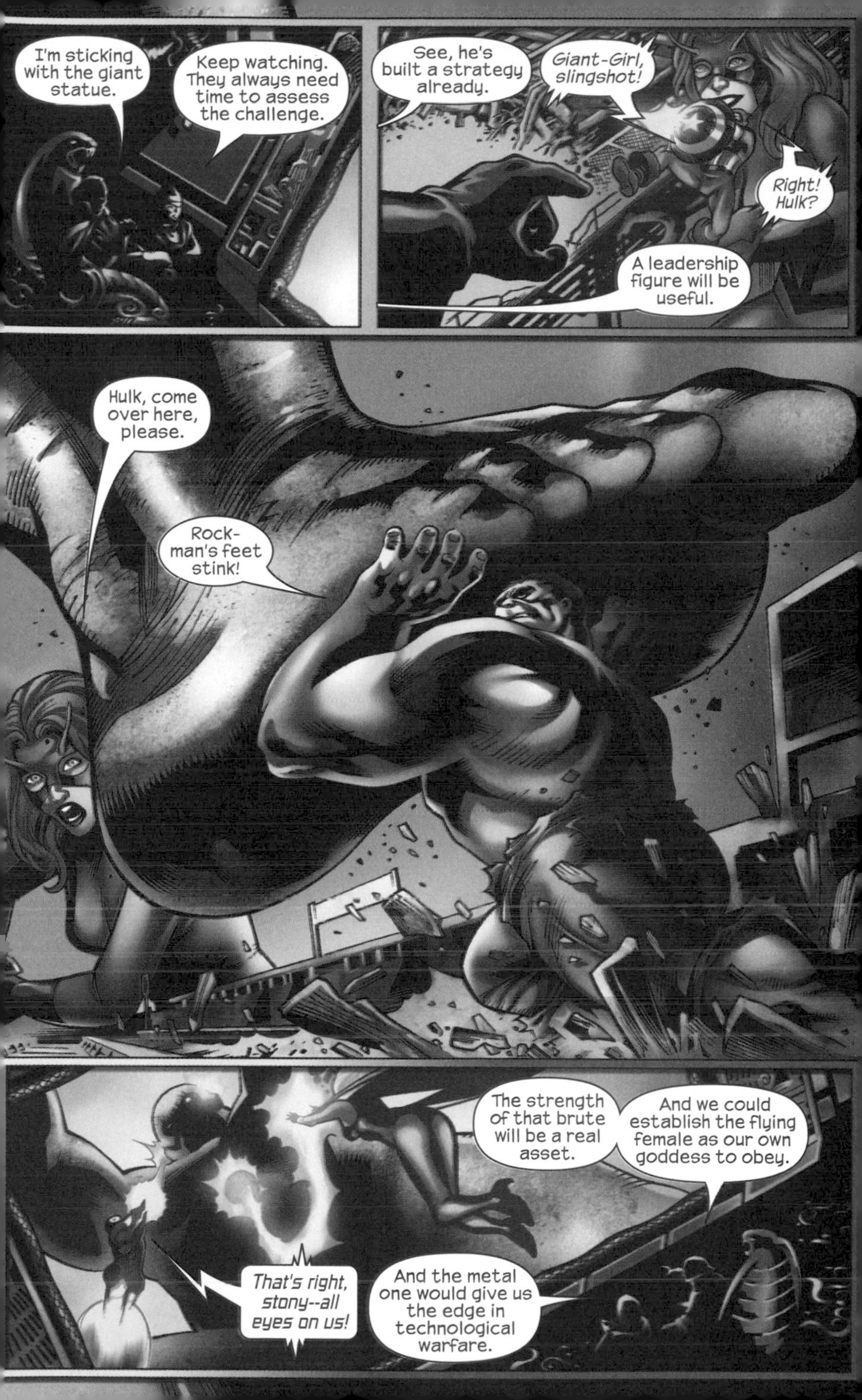

I'm sticking with the giant statue.
Keep watching. They always need time to assess the challenge.
See, he's built a strategy already.
Giant-Girl, slingshot!
Right! Hulk?
A leadership figure will be useful.
Hulk, come over here, please.
Rock-man's feet stink!
The strength of that brute will be a real asset.
And we could establish the flying female as our own goddess to obey.
That's right, stony--all eyes on us!
And the metal one would give us the edge in technological warfare.

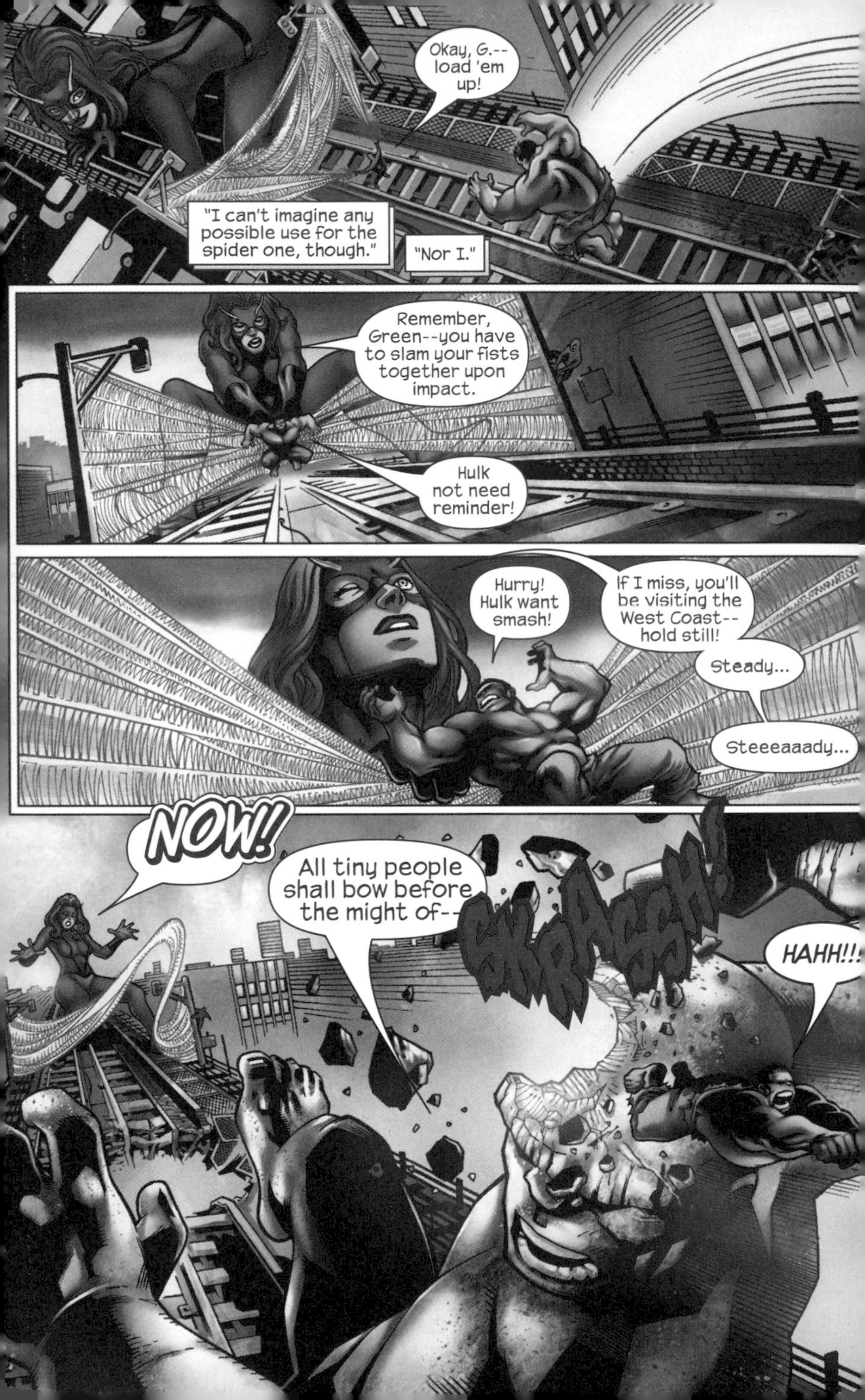
Okay, G.-- load 'em up!
"I can't imagine any possible use for the spider one, though."
"Nor I."
Remember, Green--you have to slam your fists together upon impact.
Hulk not need reminder!
Hurry! Hulk want smash!
If I miss, you'll be visiting the West Coast-- hold still!
Steady...
Steeeaaady...
NOW!
All tiny people shall bow before the might of--
SKRASSH!
HAHH!!!

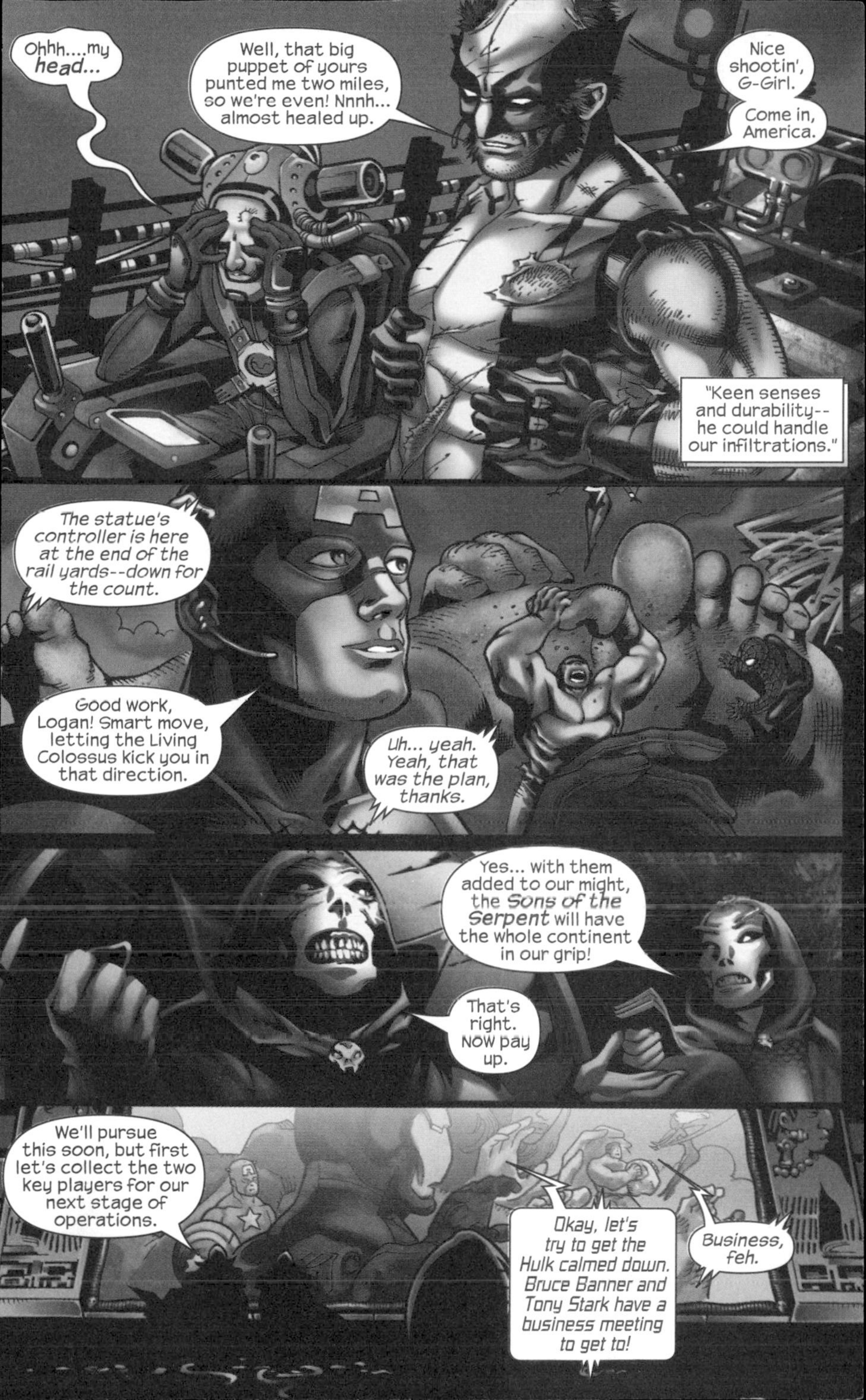
Ohhh....my head...
Well, that big puppet of yours punted me two miles, so we're even! Nnnh... almost healed up.
Nice shootin', G-Girl.
Come in, America.
"Keen senses and durability-- he could handle our infiltrations."
The statue's controller is here at the end of the rail yards--down for the count.
Good work, Logan! Smart move, letting the Living Colossus kick you in that direction.
Uh... yeah. Yeah, that was the plan, thanks.
Yes... with them added to our might, the Sons of the Serpent will have the whole continent in our grip!
That's right. Now pay up.
We'll pursue this soon, but first let's collect the two key players for our next stage of operations.
Okay, let's try to get the Hulk calmed down. Bruce Banner and Tony Stark have a business meeting to get to!
Business, feh.

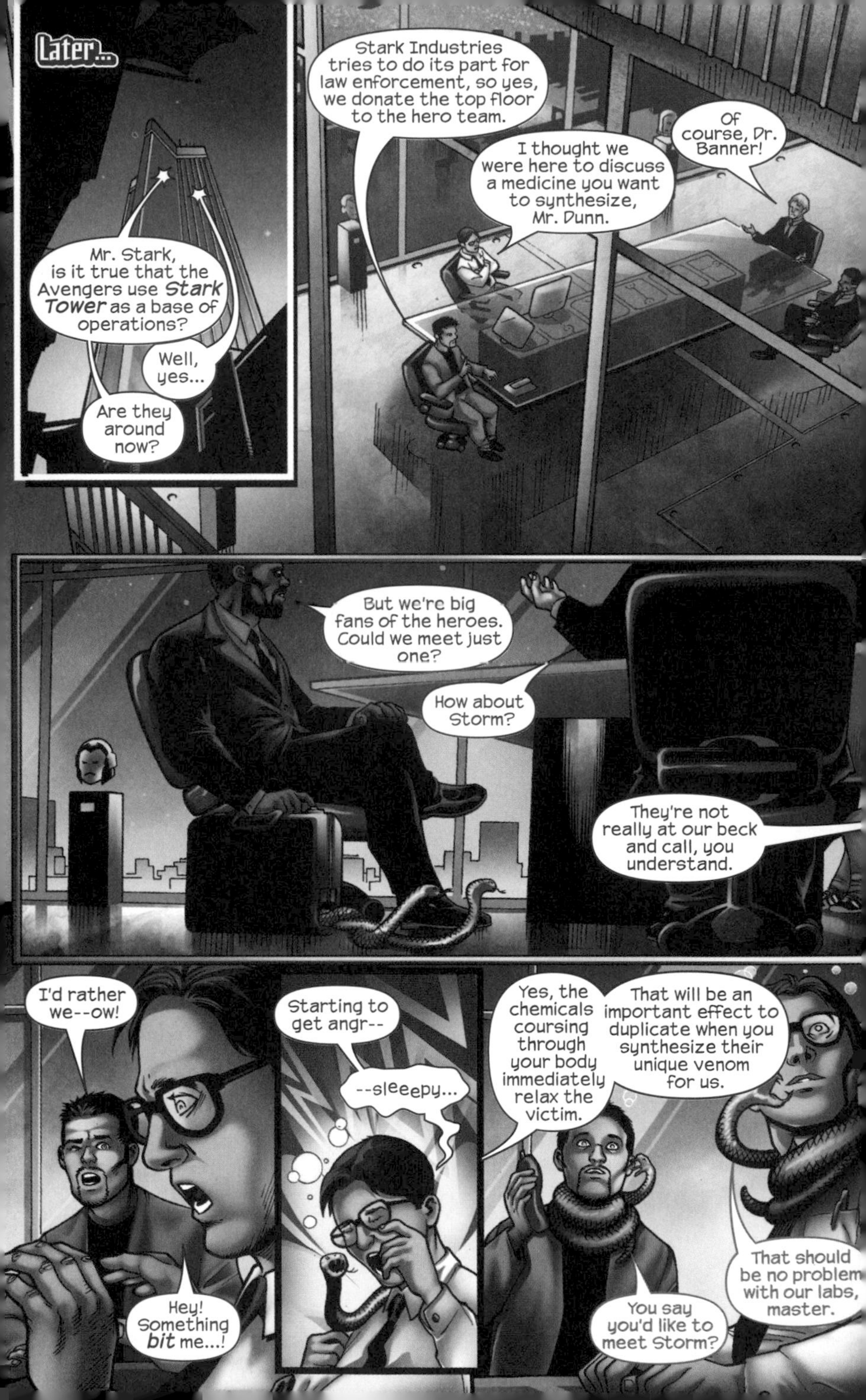
Later...
Mr. Stark, is it true that the Avengers use *Stark Tower* as a base of operations?
Well, yes...
Are they around now?
Stark Industries tries to do its part for law enforcement, so yes, we donate the top floor to the hero team.
I thought we were here to discuss a medicine you want to synthesize, Mr. Dunn.
Of course, Dr. Banner!
But we're big fans of the heroes. Could we meet just one?
How about Storm?
They're not really at our beck and call, you understand.
I'd rather we--ow!
Hey! Something *bit* me...!
Starting to get angr--
--sleeepy...
Yes, the chemicals coursing through your body immediately relax the victim.
That will be an important effect to duplicate when you synthesize their unique venom for us.
You say you'd like to meet Storm?
That should be no problem with our labs, master.

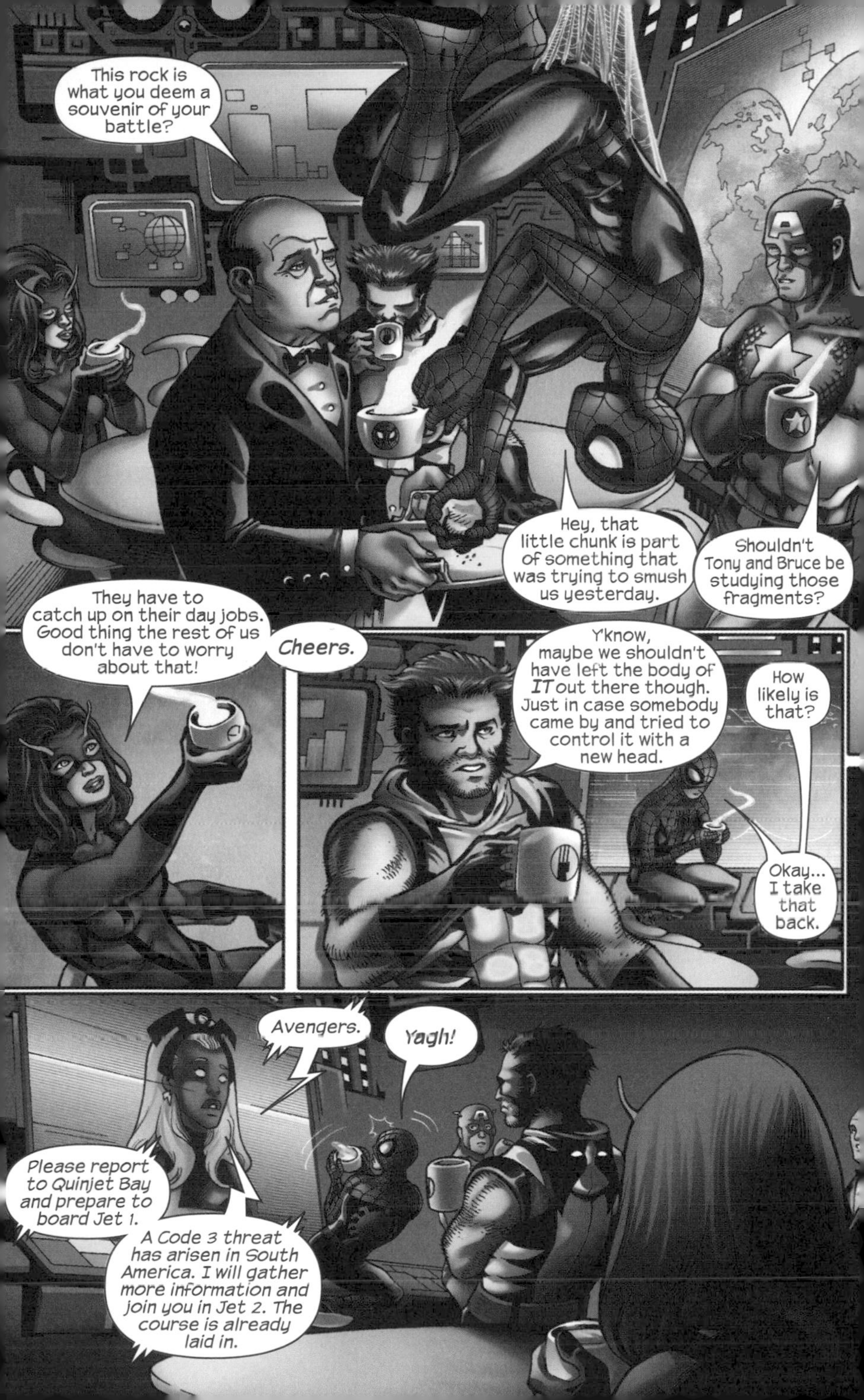

This rock is what you deem a souvenir of your battle?
Hey, that little chunk is part of something that was trying to smush us yesterday.
Shouldn't Tony and Bruce be studying those fragments?
They have to catch up on their day jobs. Good thing the rest of us don't have to worry about that!
Cheers.
Y'know, maybe we shouldn't have left the body of IT out there though. Just in case somebody came by and tried to control it with a new head.
How likely is that?
Okay... I take that back.
Avengers.
Yagh!
Please report to Quinjet Bay and prepare to board Jet 1.
A Code 3 threat has arisen in South America. I will gather more information and join you in Jet 2. The course is already laid in.

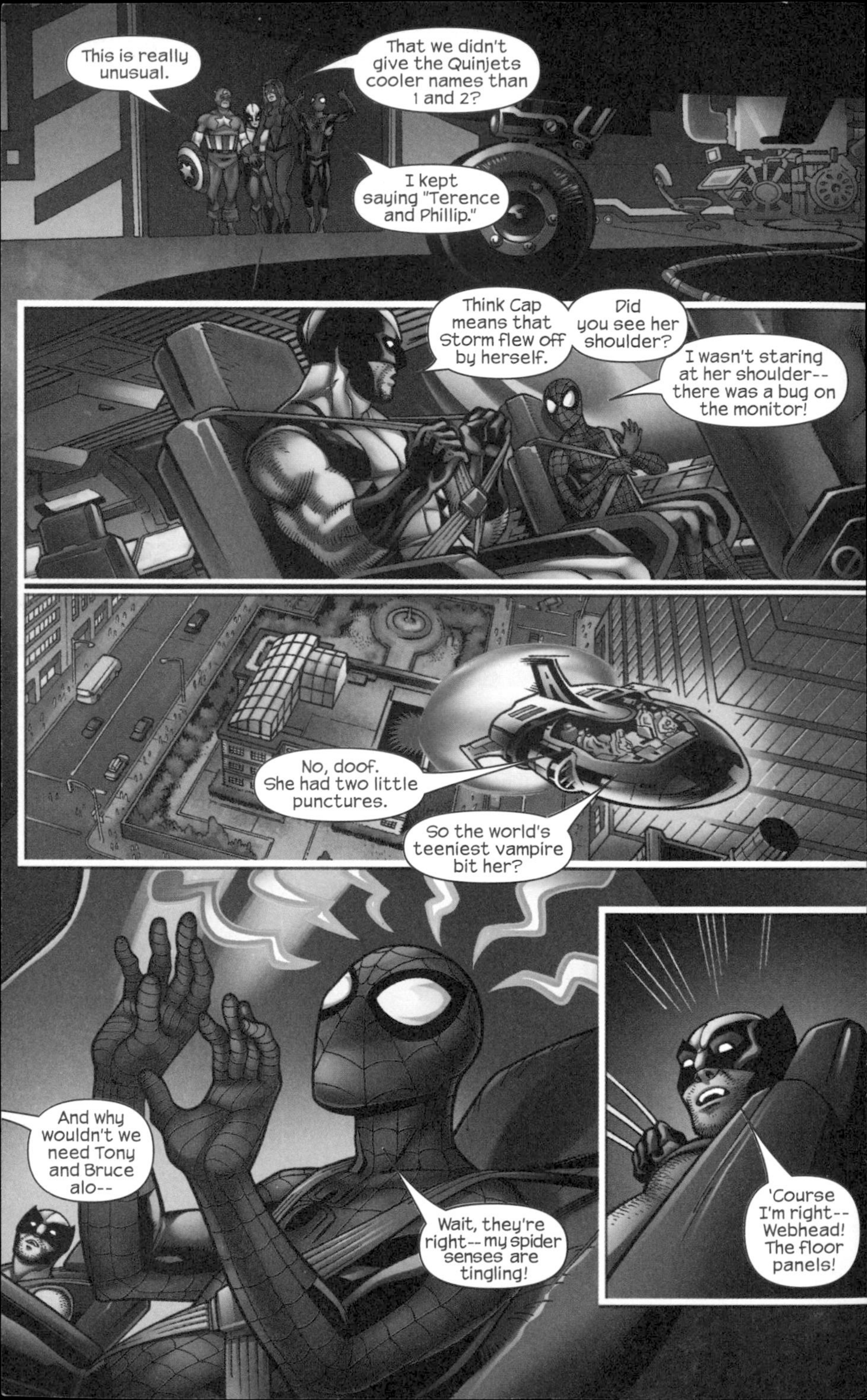
This is really unusual.
That we didn't give the Quinjets cooler names than 1 and 2?
I kept saying "Terence and Phillip."
Think Cap means that Storm flew off by herself.
Did you see her shoulder?
I wasn't staring at her shoulder-- there was a bug on the monitor!
No, doof. She had two little punctures.
So the world's teeniest vampire bit her?
And why wouldn't we need Tony and Bruce alo--
Wait, they're right-- my spider senses are tingling!
'Course I'm right-- Webhead! The floor panels!

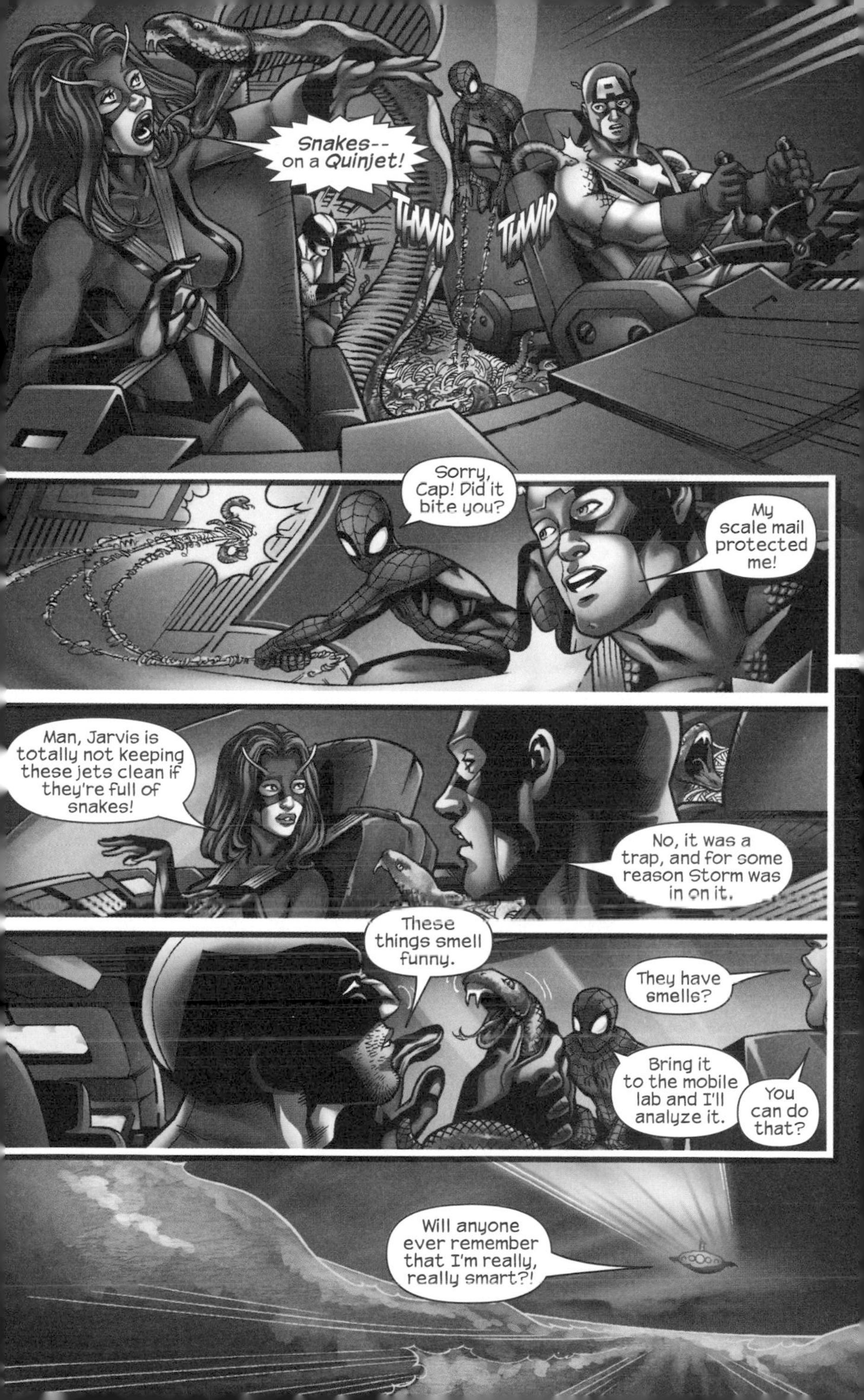
Snakes-- on a Quinjet!
THWIP
THWIP
Sorry, Cap! Did it bite you?
My scale mail protected me!
Man, Jarvis is totally not keeping these jets clean if they're full of snakes!
No, it was a trap, and for some reason Storm was in on it.
These things smell funny.
They have smells?
Bring it to the mobile lab and I'll analyze it.
You can do that?
Will anyone ever remember that I'm really, really smart?!

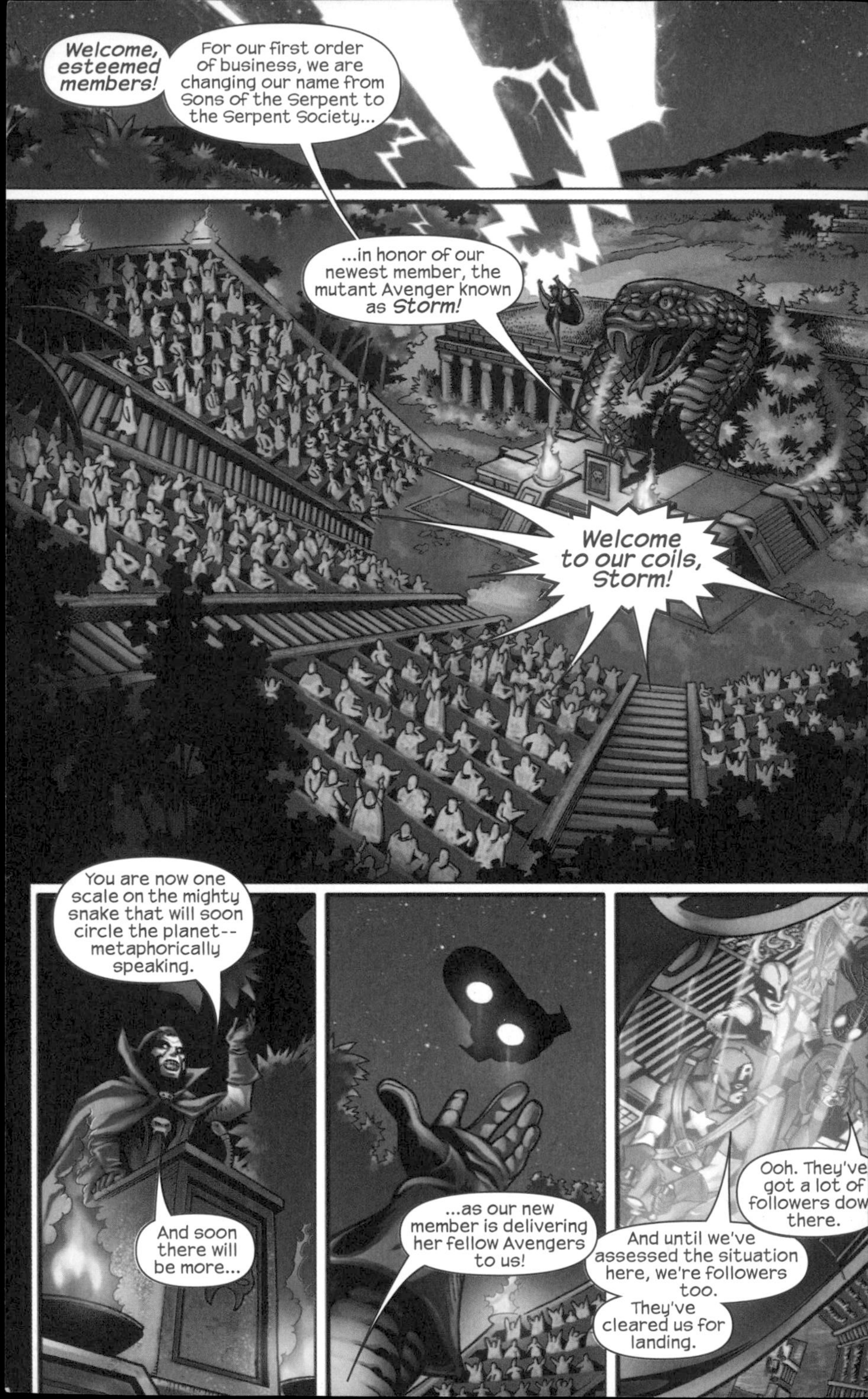
Welcome, esteemed members!
For our first order of business, we are changing our name from Sons of the Serpent to the Serpent Society...
...in honor of our newest member, the mutant Avenger known as Storm!
Welcome to our coils, Storm!
You are now one scale on the mighty snake that will soon circle the planet-- metaphorically speaking.
And soon there will be more...
...as our new member is delivering her fellow Avengers to us!
Ooh. They've got a lot of followers dow there.
And until we've assessed the situation here, we're followers too.
They've cleared us for landing.

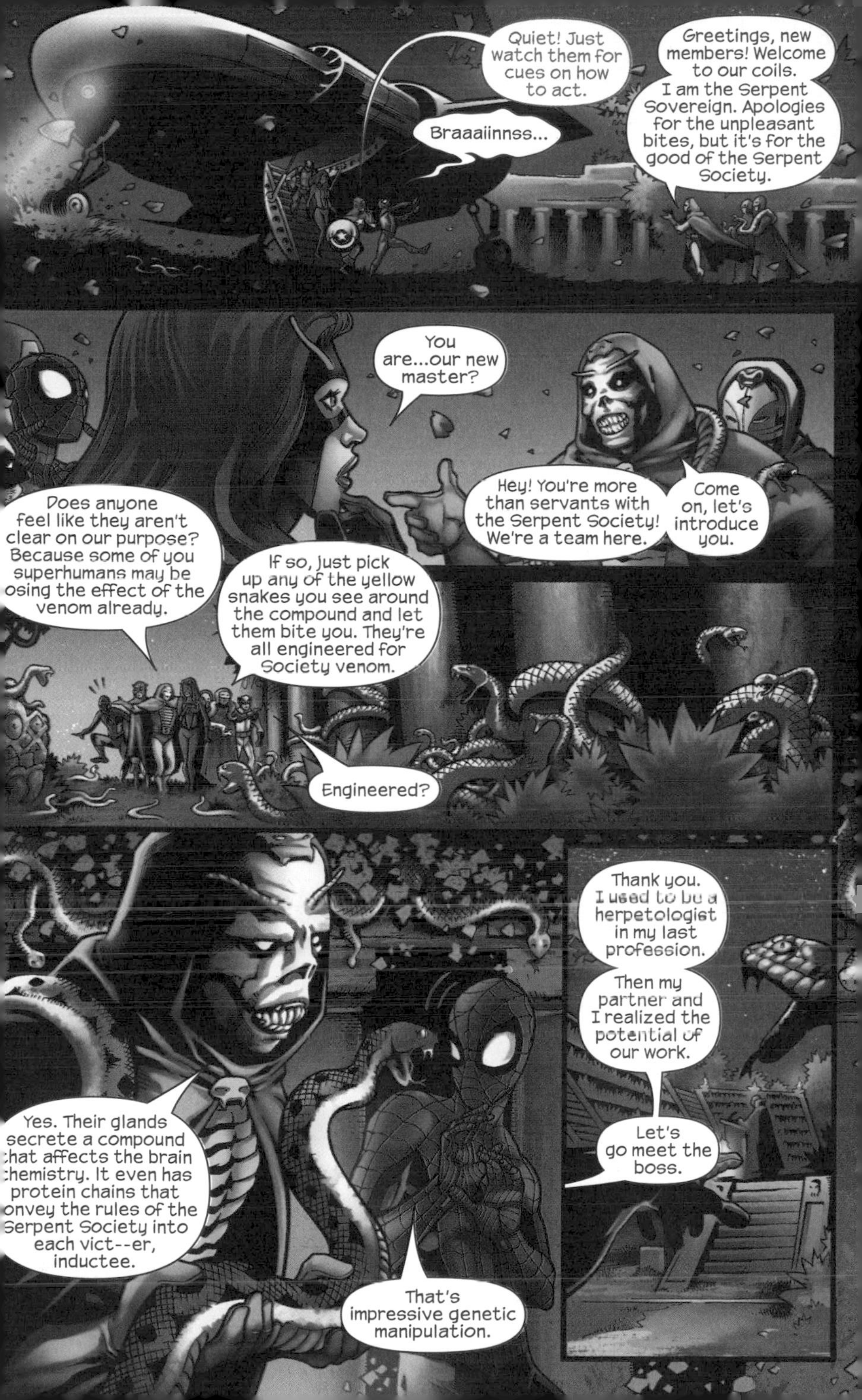
Quiet! Just watch them for cues on how to act.
Braaaiinnss...
Greetings, new members! Welcome to our coils. I am the Serpent Sovereign. Apologies for the unpleasant bites, but it's for the good of the Serpent Society.
You are...our new master?
Hey! You're more than servants with the Serpent Society! We're a team here.
Come on, let's introduce you.
Does anyone feel like they aren't clear on our purpose? Because some of you superhumans may be osing the effect of the venom already.
If so, just pick up any of the yellow snakes you see around the compound and let them bite you. They're all engineered for Society venom.
Engineered?
Yes. Their glands secrete a compound hat affects the brain hemistry. It even has protein chains that onvey the rules of the Serpent Society into each vict--er, inductee.
That's impressive genetic manipulation.
Thank you. I used to be a herpetologist in my last profession.
Then my partner and I realized the potential of our work.
Let's go meet the boss.

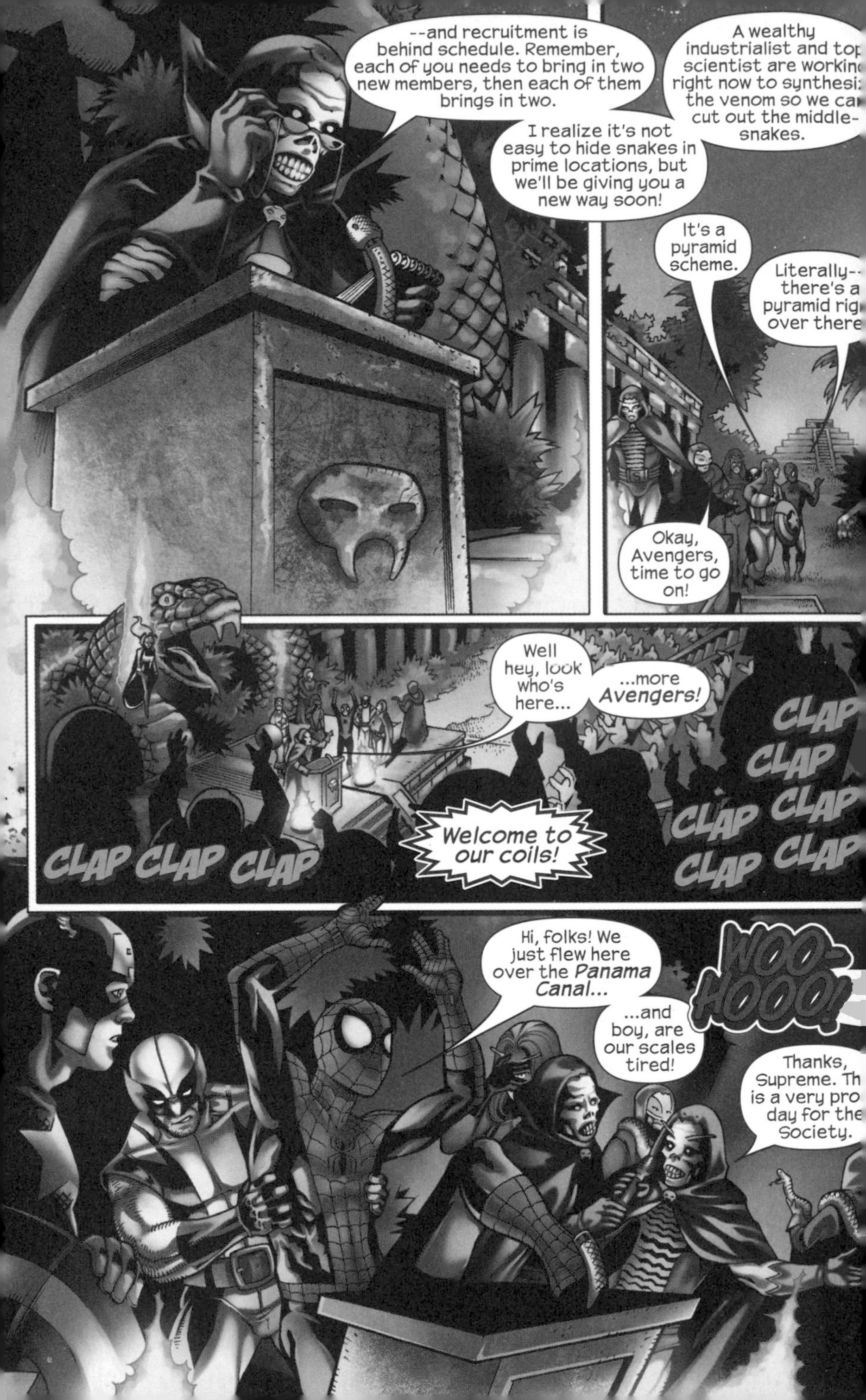
--and recruitment is behind schedule. Remember, each of you needs to bring in two new members, then each of them brings in two.
I realize it's not easy to hide snakes in prime locations, but we'll be giving you a new way soon!
A wealthy industrialist and top scientist are workin right now to synthesi the venom so we ca cut out the middle-snakes.
It's a pyramid scheme.
Literally-- there's a pyramid rig over there
Okay, Avengers, time to go on!
Well hey, look who's here...
...more Avengers!
CLAP CLAP CLAP
Welcome to our coils!
CLAP CLAP CLAP CLAP CLAP CLAP
Hi, folks! We just flew here over the Panama Canal...
...and boy, are our scales tired!
WOO-HOOO!
Thanks, Supreme. Th is a very pro day for the Society.

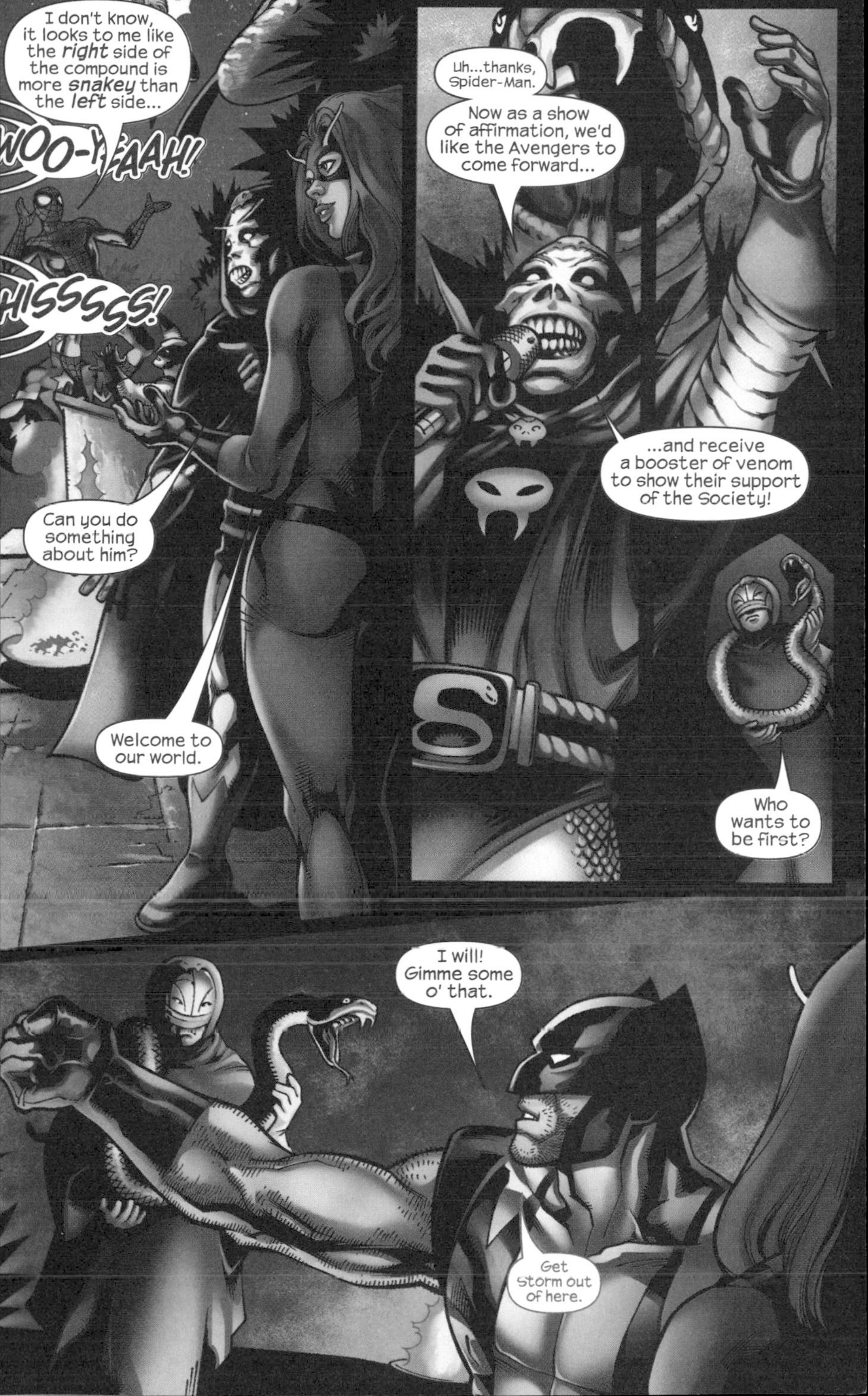
I don't know, it looks to me like the right side of the compound is more snakey than the left side...
WOO-YEAAH!
HISSSSSS!
Can you do something about him?
Welcome to our world.
Uh...thanks, Spider-Man.
Now as a show of affirmation, we'd like the Avengers to come forward...
...and receive a booster of venom to show their support of the Society!
Who wants to be first?
I will! Gimme some o' that.
Get Storm out of here.

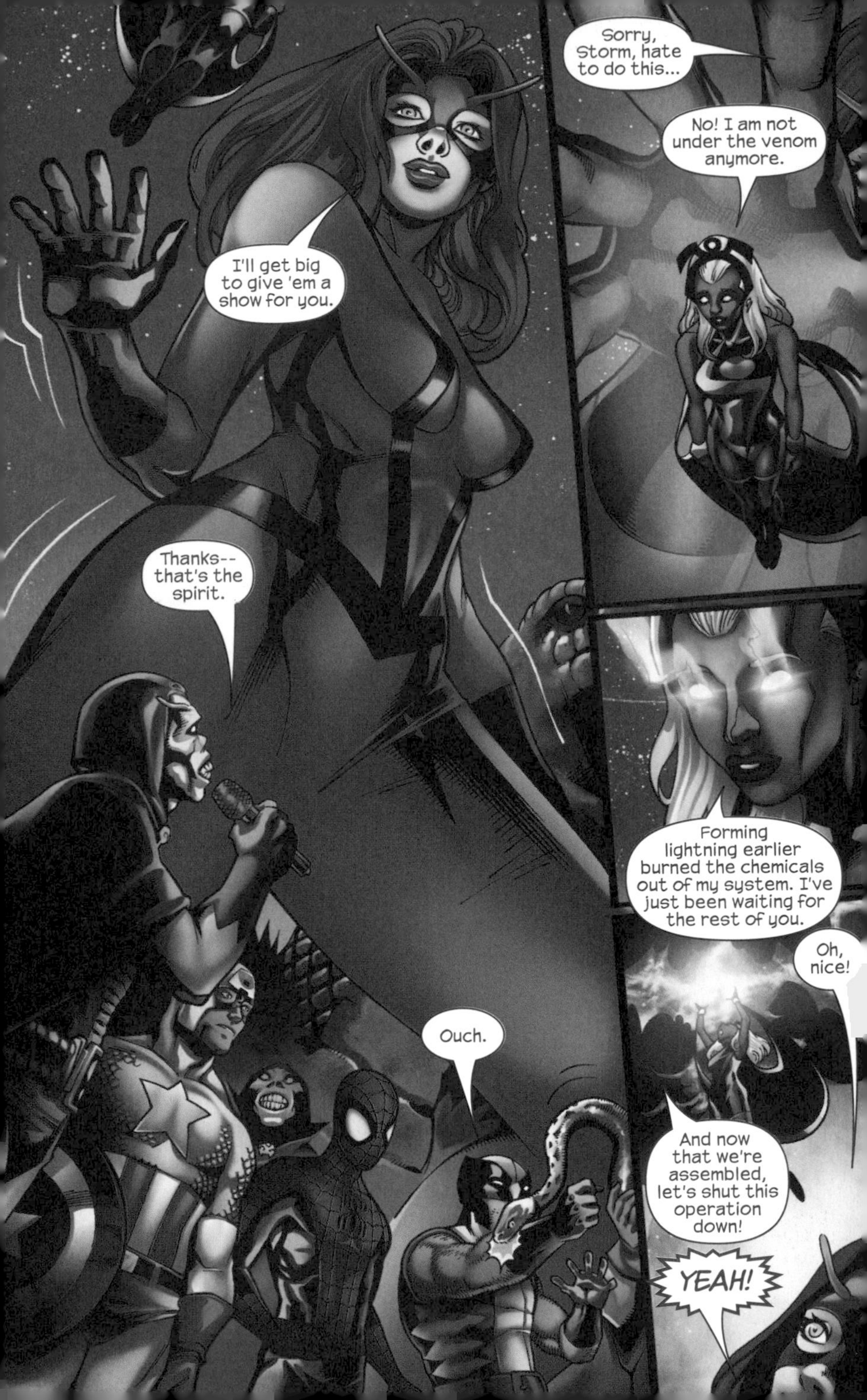
I'll get big to give 'em a show for you.
Thanks--that's the spirit.
Ouch.
Sorry, Storm, hate to do this...
No! I am not under the venom anymore.
Forming lightning earlier burned the chemicals out of my system. I've just been waiting for the rest of you.
Oh, nice!
And now that we're assembled, let's shut this operation down!
YEAH!

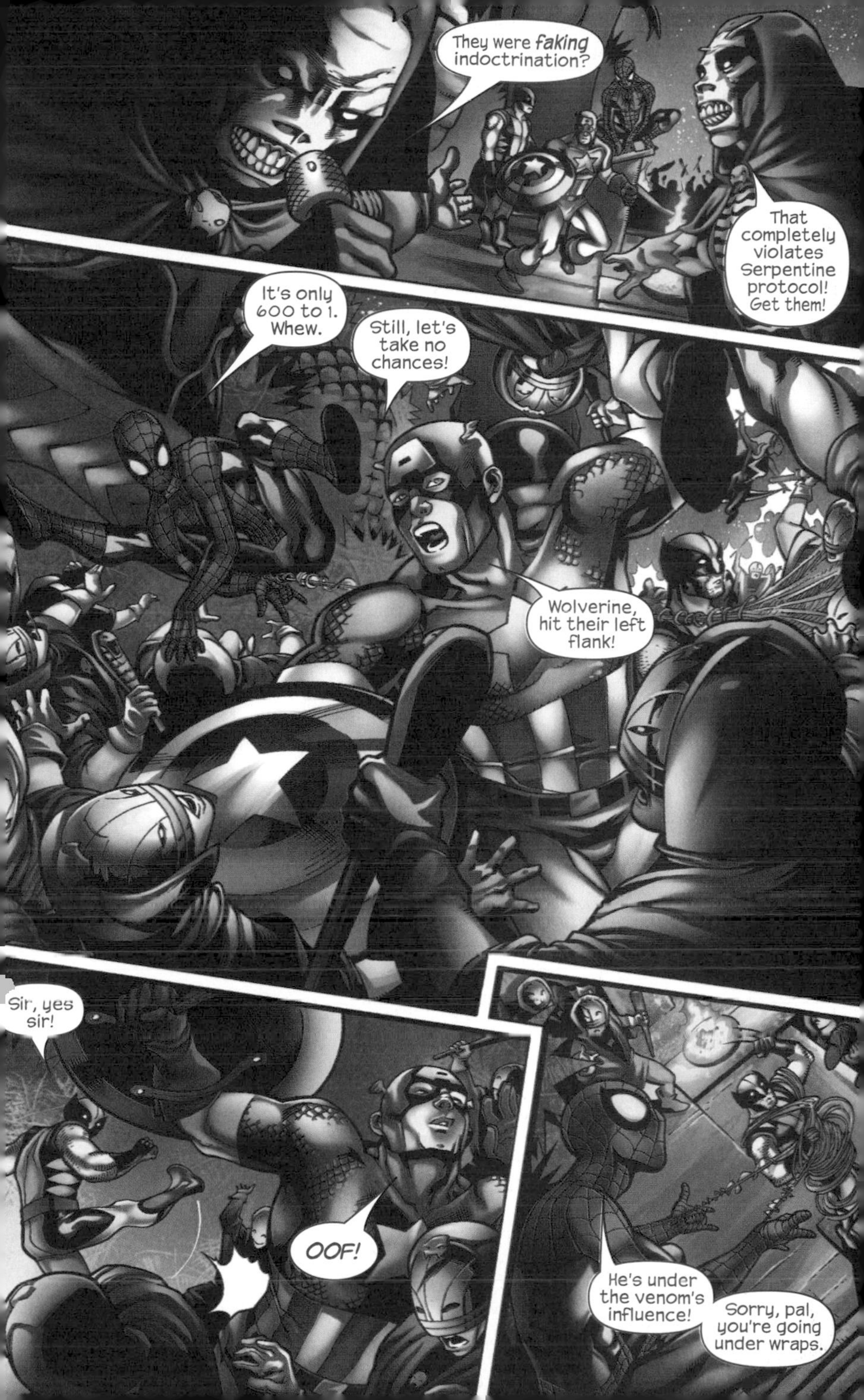

They were *faking* indoctrination?
That completely violates Serpentine protocol! Get them!
It's only 600 to 1. Whew.
Still, let's take no chances!
Wolverine, hit their left flank!
Sir, yes sir!
OOF!
He's under the venom's influence!
Sorry, pal, you're going under wraps.

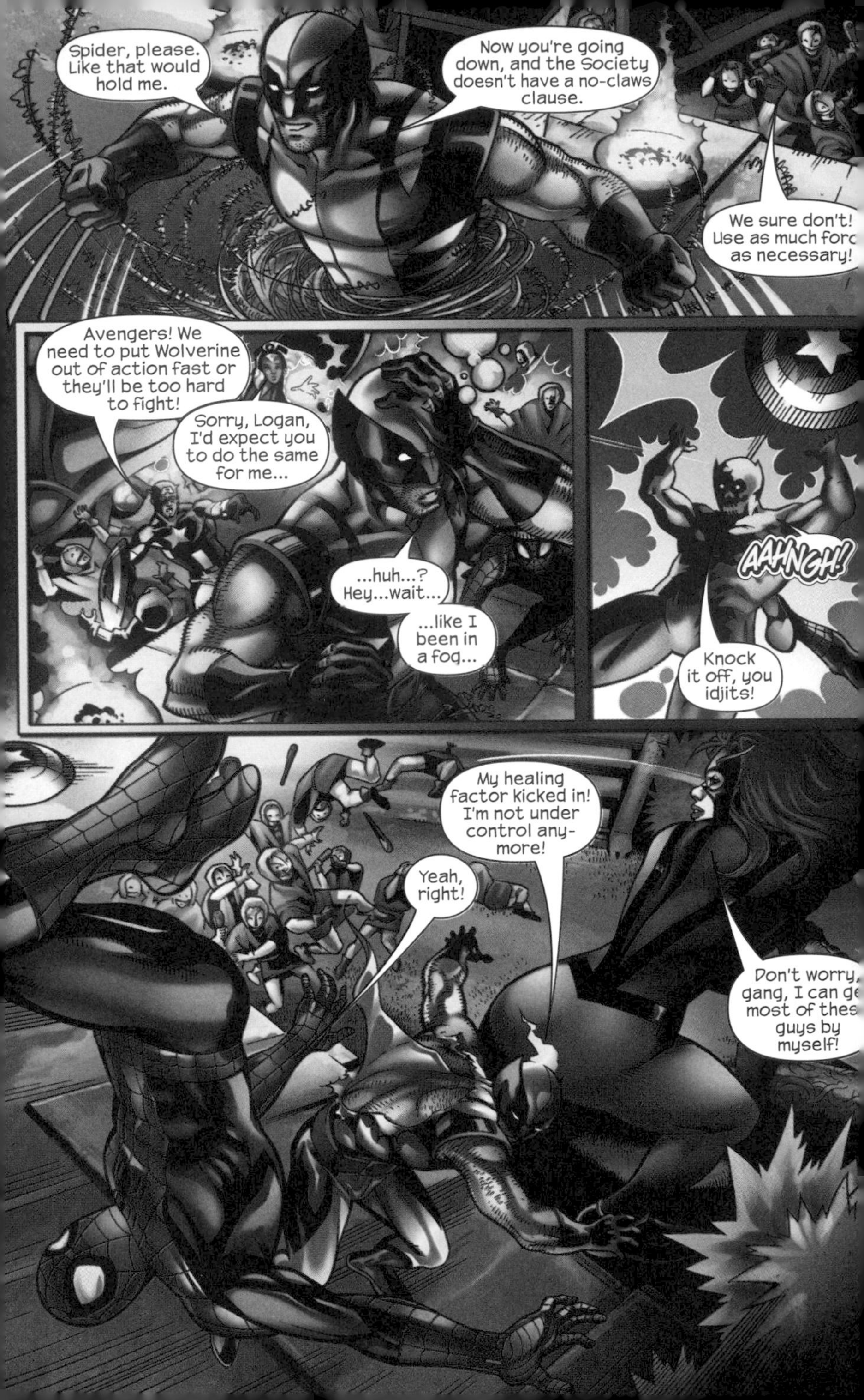
Spider, please. Like that would hold me.
Now you're going down, and the Society doesn't have a no-claws clause.
We sure don't! Use as much forc as necessary!
Avengers! We need to put Wolverine out of action fast or they'll be too hard to fight!
Sorry, Logan, I'd expect you to do the same for me...
...huh...? Hey...wait...
...like I been in a fog...
AAHNGH!
Knock it off, you idjits!
My healing factor kicked in! I'm not under control any-more!
Yeah, right!
Don't worry, gang, I can ge most of thes guys by myself!

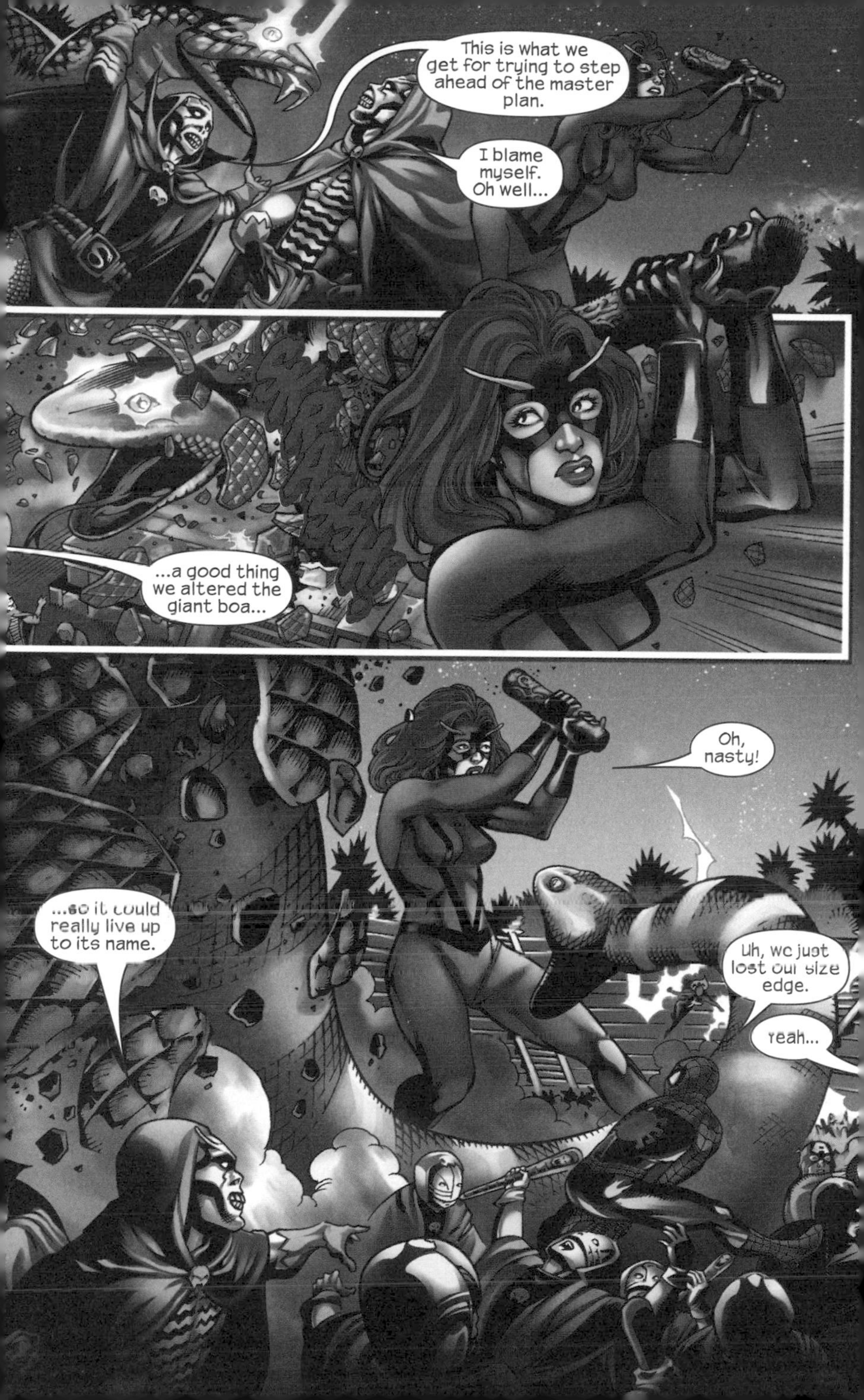
This is what we get for trying to step ahead of the master plan.
I blame myself. Oh well...
...a good thing we altered the giant boa...
Oh, nasty!
...so it could really live up to its name.
Uh, we just lost our size edge.
Yeah...

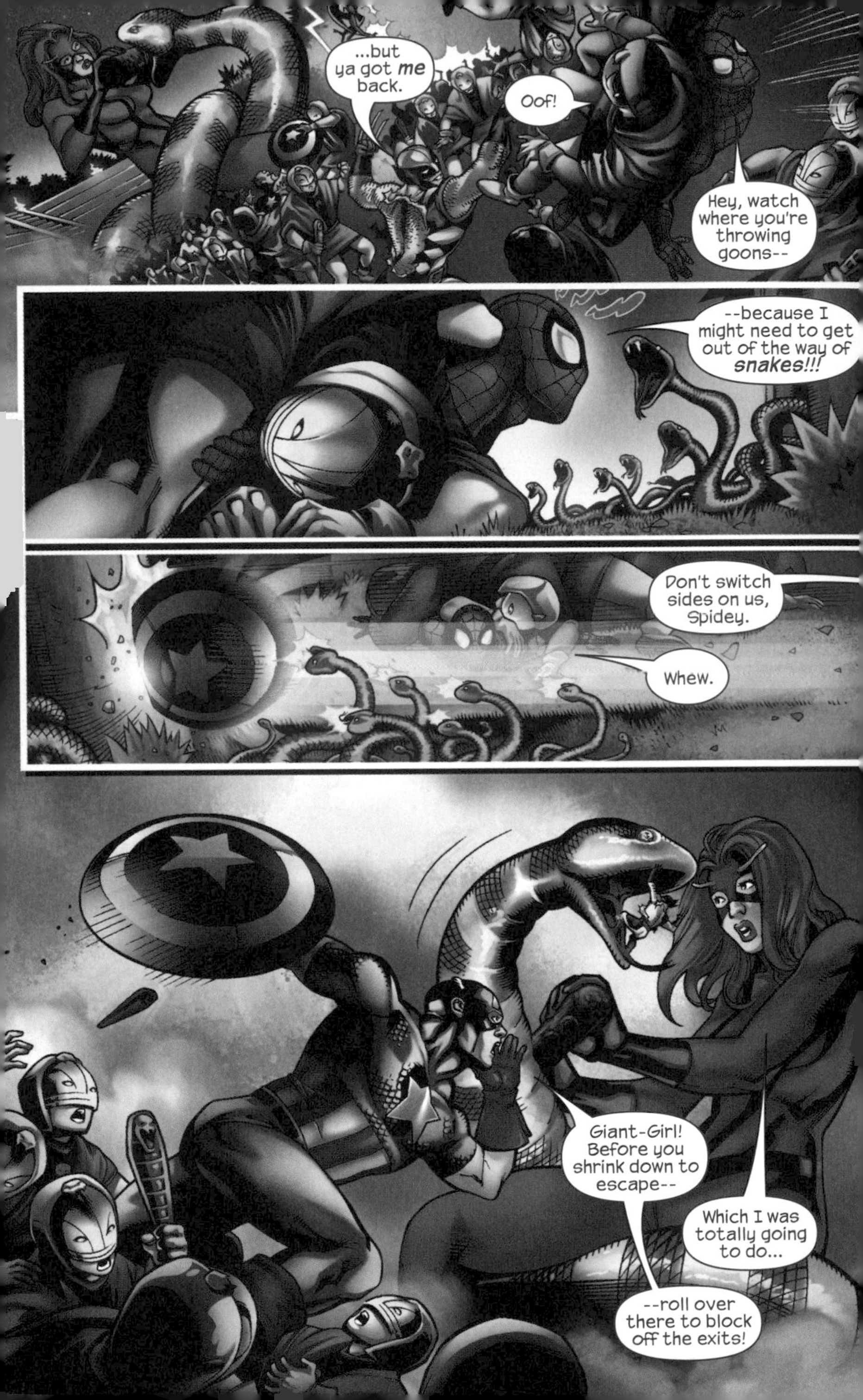
...but ya got *me* back.
Oof!
Hey, watch where you're throwing goons--
--because I might need to get out of the way of ***snakes!!!***
Don't switch sides on us, Spidey.
Whew.
Giant-Girl! Before you shrink down to escape--
Which I was totally going to do...
--roll over there to block off the exits!

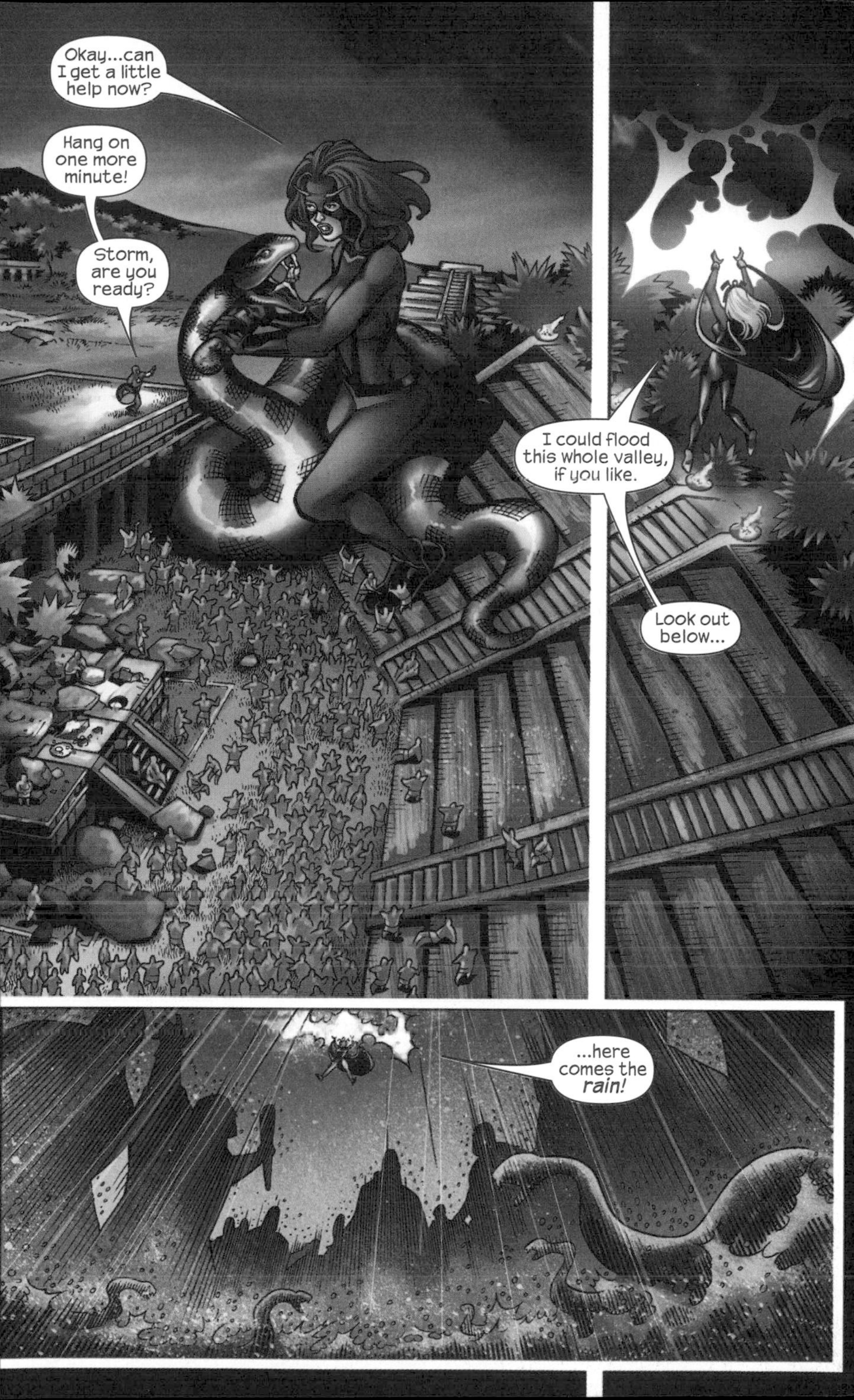

Okay...can I get a little help now?
Hang on one more minute!
Storm, are you ready?
I could flood this whole valley, if you like.
Look out below...
...here comes the *rain!*

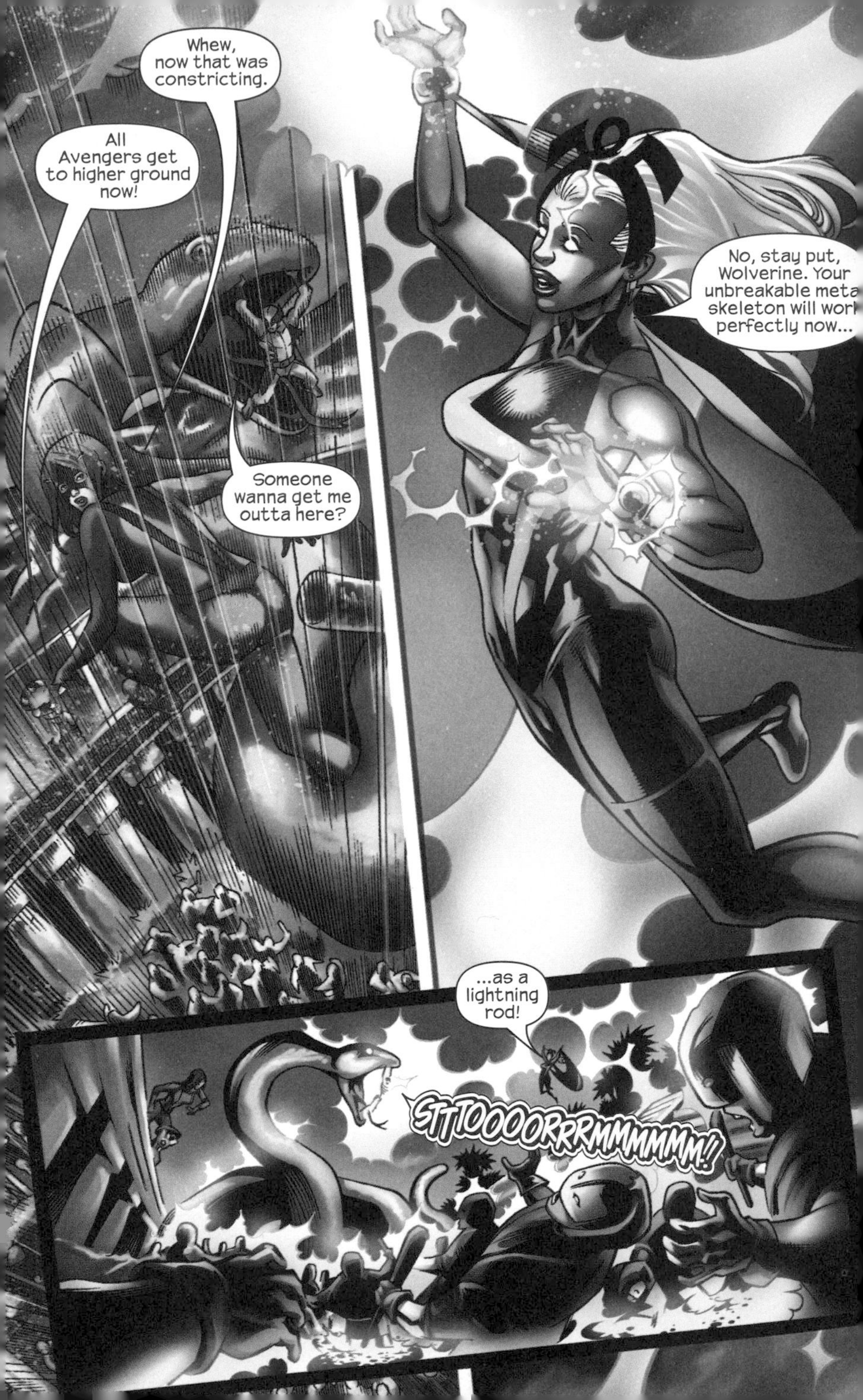
All Avengers get to higher ground now!
Whew, now that was constricting.
Someone wanna get me outta here?
No, stay put, Wolverine. Your unbreakable meta skeleton will work perfectly now...
...as a lightning rod!
STTOOOORRRMMMMMM!!

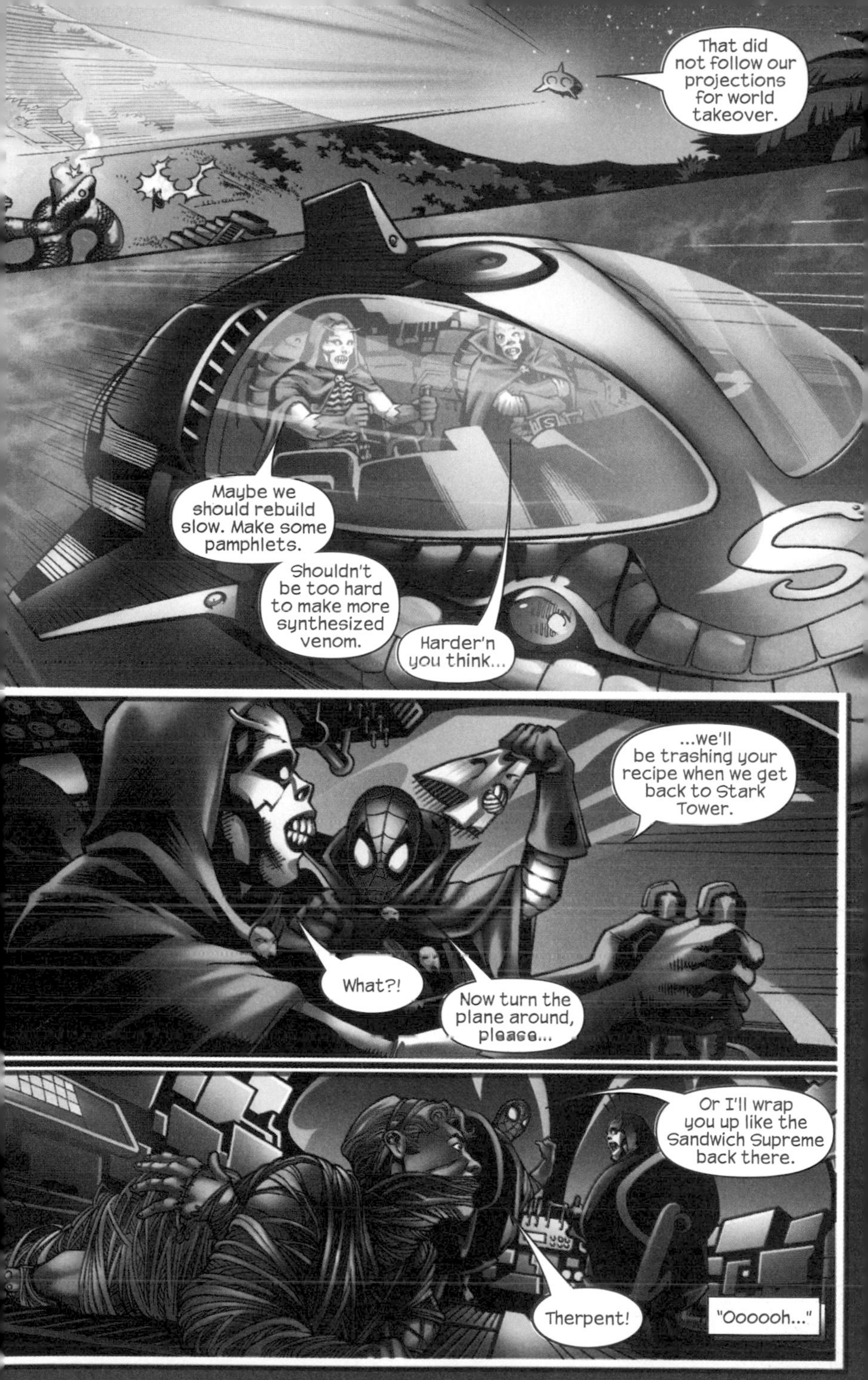
That did not follow our projections for world takeover.
Maybe we should rebuild slow. Make some pamphlets.
Shouldn't be too hard to make more synthesized venom.
Harder'n you think...
...we'll be trashing your recipe when we get back to Stark Tower.
What?!
Now turn the plane around, please...
Or I'll wrap you up like the Sandwich Supreme back there.
Therpent!
"Oooooh..."

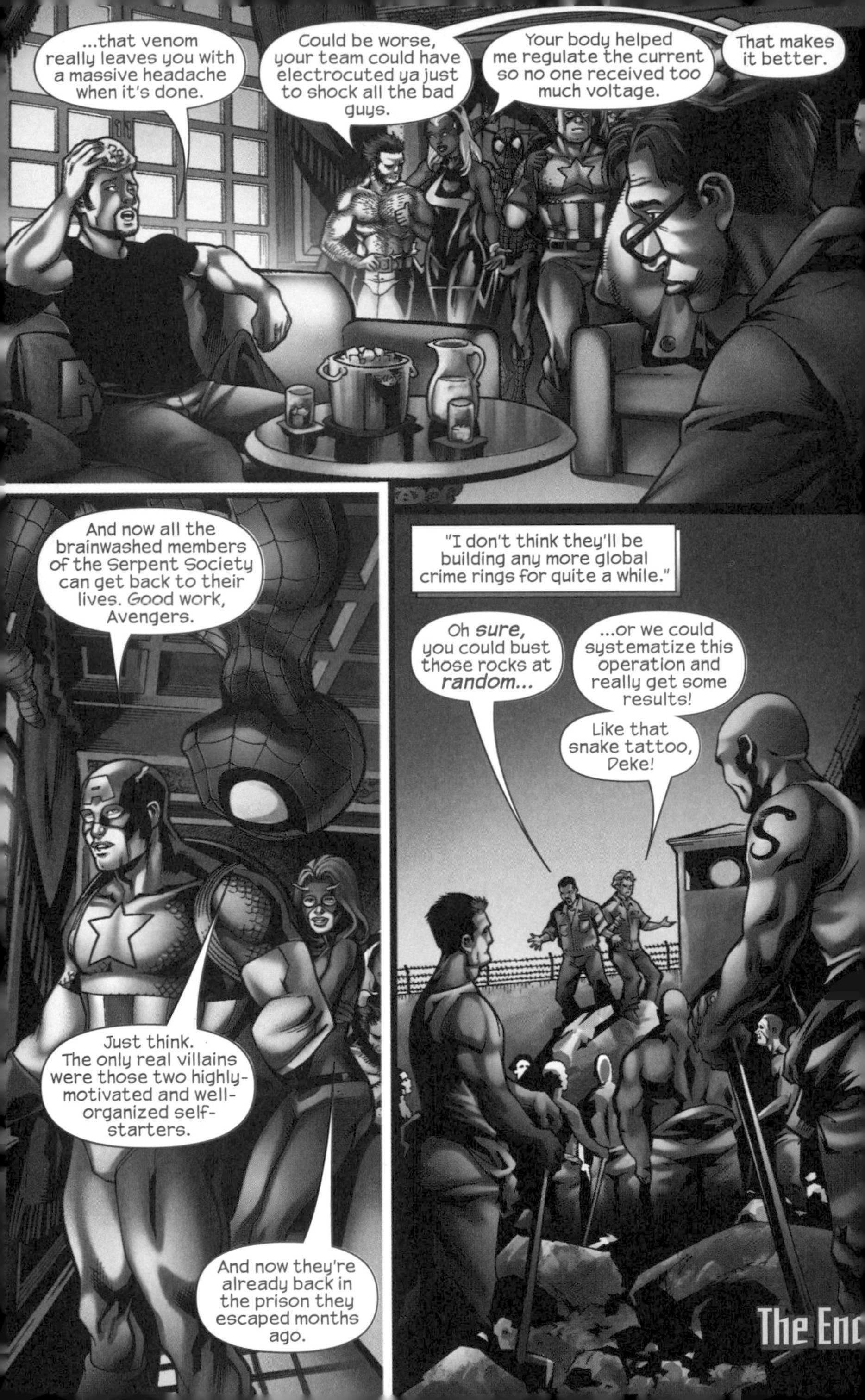
...that venom really leaves you with a massive headache when it's done.
Could be worse, your team could have electrocuted ya just to shock all the bad guys.
Your body helped me regulate the current so no one received too much voltage.
That makes it better.
And now all the brainwashed members of the Serpent Society can get back to their lives. Good work, Avengers.
Just think. The only real villains were those two highly-motivated and well-organized self-starters.
And now they're already back in the prison they escaped months ago.
"I don't think they'll be building any more global crime rings for quite a while."
Oh sure, you could bust those rocks at random...
...or we could systematize this operation and really get some results!
Like that snake tattoo, Deke!

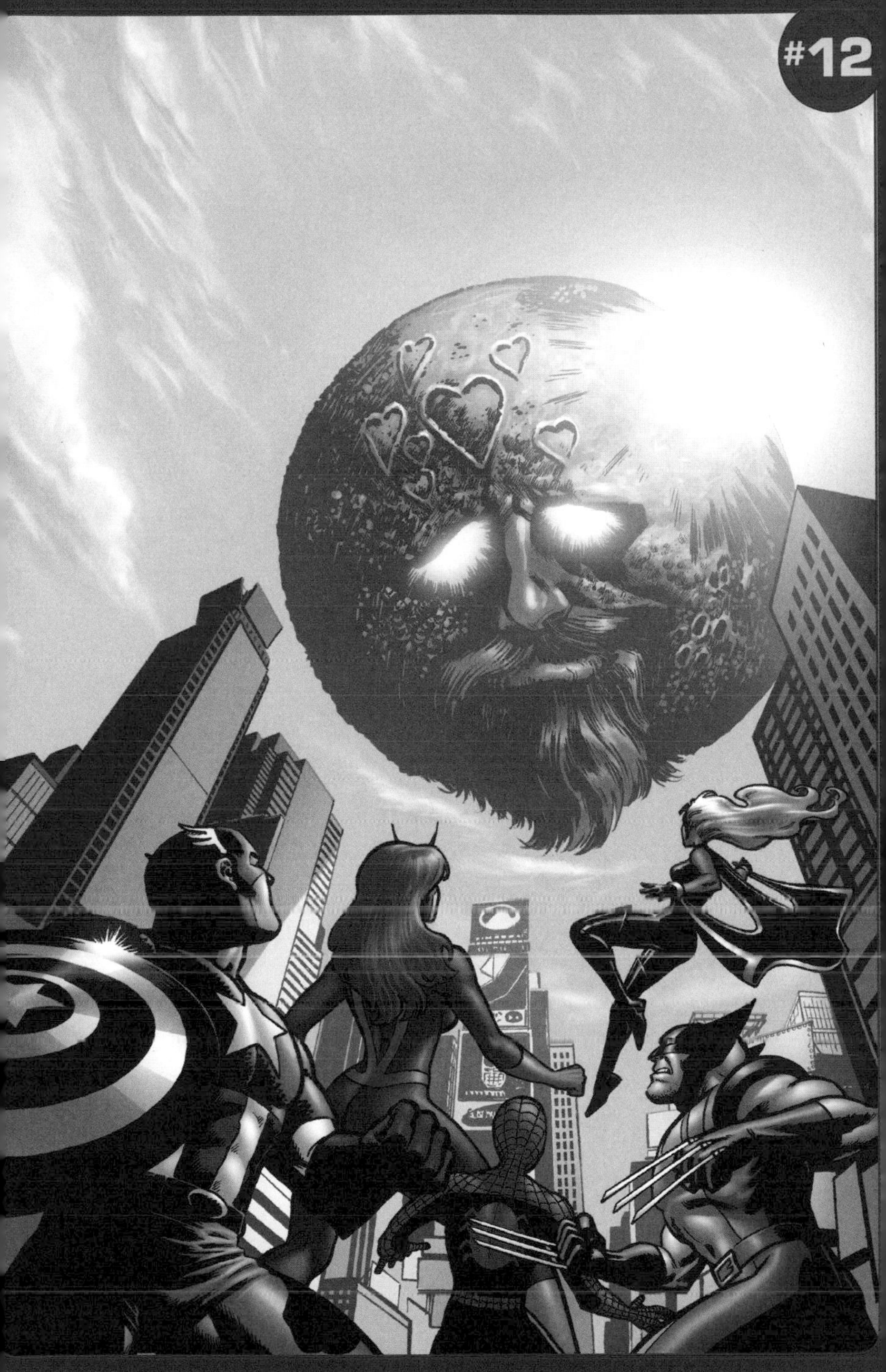
#12

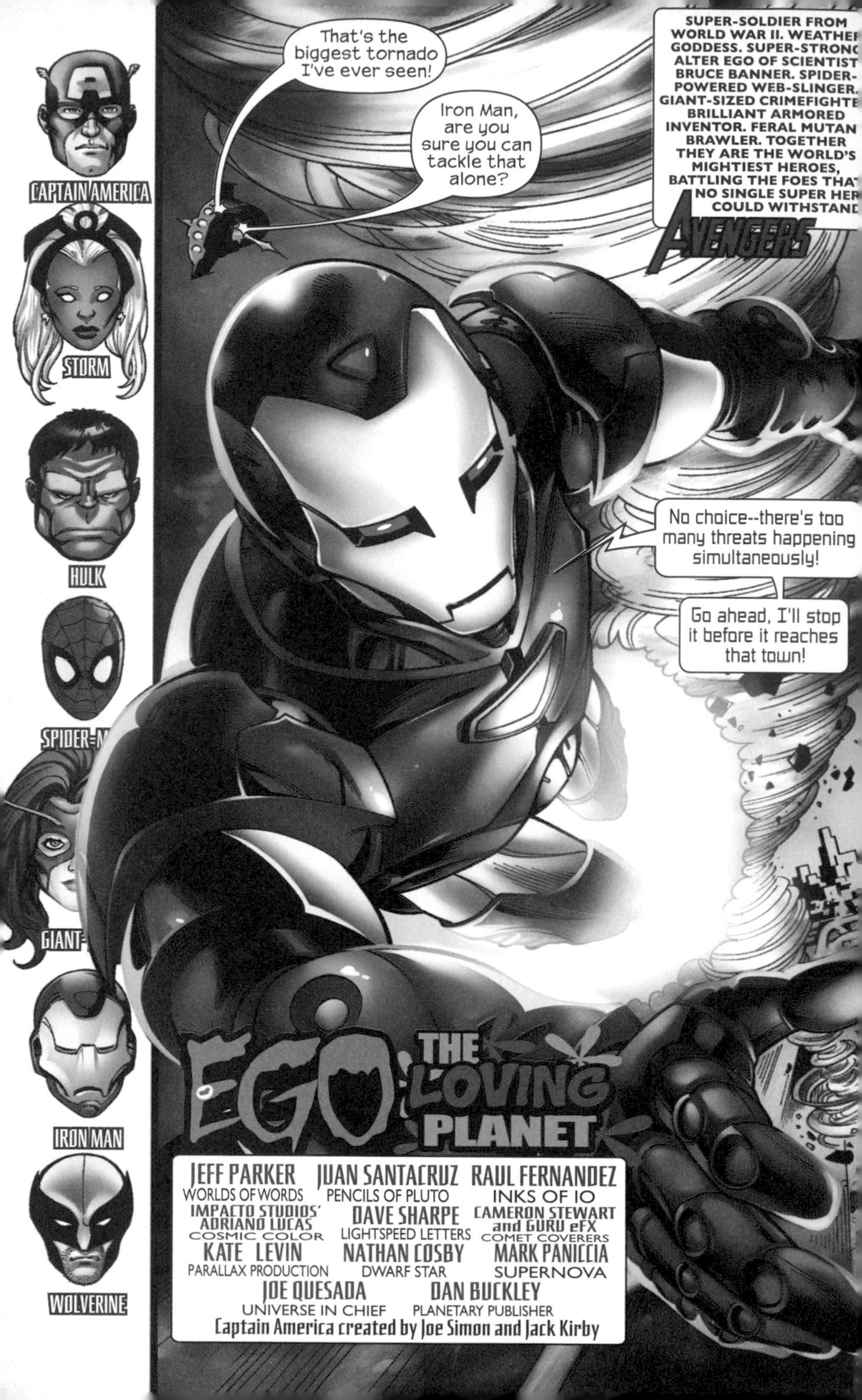
CAPTAIN AMERICA
STORM
HULK
SPIDER-M
GIANT-
IRON MAN
WOLVERINE
SUPER-SOLDIER FROM WORLD WAR II. WEATHE GODDESS. SUPER-STRON ALTER EGO OF SCIENTIST BRUCE BANNER. SPIDER-POWERED WEB-SLINGER. GIANT-SIZED CRIMEFIGHT BRILLIANT ARMORED INVENTOR. FERAL MUTAN BRAWLER. TOGETHER THEY ARE THE WORLD'S MIGHTIEST HEROES, BATTLING THE FOES THA NO SINGLE SUPER HER COULD WITHSTAN
AVENGERS
That's the biggest tornado I've ever seen!
Iron Man, are you sure you can tackle that alone?
No choice--there's too many threats happening simultaneously!
Go ahead, I'll stop it before it reaches that town!
EGO THE LOVING PLANET
JEFF PARKER WORLDS OF WORDS
JUAN SANTACRUZ PENCILS OF PLUTO
RAUL FERNANDEZ INKS OF IO
IMPACTO STUDIOS' ADRIANO LUCAS COSMIC COLOR
DAVE SHARPE LIGHTSPEED LETTERS
CAMERON STEWART and GURU eFX COMET COVERERS
KATE LEVIN PARALLAX PRODUCTION
NATHAN COSBY DWARF STAR
MARK PANICCIA SUPERNOVA
JOE QUESADA UNIVERSE IN CHIEF
DAN BUCKLEY PLANETARY PUBLISHER
Captain America created by Joe Simon and Jack Kirby

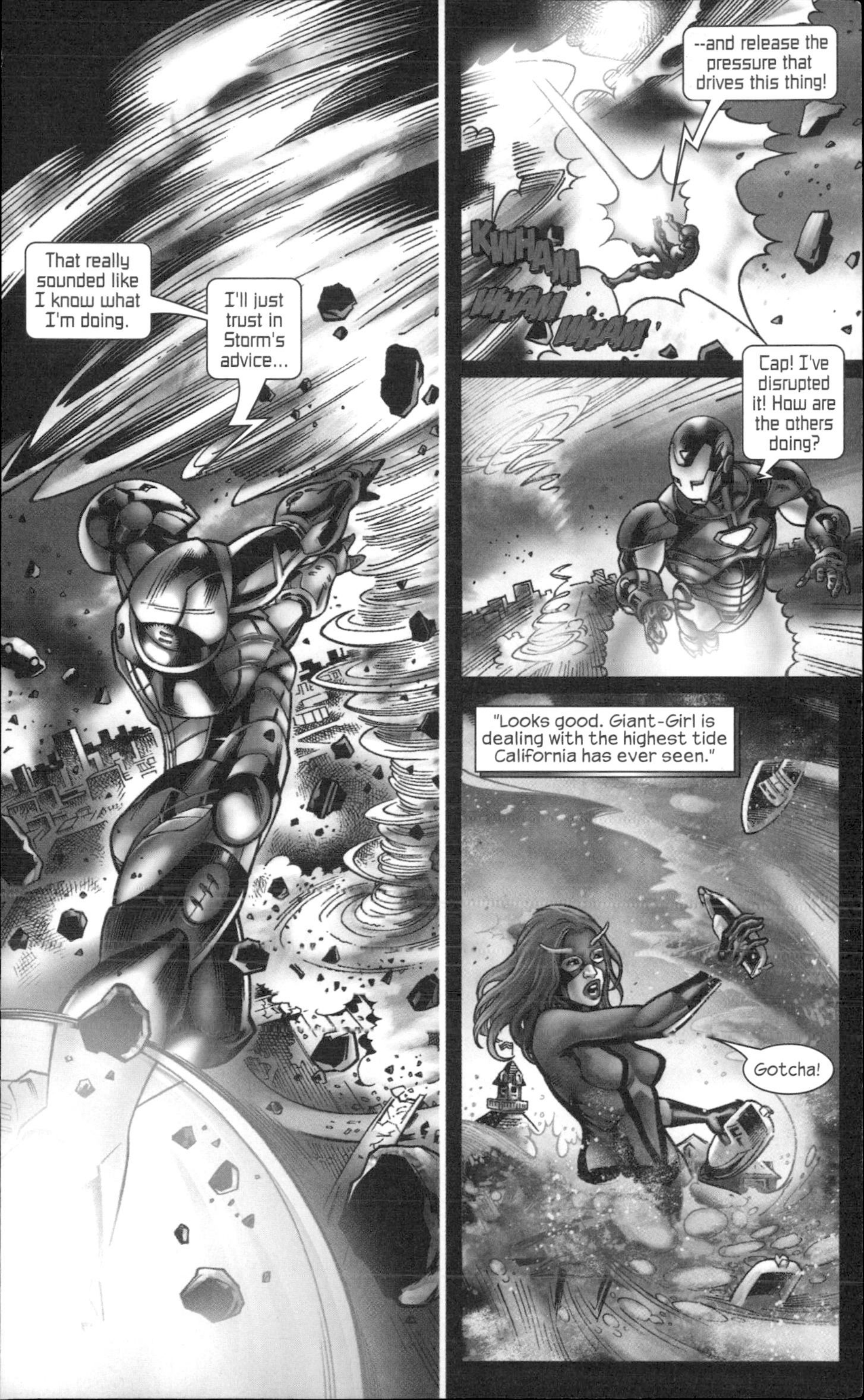
That really sounded like I know what I'm doing.
I'll just trust in Storm's advice...
--and release the pressure that drives this thing!
KWHAM
WHAM
WHAM
Cap! I've disrupted it! How are the others doing?
"Looks good. Giant-Girl is dealing with the highest tide California has ever seen."
Gotcha!

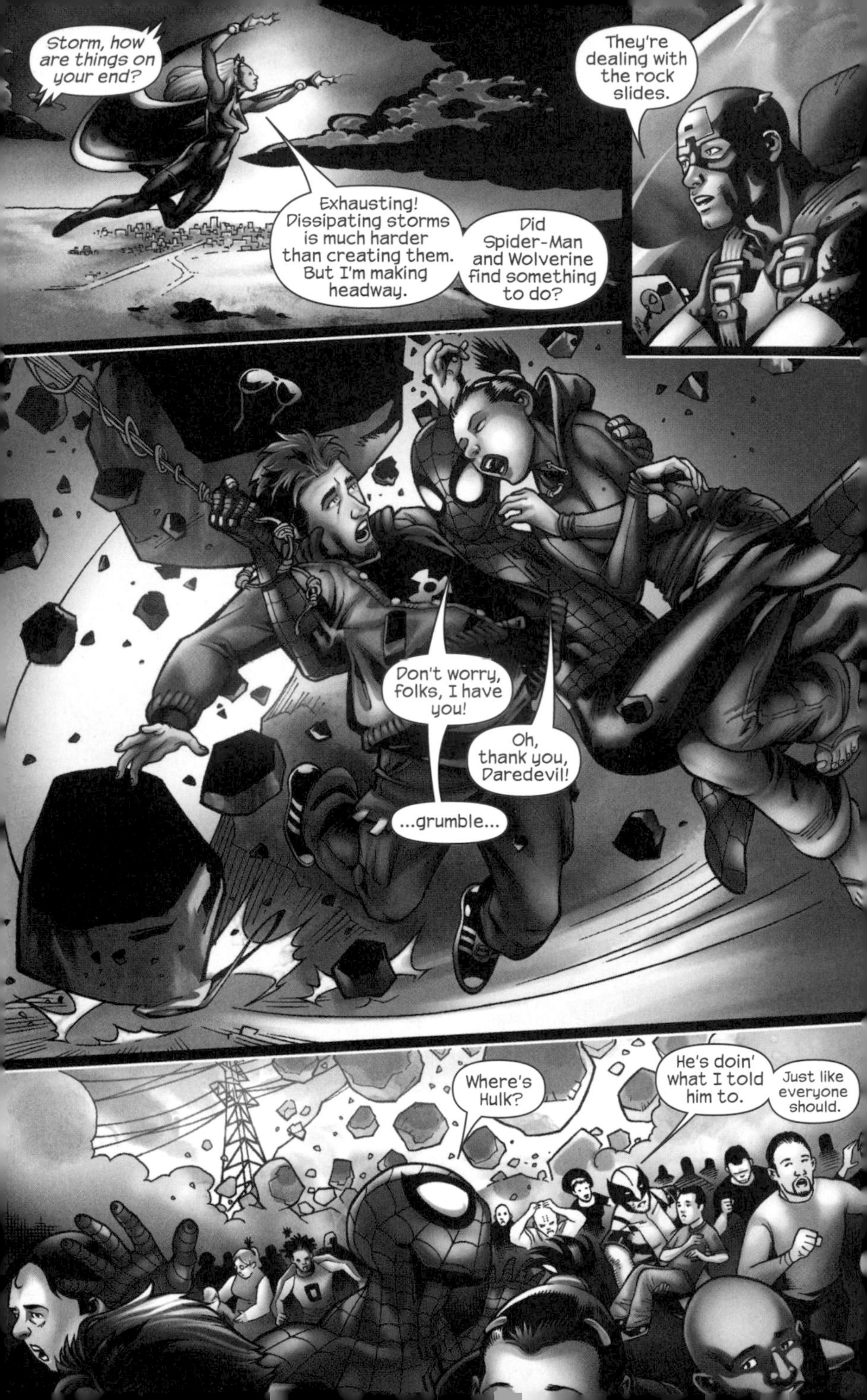
Storm, how are things on your end?
They're dealing with the rock slides.
Exhausting! Dissipating storms is much harder than creating them. But I'm making headway.
Did Spider-Man and Wolverine find something to do?
Don't worry, folks, I have you!
Oh, thank you, Daredevil!
...grumble...
Where's Hulk?
He's doin' what I told him to.
Just like everyone should.

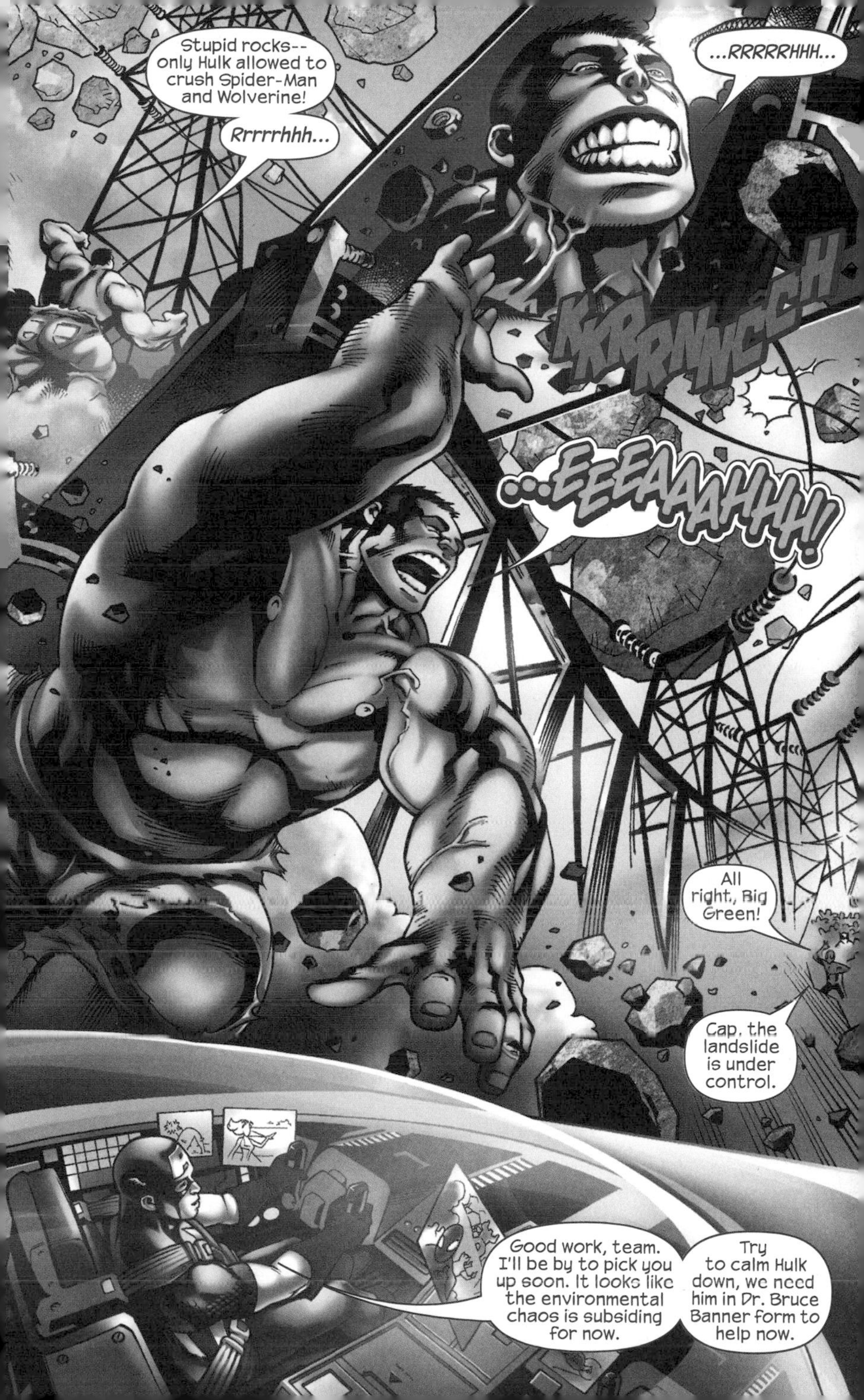
Stupid rocks-- only Hulk allowed to crush Spider-Man and Wolverine!
Rrrrhhh...
...RRRRRHHH...
KKRRNNCCH
...EEEAAAAHHH!!
All right, Big Green!
Cap, the landslide is under control.
Good work, team. I'll be by to pick you up soon. It looks like the environmental chaos is subsiding for now.
Try to calm Hulk down, we need him in Dr. Bruce Banner form to help now.

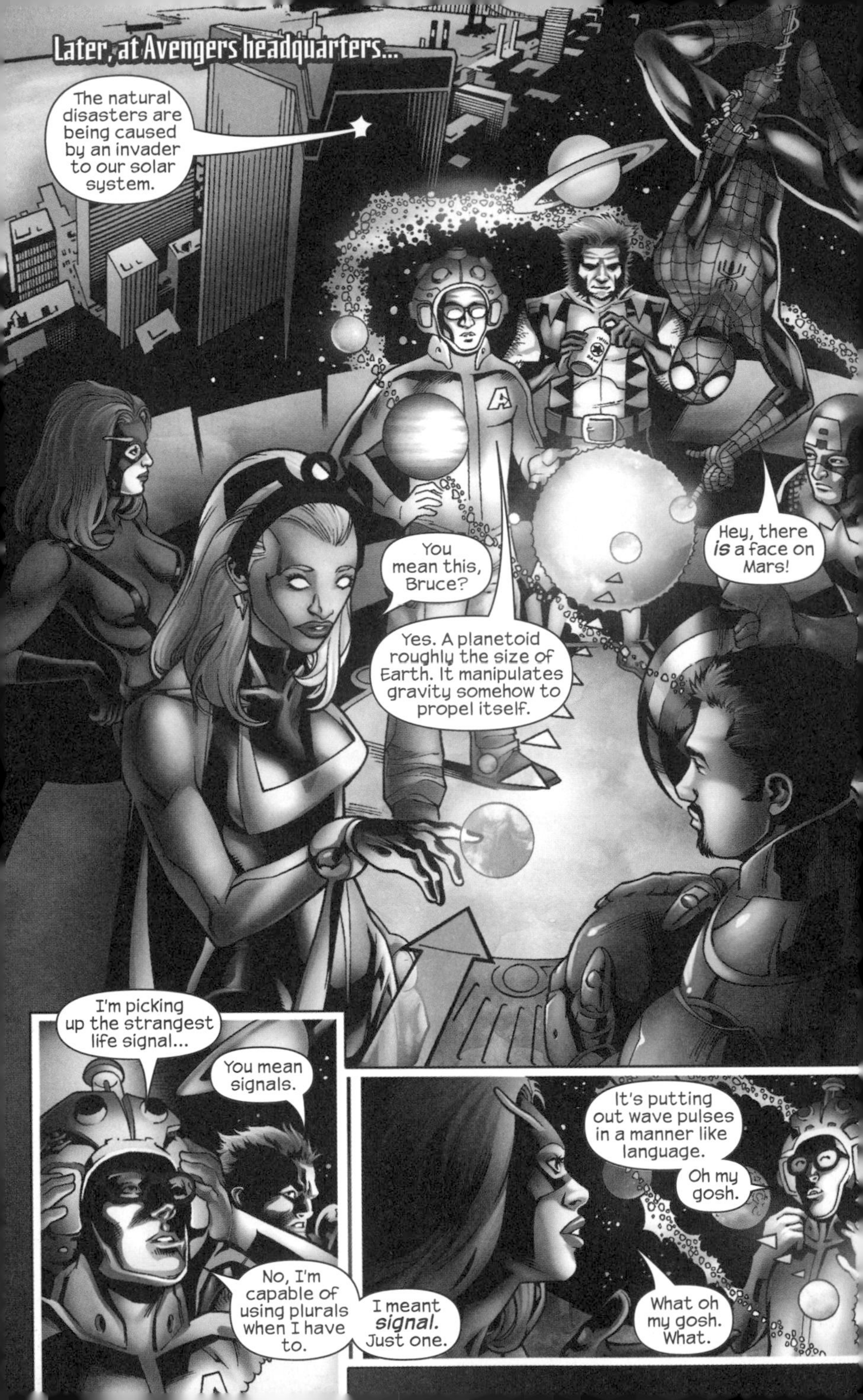
Later, at Avengers headquarters...
The natural disasters are being caused by an invader to our solar system.
You mean this, Bruce?
Yes. A planetoid roughly the size of Earth. It manipulates gravity somehow to propel itself.
Hey, there *is* a face on Mars!
I'm picking up the strangest life signal...
You mean signals.
No, I'm capable of using plurals when I have to.
I meant *signal.* Just one.
It's putting out wave pulses in a manner like language.
Oh my gosh.
What oh my gosh. What.

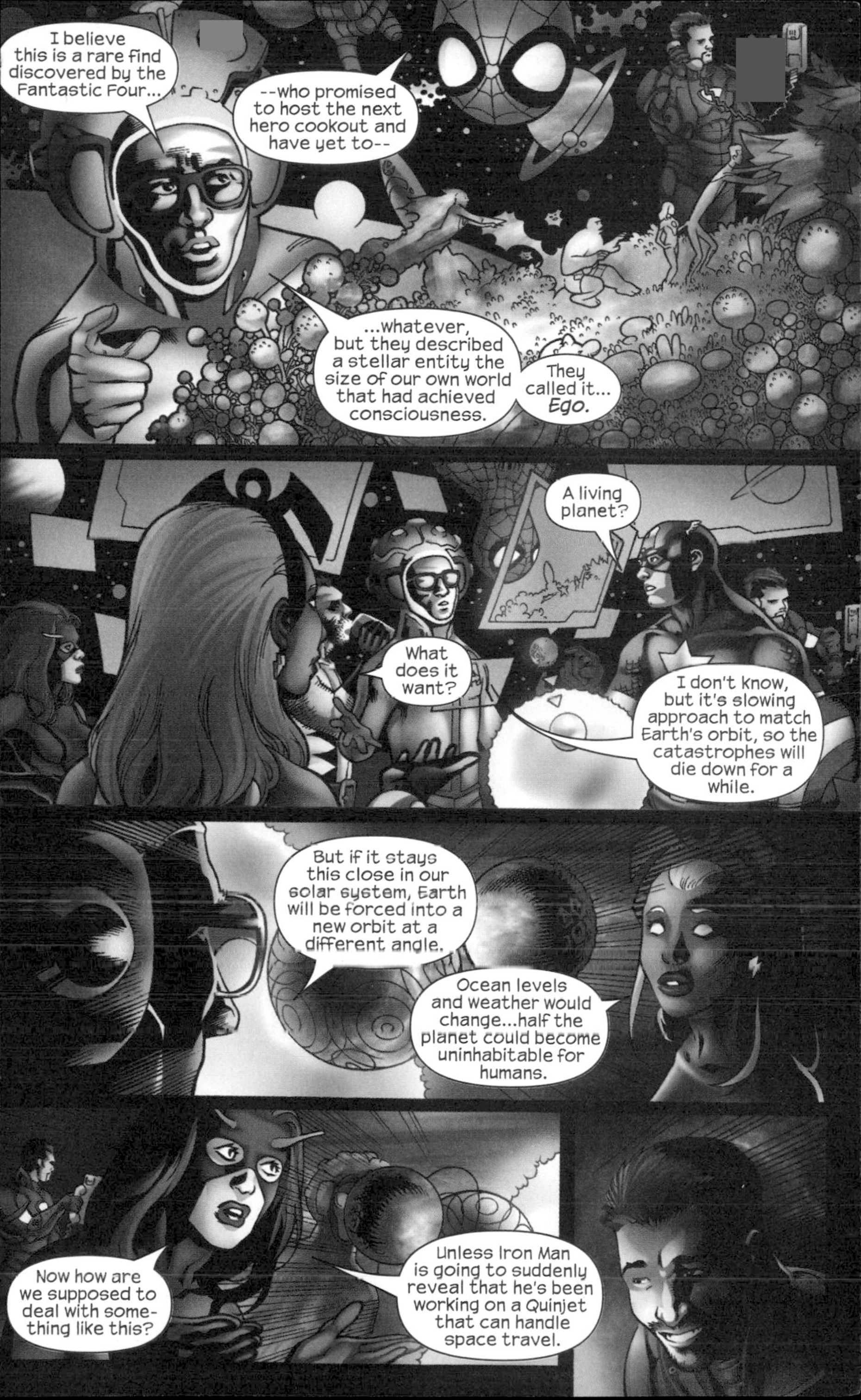
I believe this is a rare find discovered by the Fantastic Four...
--who promised to host the next hero cookout and have yet to--
...whatever, but they described a stellar entity the size of our own world that had achieved consciousness.
They called it... *Ego.*
A living planet?
What does it want?
I don't know, but it's slowing approach to match Earth's orbit, so the catastrophes will die down for a while.
But if it stays this close in our solar system, Earth will be forced into a new orbit at a different angle.
Ocean levels and weather would change...half the planet could become uninhabitable for humans.
Now how are we supposed to deal with some-thing like this?
Unless Iron Man is going to suddenly reveal that he's been working on a Quinjet that can handle space travel.

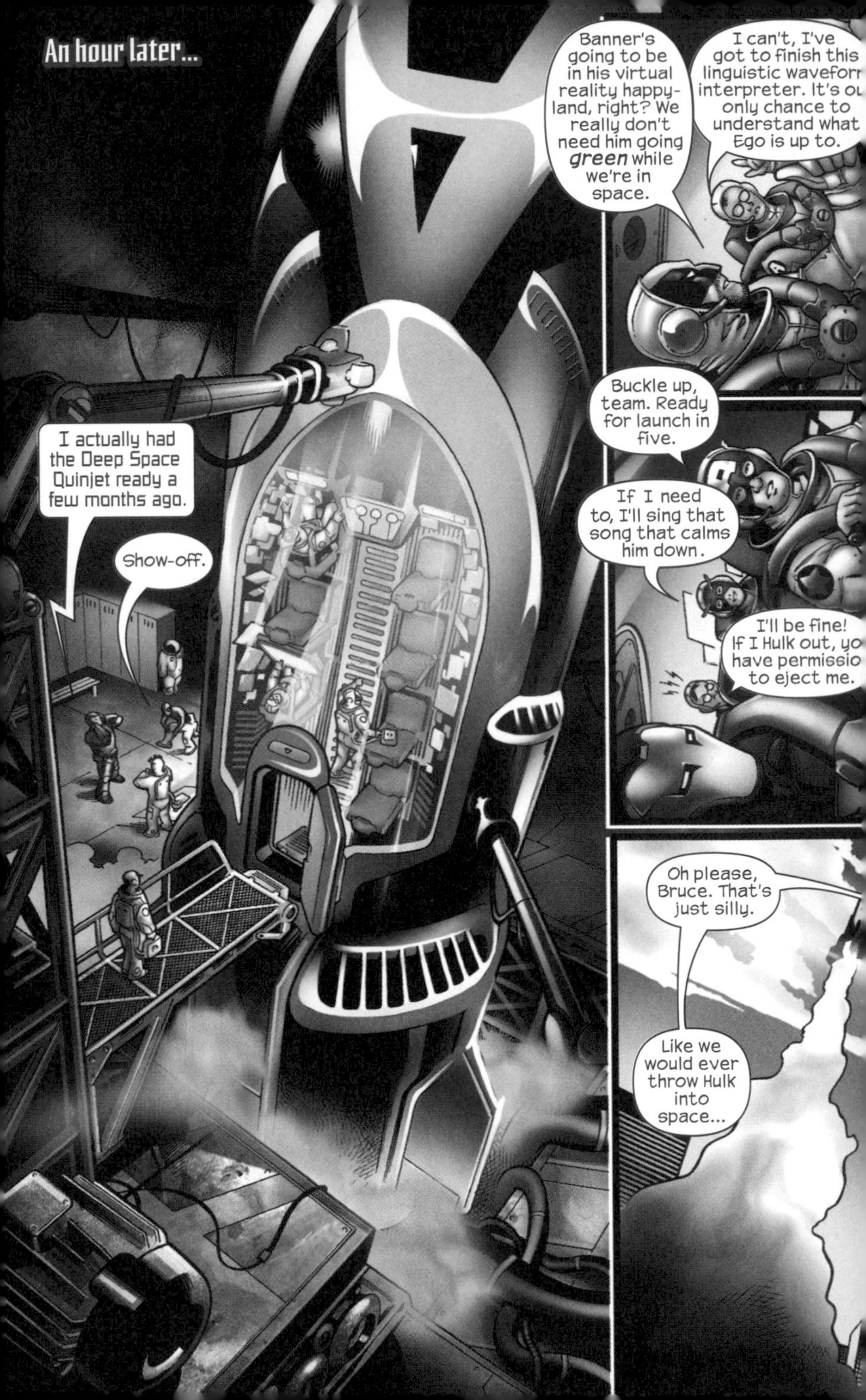
An hour later...
I actually had the Deep Space Quinjet ready a few months ago.
Show-off.
Banner's going to be in his virtual reality happy-land, right? We really don't need him going *green* while we're in space.
I can't, I've got to finish this linguistic waveforr interpreter. It's ou only chance to understand what Ego is up to.
Buckle up, team. Ready for launch in five.
If I need to, I'll sing that song that calms him down.
I'll be fine! If I Hulk out, yo have permissio to eject me.
Oh please, Bruce. That's just silly.
Like we would ever throw Hulk into space...

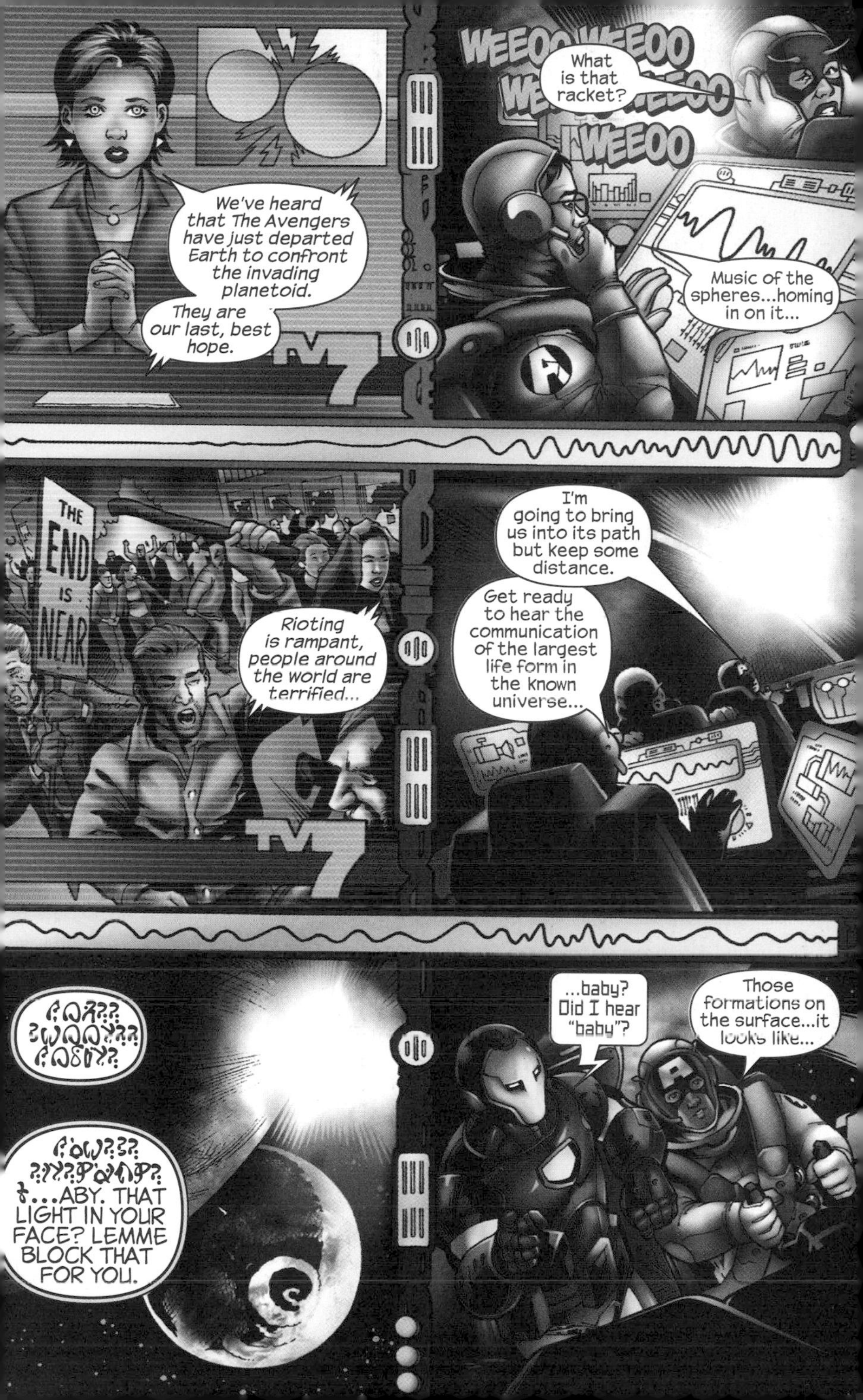
We've heard that The Avengers have just departed Earth to confront the invading planetoid.
They are our last, best hope.
TV7
WEEOO WEEOO
What is that racket?
WEEOO
Music of the spheres...homing in on it...
THE END IS NEAR
Rioting is rampant, people around the world are terrified...
TV7
I'm going to bring us into its path but keep some distance.
Get ready to hear the communication of the largest life form in the known universe...
...ABY. THAT LIGHT IN YOUR FACE? LEMME BLOCK THAT FOR YOU.
...baby? Did I hear "baby"?
Those formations on the surface...it looks like...

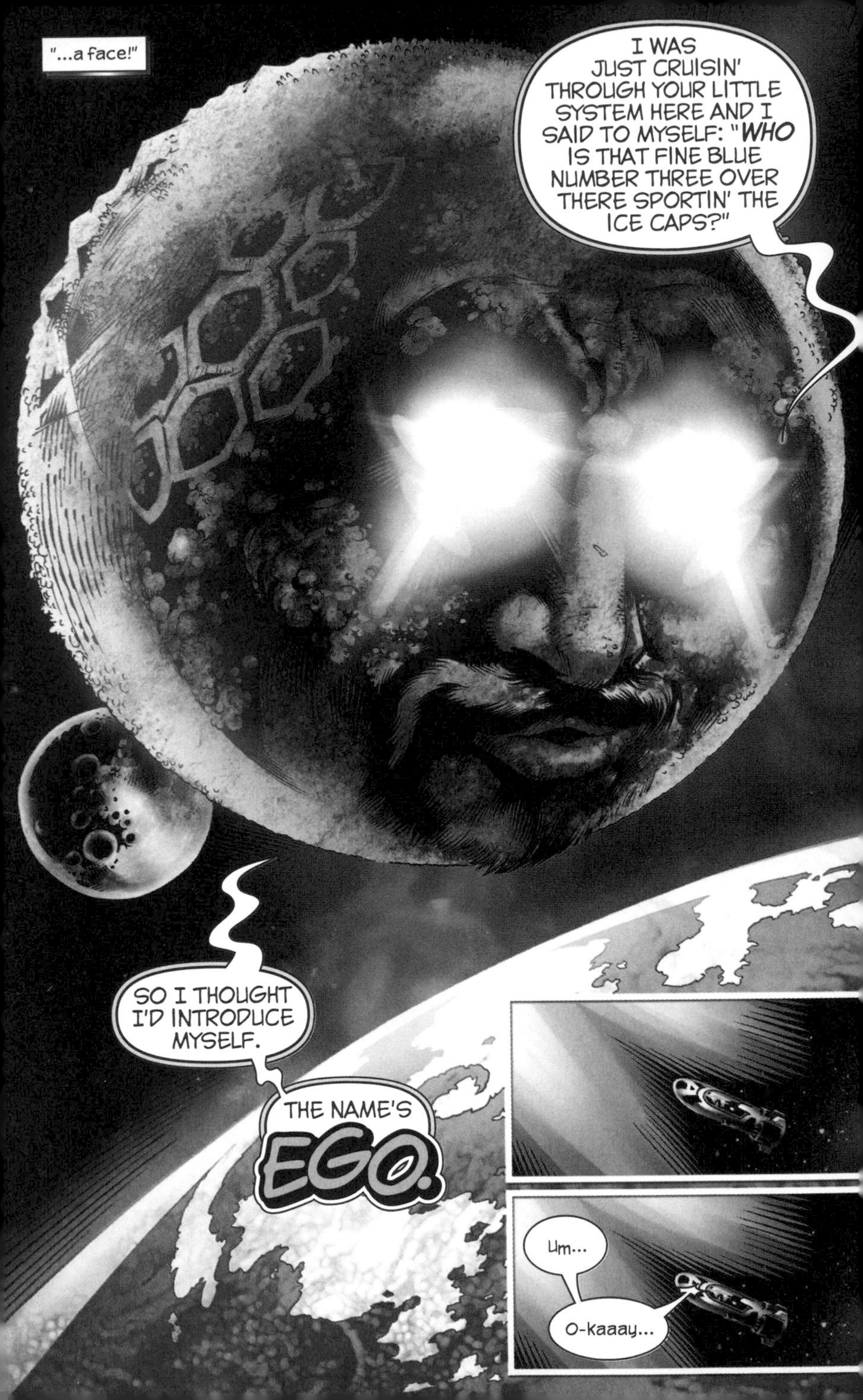
"...a face!"
I WAS JUST CRUISIN' THROUGH YOUR LITTLE SYSTEM HERE AND I SAID TO MYSELF: "WHO IS THAT FINE BLUE NUMBER THREE OVER THERE SPORTIN' THE ICE CAPS?"
SO I THOUGHT I'D INTRODUCE MYSELF.
THE NAME'S
EGO.
Um...
O-kaaay...

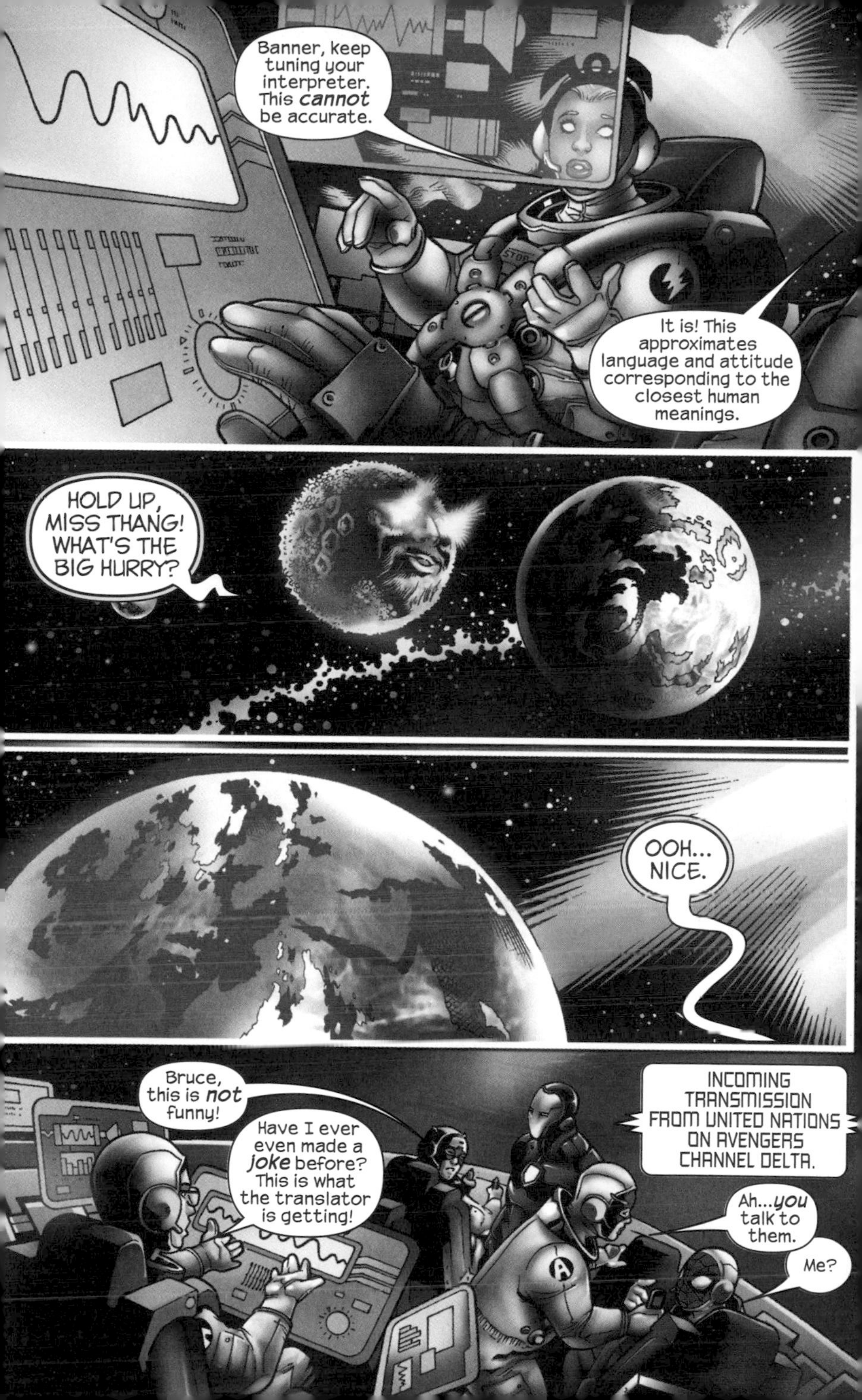
Banner, keep tuning your interpreter. This cannot be accurate.
It is! This approximates language and attitude corresponding to the closest human meanings.
HOLD UP, MISS THANG! WHAT'S THE BIG HURRY?
OOH... NICE.
Bruce, this is not funny!
Have I ever even made a joke before? This is what the translator is getting!
INCOMING TRANSMISSION FROM UNITED NATIONS ON AVENGERS CHANNEL DELTA.
Ah...you talk to them.
Me?

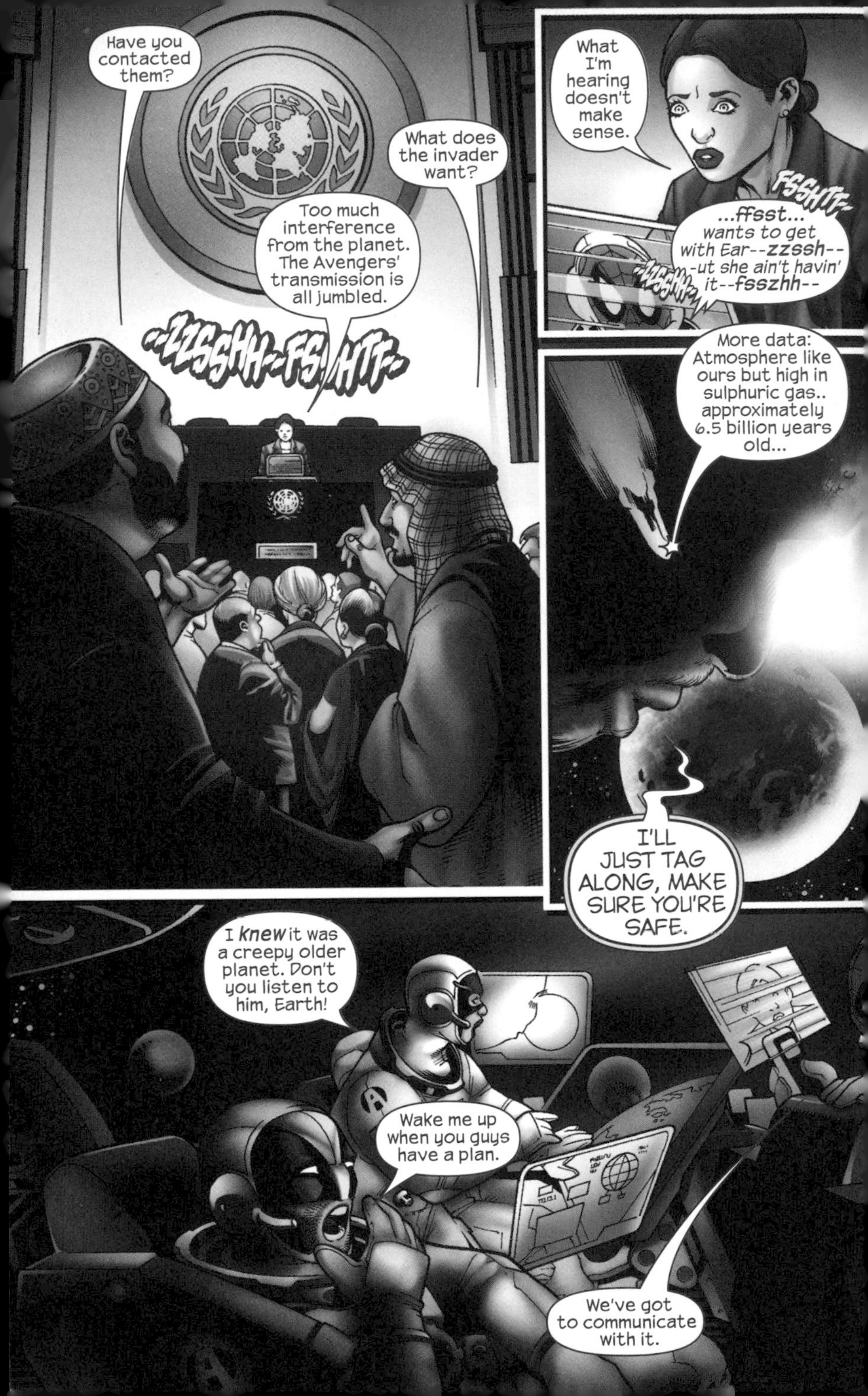
Have you contacted them?
What does the invader want?
Too much interference from the planet. The Avengers' transmission is all jumbled.
--ZZSSHH--FS/HIT--
What I'm hearing doesn't make sense.
FSSHIT--
...ffsst... wants to get with Ear--zzssh-- -ut she ain't havin' it--fsszhh--
--ZZSSHH--
More data: Atmosphere like ours but high in sulphuric gas.. approximately 6.5 billion years old...
I'LL JUST TAG ALONG, MAKE SURE YOU'RE SAFE.
I *knew* it was a creepy older planet. Don't you listen to him, Earth!
Wake me up when you guys have a plan.
We've got to communicate with it.

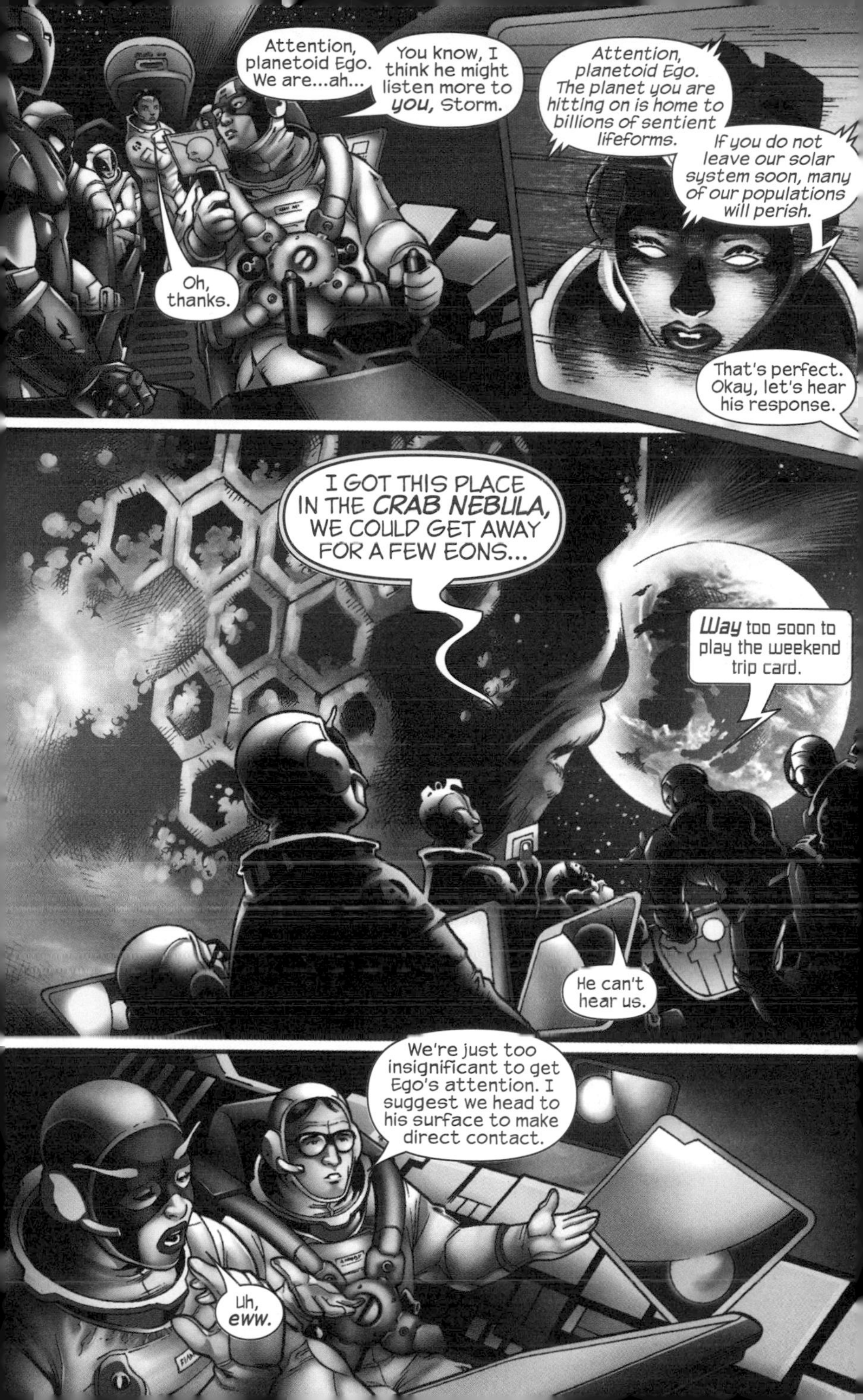
Attention, planetoid Ego. We are...ah...
You know, I think he might listen more to *you*, Storm.
Oh, thanks.
Attention, planetoid Ego. The planet you are hitting on is home to billions of sentient lifeforms.
If you do not leave our solar system soon, many of our populations will perish.
That's perfect. Okay, let's hear his response.
I GOT THIS PLACE IN THE *CRAB NEBULA,* WE COULD GET AWAY FOR A FEW EONS...
Way too soon to play the weekend trip card.
He can't hear us.
We're just too insignificant to get Ego's attention. I suggest we head to his surface to make direct contact.
Uh, *eww.*

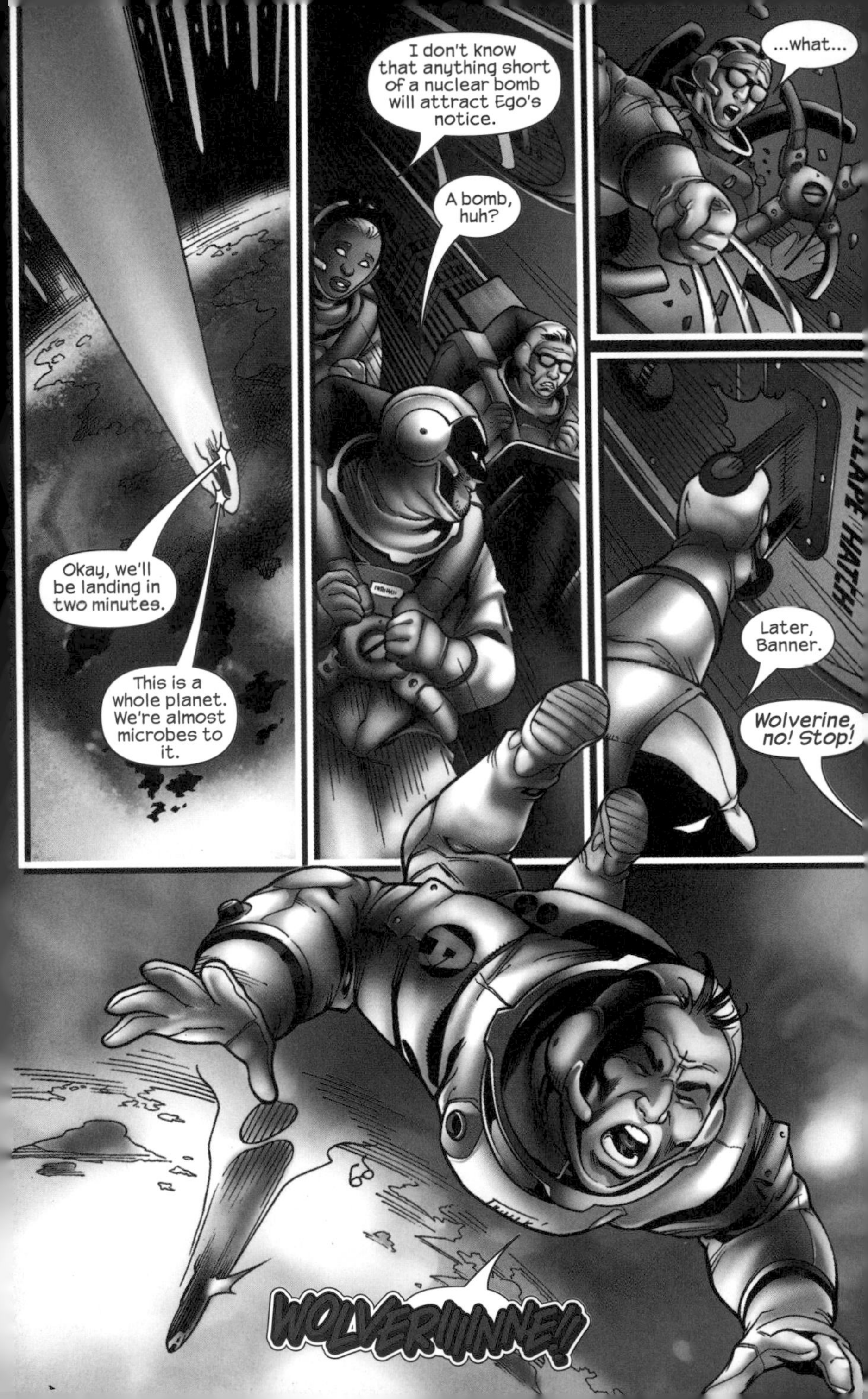
Okay, we'll be landing in two minutes.
This is a whole planet. We're almost microbes to it.
I don't know that anything short of a nuclear bomb will attract Ego's notice.
A bomb, huh?
...what...
Later, Banner.
Wolverine, no! Stop!
WOLVERIIIINNE!

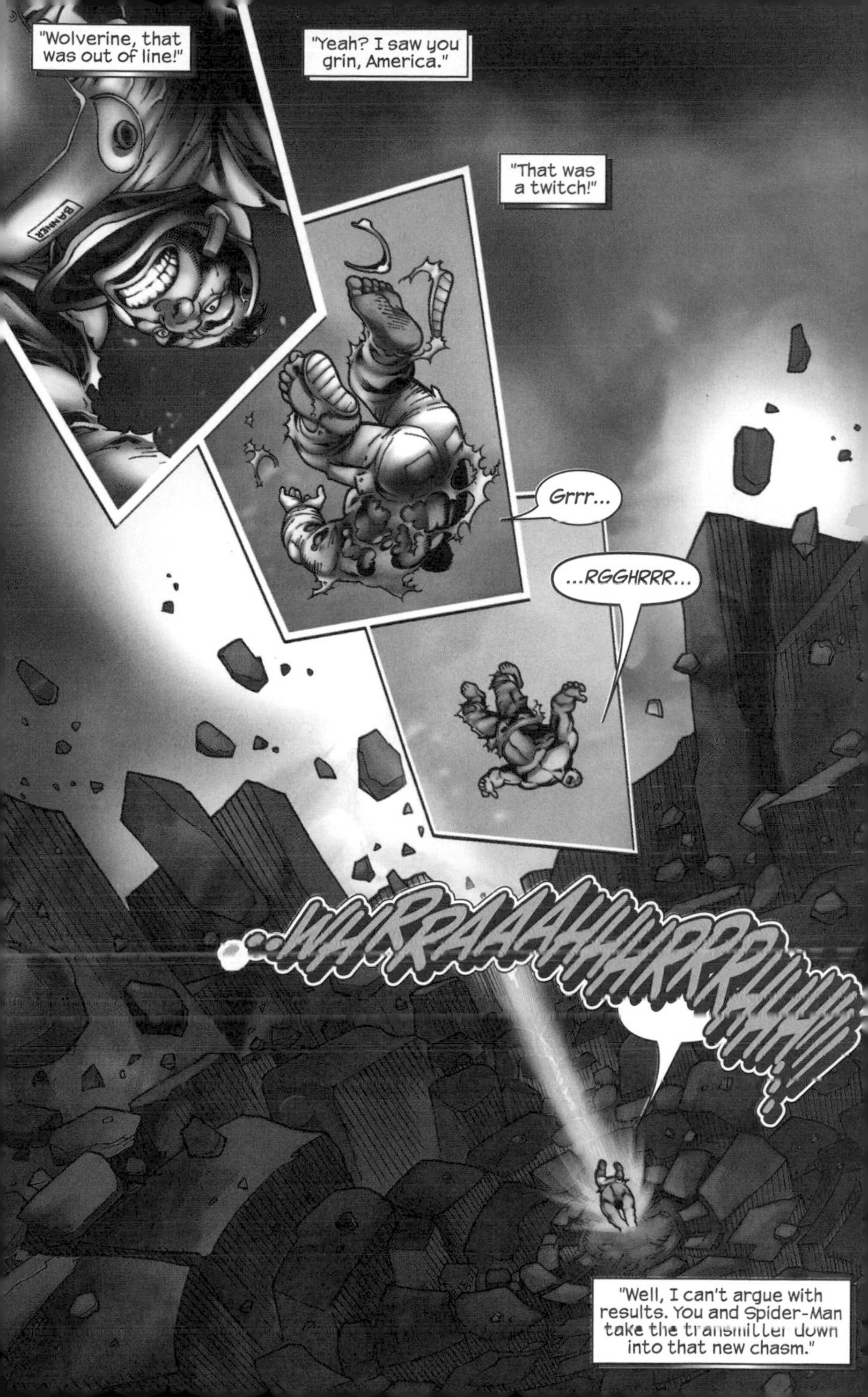
"Wolverine, that was out of line!"
"Yeah? I saw you grin, America."
"That was a twitch!"
Grrr...
...RGGHRRR...
...WHRRAAAHHHRRRAHH!!
"Well, I can't argue with results. You and Spider-Man take the transmitter down into that new chasm."

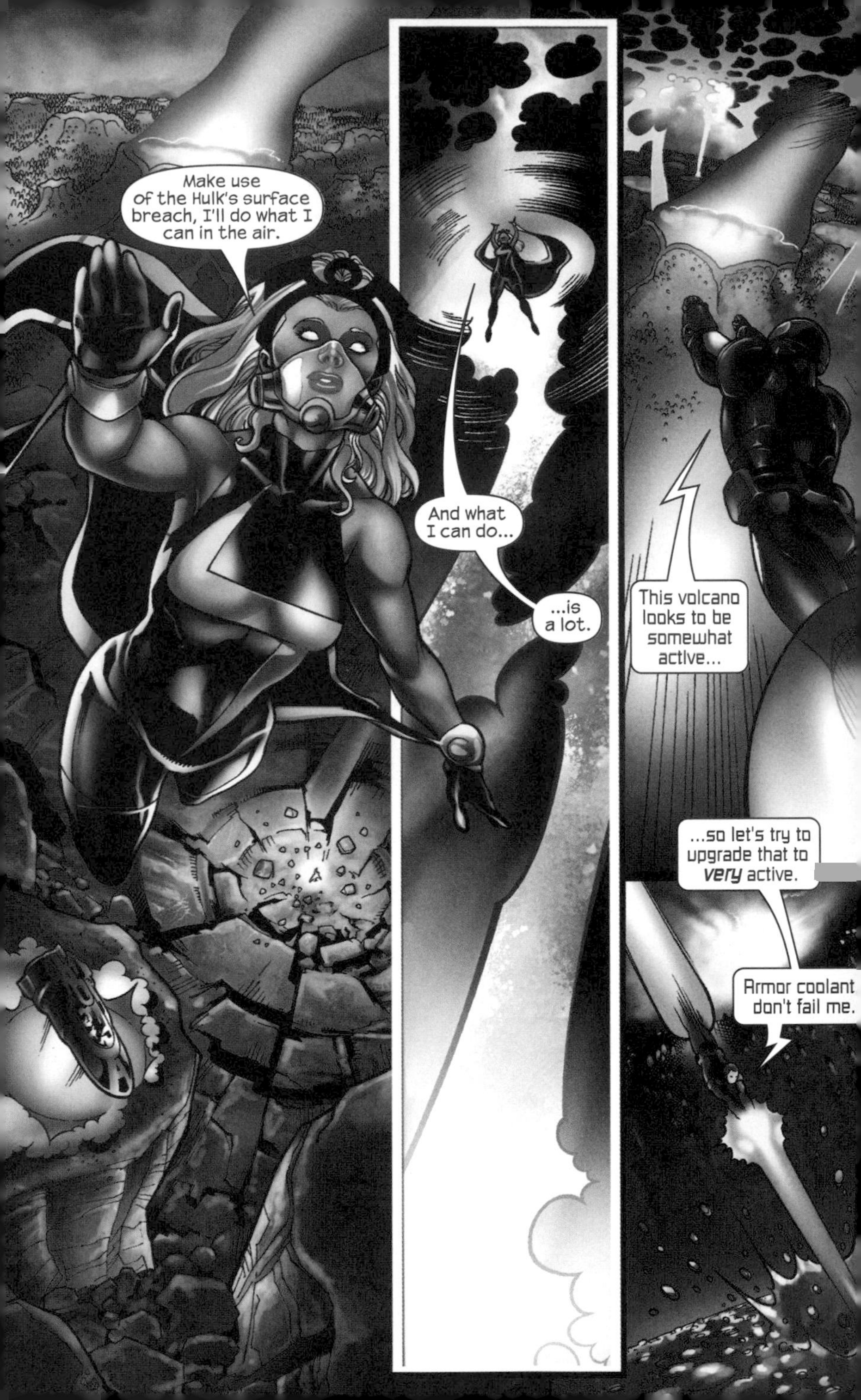
Make use of the Hulk's surface breach, I'll do what I can in the air.
And what I can do...
...is a lot.
This volcano looks to be somewhat active...
...so let's try to upgrade that to *very* active.
Armor coolant don't fail me.

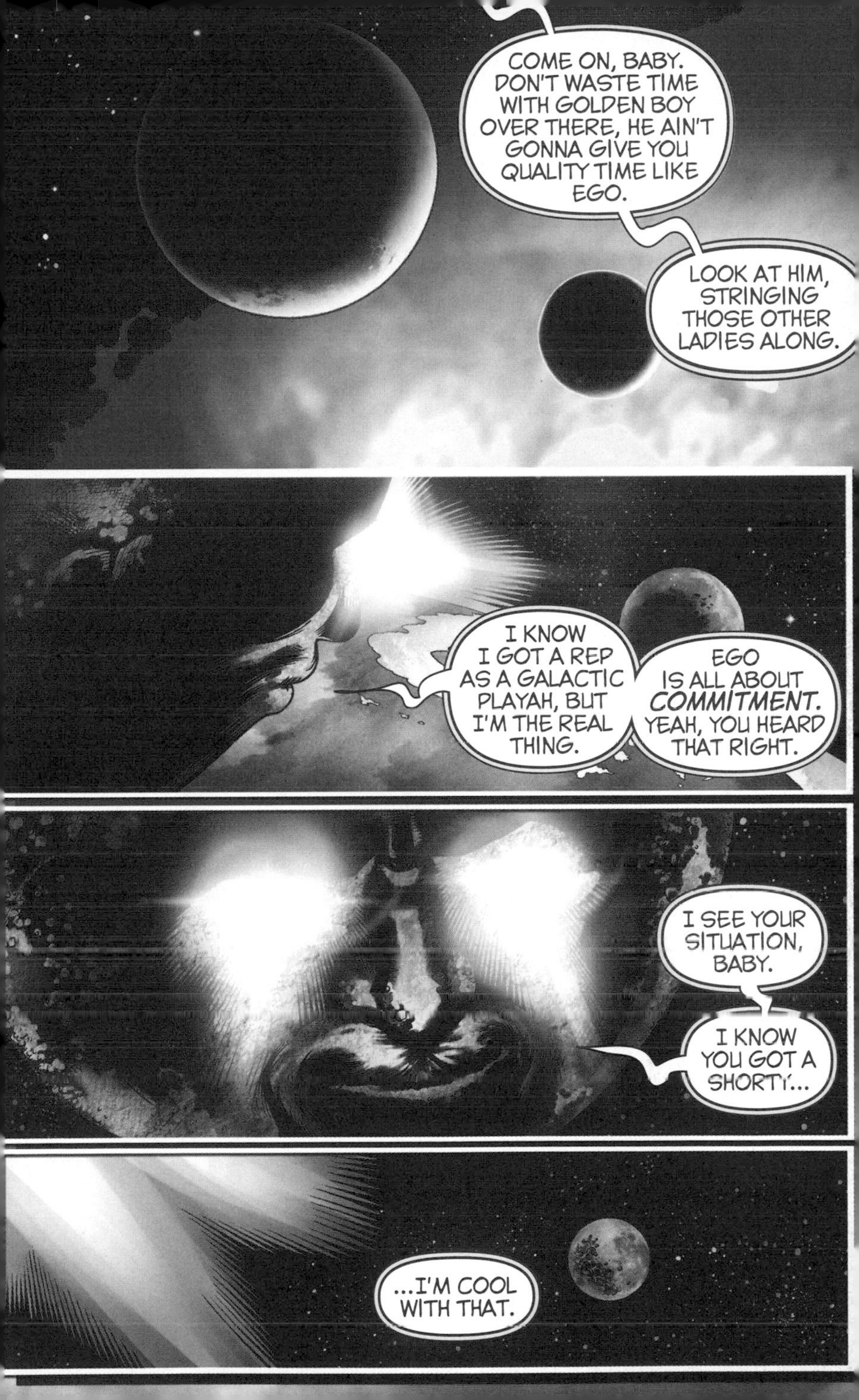
COME ON, BABY. DON'T WASTE TIME WITH GOLDEN BOY OVER THERE, HE AIN'T GONNA GIVE YOU QUALITY TIME LIKE EGO.
LOOK AT HIM, STRINGING THOSE OTHER LADIES ALONG.
I KNOW I GOT A REP AS A GALACTIC PLAYAH, BUT I'M THE REAL THING.
EGO IS ALL ABOUT *COMMITMENT*. YEAH, YOU HEARD THAT RIGHT.
I SEE YOUR SITUATION, BABY.
I KNOW YOU GOT A SHORTY...
...I'M COOL WITH THAT.

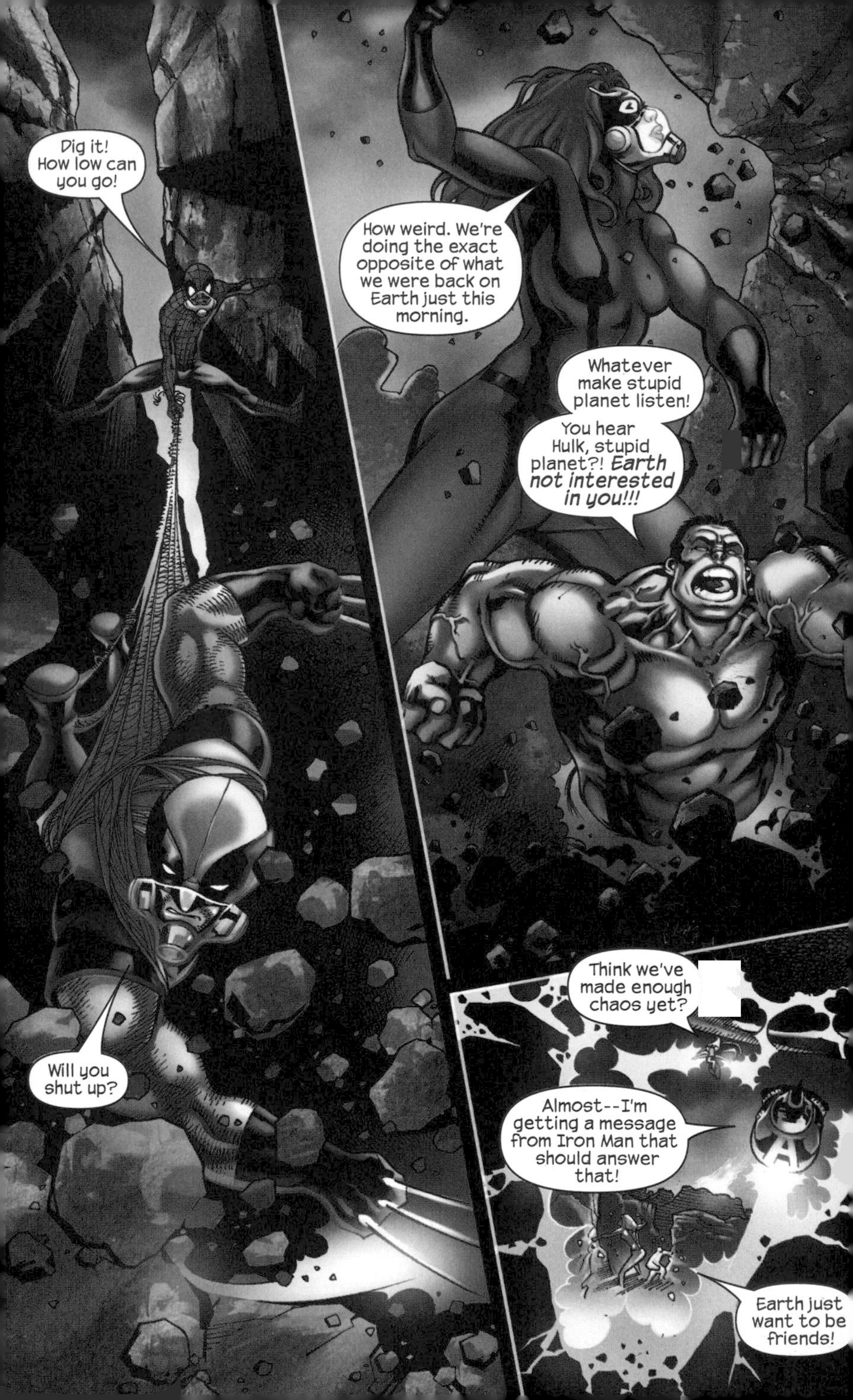
Dig it! How low can you go!
Will you shut up?
How weird. We're doing the exact opposite of what we were back on Earth just this morning.
Whatever make stupid planet listen!
You hear Hulk, stupid planet?! *Earth not interested in you!!!*
Think we've made enough chaos yet?
Almost--I'm getting a message from Iron Man that should answer that!
Earth just want to be friends!

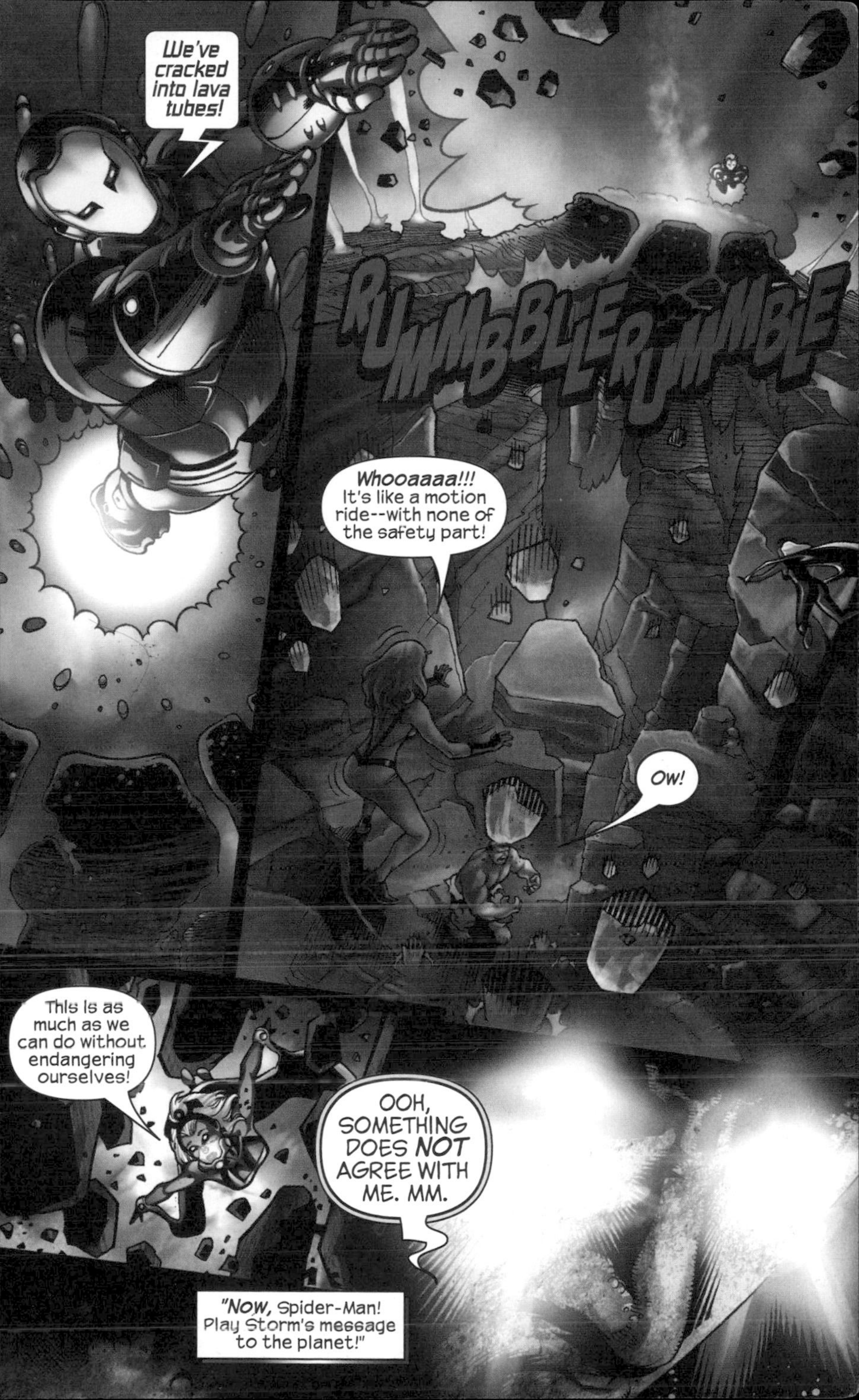
We've cracked into lava tubes!
RUMMBBLLERUMMBLE
Whooaaaa!!! It's like a motion ride--with none of the safety part!
Ow!
This is as much as we can do without endangering ourselves!
OOH, SOMETHING DOES NOT AGREE WITH ME. MM.
"NOW, Spider-Man! Play Storm's message to the planet!"

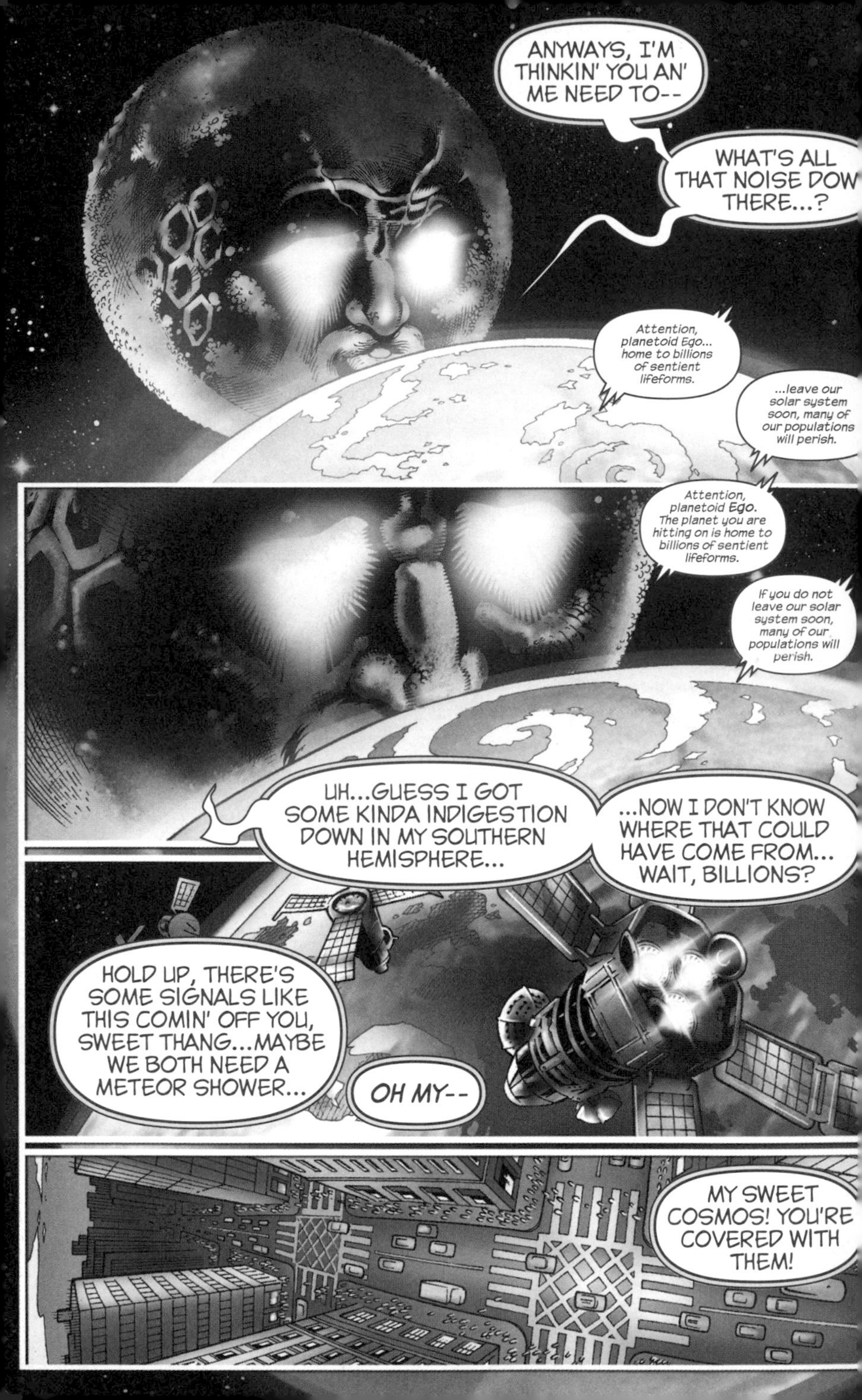
ANYWAYS, I'M THINKIN' YOU AN' ME NEED TO--
WHAT'S ALL THAT NOISE DOW THERE...?
Attention, planetoid Ego... home to billions of sentient lifeforms.
...leave our solar system soon, many of our populations will perish.
Attention, planetoid Ego. The planet you are hitting on is home to billions of sentient lifeforms.
If you do not leave our solar system soon, many of our populations will perish.
UH...GUESS I GOT SOME KINDA INDIGESTION DOWN IN MY SOUTHERN HEMISPHERE...
...NOW I DON'T KNOW WHERE THAT COULD HAVE COME FROM... WAIT, BILLIONS?
HOLD UP, THERE'S SOME SIGNALS LIKE THIS COMIN' OFF YOU, SWEET THANG...MAYBE WE BOTH NEED A METEOR SHOWER...
OH MY--
MY SWEET COSMOS! YOU'RE COVERED WITH THEM!

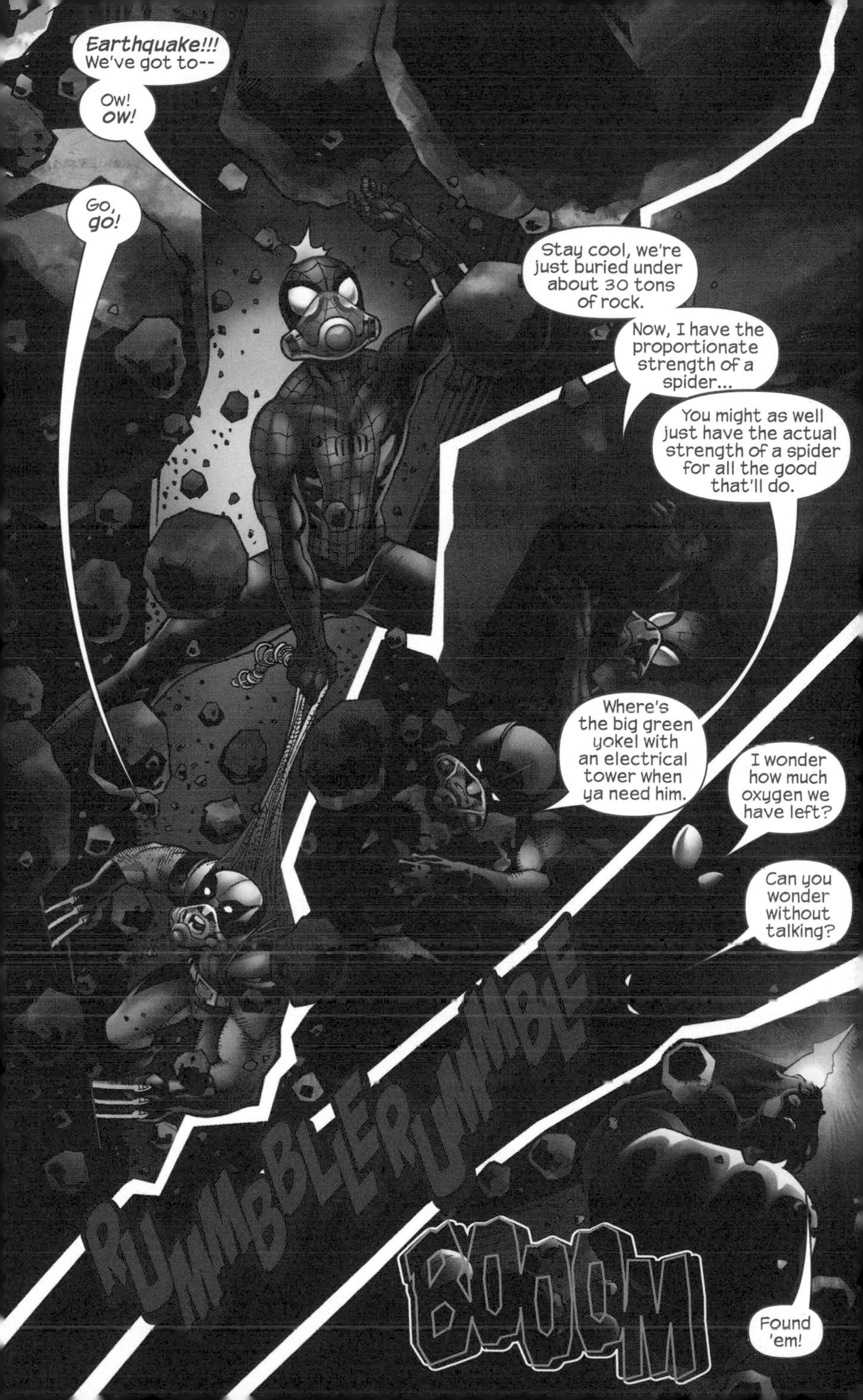
Earthquake!!! We've got to--
Ow! OW!
Go, go!
Stay cool, we're just buried under about 30 tons of rock.
Now, I have the proportionate strength of a spider...
You might as well just have the actual strength of a spider for all the good that'll do.
Where's the big green yokel with an electrical tower when ya need him.
I wonder how much oxygen we have left?
Can you wonder without talking?
RUMMBLERUMBLE
BOOOOM
Found 'em!

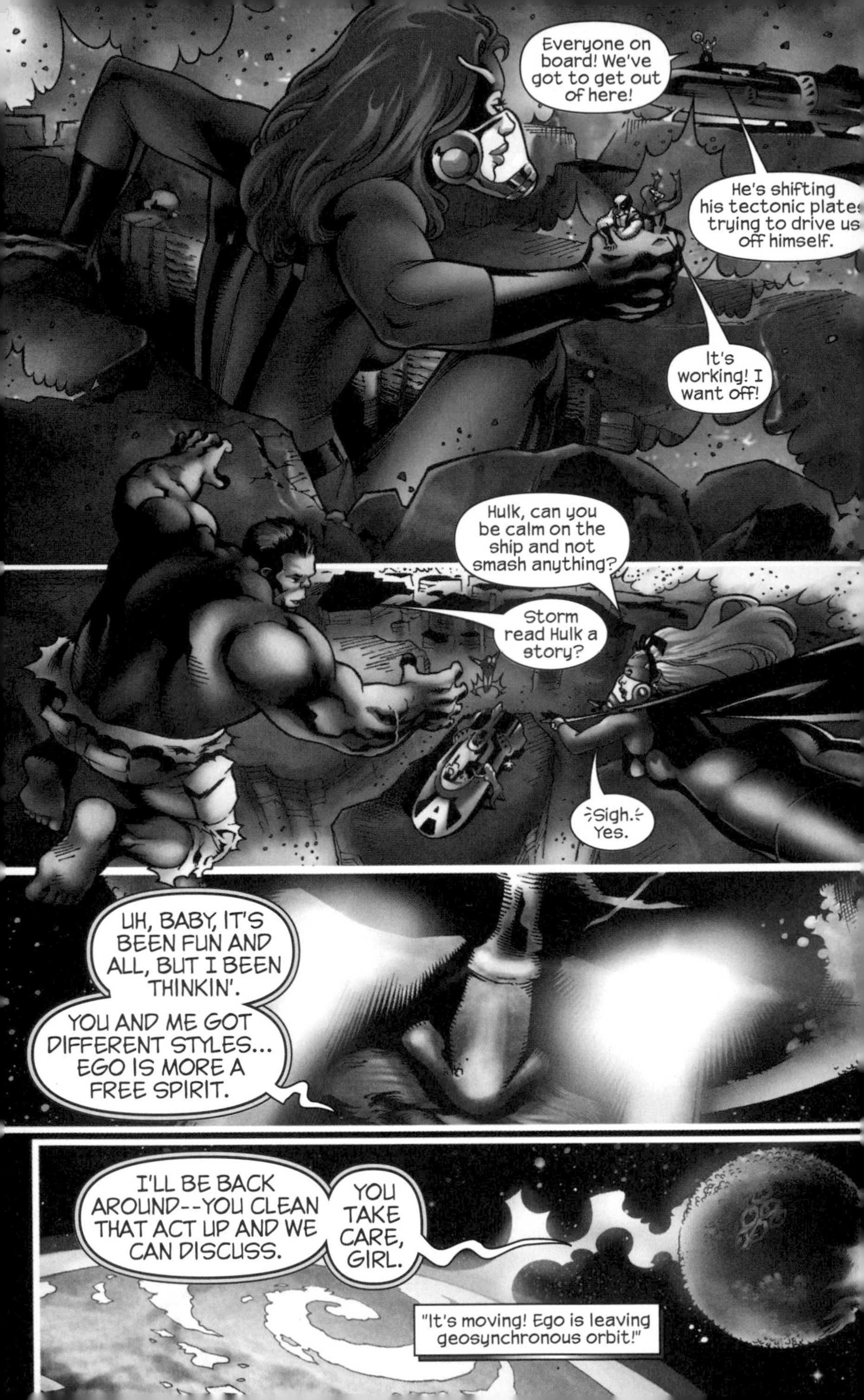
Everyone on board! We've got to get out of here!
He's shifting his tectonic plates trying to drive us off himself.
It's working! I want off!
Hulk, can you be calm on the ship and not smash anything?
Storm read Hulk a story?
Sigh. Yes.
UH, BABY, IT'S BEEN FUN AND ALL, BUT I BEEN THINKIN'.
YOU AND ME GOT DIFFERENT STYLES... EGO IS MORE A FREE SPIRIT.
I'LL BE BACK AROUND--YOU CLEAN THAT ACT UP AND WE CAN DISCUSS.
YOU TAKE CARE, GIRL.
"It's moving! Ego is leaving geosynchronous orbit!"

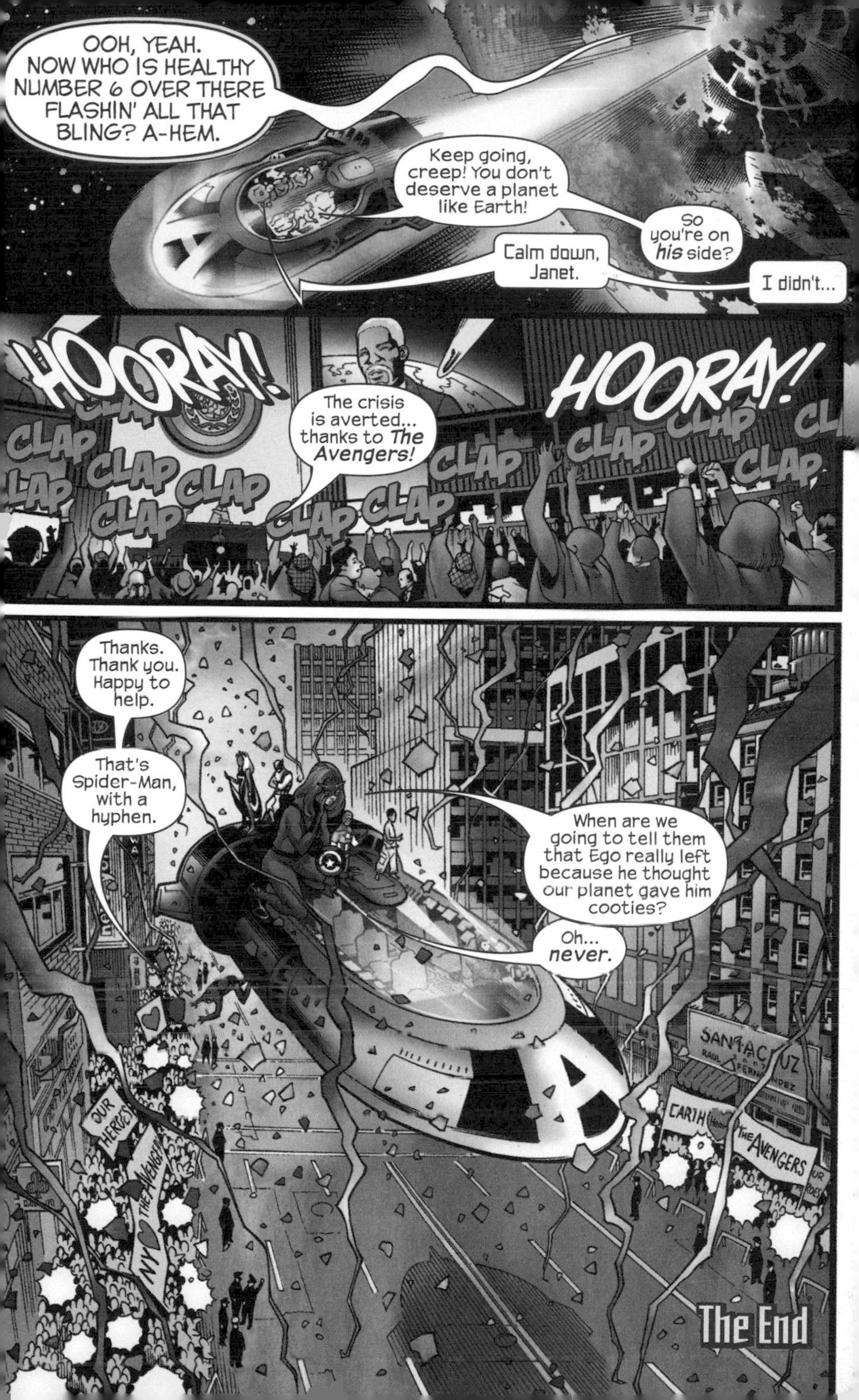
OOH, YEAH. NOW WHO IS HEALTHY NUMBER 6 OVER THERE FLASHIN' ALL THAT BLING? A-HEM.
Keep going, creep! You don't deserve a planet like Earth!
So you're on *his* side?
Calm down, Janet.
I didn't...
HOORAY!
The crisis is averted... thanks to *The Avengers!*
HOORAY!
CLAP CLAP CLAP CLAP CLAP CLAP CLAP CLAP CLAP CLAP CLAP
Thanks. Thank you. Happy to help.
That's Spider-Man, with a hyphen.
When are we going to tell them that Ego really left because he thought our planet gave him cooties?
Oh... *never.*
OUR HEROES
THE AVENGERS
The End

THE AVENGERS
BIZARRE ADVENTURES

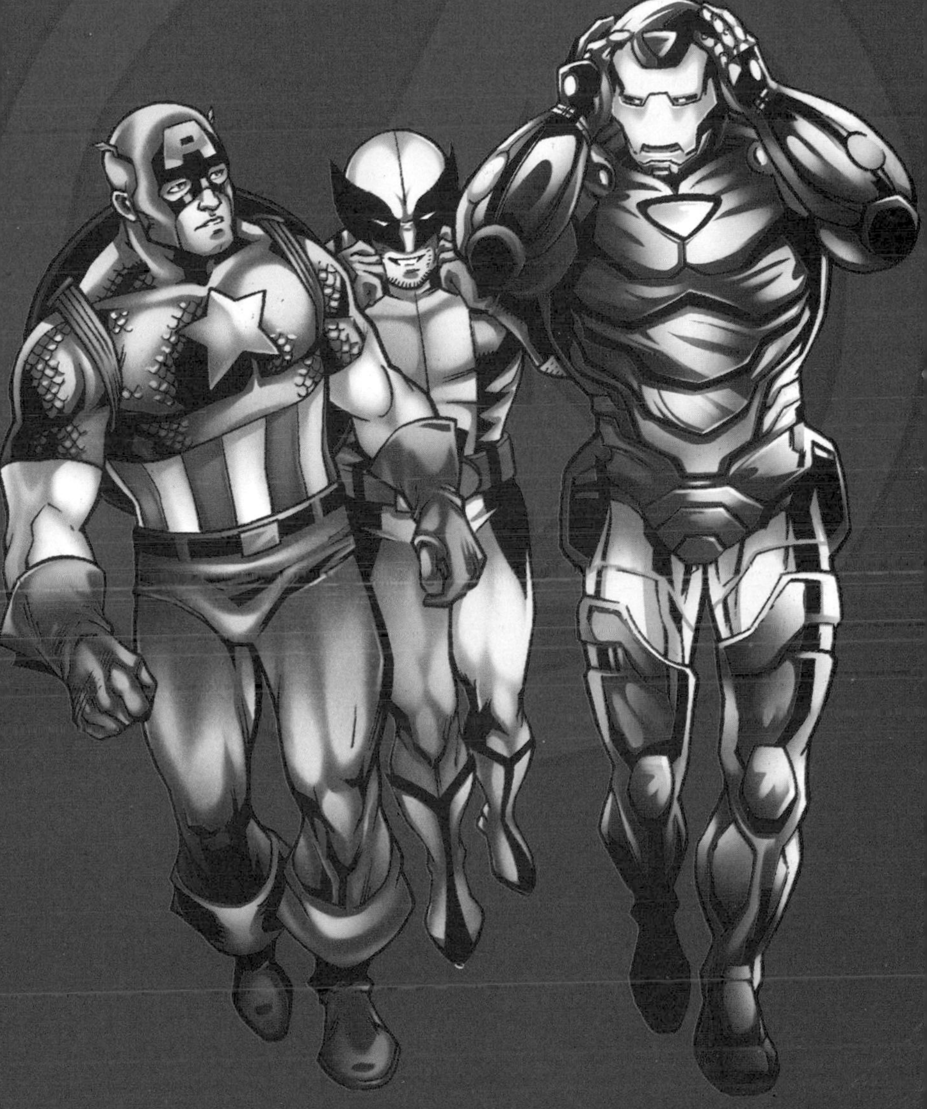

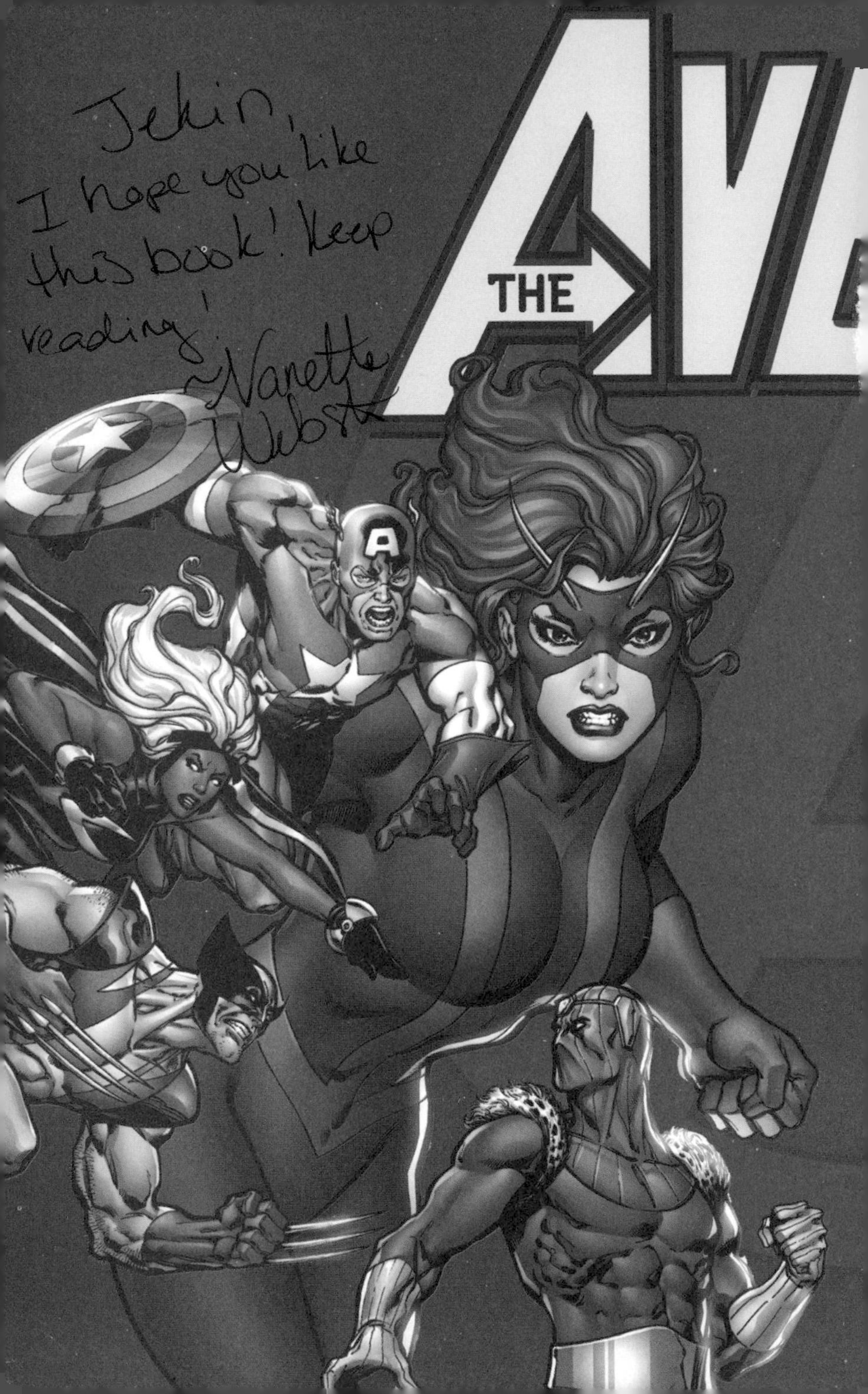
THE
Jekin,
I hope you like
this book! Keep
reading!
~Nanette
Webst